LONE STAR BRIDE

Carolyn Davidson

MILLS & BOON

All the ⬚⬚⬚⬚⬚⬚⬚⬚⬚⬚⬚⬚⬚⬚⬚⬚⬚⬚ igination of the a⬚⬚ ⬚⬚⬚⬚⬚⬚⬚⬚⬚⬚ g the same na⬚⬚ ⬚⬚⬚⬚⬚⬚ ⬚⬚⬚ ⬚⬚⬚⬚⬚⬚ ⬚⬚⬚⬚⬚⬚⬚ ⬚⬚ individu⬚⬚ ⬚⬚⬚⬚ ⬚⬚ ⬚⬚⬚⬚⬚⬚⬚ ⬚⬚⬚ ⬚⬚ ⬚⬚ ⬚⬚⬚⬚⬚⬚ s are pure inv⬚⬚⬚⬚

All Rig⬚⬚ ⬚⬚⬚⬚⬚⬚ including the right of reproduction in whole or in part i⬚ ⬚⬚⬚ form. This ⬚⬚⬚⬚⬚ ⬚⬚⬚⬚⬚⬚⬚⬚⬚ ⬚⬚⬚⬚⬚⬚⬚⬚ with Harlequ⬚⬚ Enterprises II BV/S.à.⬚⬚⬚ ⬚⬚⬚ ⬚⬚⬚⬚⬚⬚ publi⬚⬚⬚⬚on or any par⬚ ⬚⬚⬚⬚⬚⬚⬚⬚⬚⬚ ⬚⬚⬚⬚⬚⬚⬚⬚ ⬚⬚ ⬚⬚⬚⬚⬚⬚⬚⬚⬚⬚⬚ ⬚⬚ ⬚⬚⬚ form or by a⬚⬚ ⬚⬚⬚⬚⬚⬚⬚⬚⬚ ⬚⬚ ⬚⬚⬚⬚⬚⬚⬚⬚⬚⬚ including photocopying, recordi⬚⬚ ⬚⬚⬚⬚⬚⬚⬚ ⬚⬚ ⬚⬚ ⬚⬚⬚⬚⬚⬚⬚⬚⬚⬚ ⬚⬚⬚⬚⬚⬚⬚ ⬚⬚⬚⬚⬚⬚ ⬚⬚⬚⬚⬚wise, without ⬚⬚ ⬚⬚⬚⬚⬚⬚ permission of the publisher.

This bo⬚⬚ ⬚⬚ ⬚⬚⬚⬚ subject to the condition that it shall not, by way of trade or otherwise, be lent, resold ⬚⬚⬚⬚⬚ ⬚⬚⬚ ⬚⬚⬚⬚ ⬚⬚⬚⬚⬚⬚ circulated without the prior consent of the publisher in any form of binding or cover other than that in which it is ⬚⬚⬚⬚⬚⬚⬚⬚ ⬚⬚⬚ ⬚⬚⬚⬚⬚⬚ ⬚ similar condition including this condition ⬚⬚⬚⬚⬚ ⬚⬚⬚⬚⬚⬚⬚ ⬚⬚ ⬚⬚⬚ subsequent purchaser.

® and TM are trademarks owned ⬚⬚ ⬚⬚⬚ ⬚⬚⬚ ⬚⬚ ⬚⬚⬚ trademark owner and/or its licensee. Trademarks marked with ® are registered with the United Kingdom Patent Office and/or the Office for Harmonisation in the Internal Market and in other countries.

First published in Great Britain 2010
Harlequin Mills & Boon Limited,
Eton House, 18-24 Paradise Road, Richmond, Surrey TW9 1SR

© Carolyn Davidson 2006

ISBN: 978 0 263 87581 2

Harlequin Mills & Boon policy is to use papers that are natural,
renewable and recyclable products and made from wood grown in
sustainable forests. The logging and manufacturing process conform
to the legal environmental regulations of the country of origin.

Printed and bound in Spain
by Litografia Rosés, S.A., Barcelona

Reading, writing and research—**Carolyn Davidson**'s life in three simple words. At least that area of her life having to do with her career as a historical romance author. The rest of her time is divided among husband, family and travel—her husband, of course, holding top priority in her busy schedule. Then there is their church, and the church choir in which they participate. Their sons and daughters, along with assorted spouses, are spread across the eastern half of America, together with numerous grandchildren. Carolyn welcomes mail at her post office box, PO Box 2757, Goose Creek, SC 29445, USA.

Recent novels by the same author:

A MARRIAGE BY CHANCE
THE TEXAN
TEMPTING A TEXAN
STORMWALKER'S WOMAN
   (short story in *One Starry Christmas*)
TEXAS GOLD
THE MARRIAGE AGREEMENT
ABANDONED
   (short story in *Wed Under Western Skies*)
TEXAS LAWMAN
OKLAHOMA SWEETHEART
A CHRISTMAS CHILD
   (short story in *The Magic of Christmas*)

and in Mills & Boon® Super Historical Romance:

REDEMPTION
HAVEN
THE OUTLAW'S BRIDE
THE BRIDE

Reasons for a dedication are many and varied.
This one is due to the presence of a bona fide angel
in our family. Alexis Davidson will probably never be
aware of the influence she will have on the lives
of those around her, yet it will be felt by all who
love her. She is our baby, our own grandchild
and great-grandchild, and as such she is precious.
So, to our Lexy this book is dedicated,
with all the love this grandma's heart can hold.

And to Mr. Ed, who loves me.

Prologue

Benning, Texas, Spring 1895

"I heard you're looking for a deputy." James Webster stood in the doorway of the local lawman's office, presenting himself as a candidate for the job.

The sheriff, Brace Caulfield, nodded and waved a hand at the stranger. "Have a seat and tell me your qualifications, son." The young man was dressed for the trail, his boots dusty, his clothing clean but well worn. And on his face he wore the look of a man who had lived through a heap of problems.

James took off his hat and did as instructed, bringing forth an envelope from his pack before he sat it on the floor. He handed it to the sheriff and then sat, his long legs stretching halfway across to the desk. "I'm James Webster, and I brought this for you to look at. It will give you an idea of what I've been up to for the past few years."

Sheriff Caulfield opened the envelope and raised his eyes to James. "Would this be a recommendation? Have you been a lawman before?"

James shook his head. "No, but I'm a good man with a gun. I'm honest, big enough to stop any fights that might take place where a show of strength is required and I need a job."

The sheriff bent his head over the letter he'd been offered and then handed it to the man across the desk from him. "Read this aloud for me, son. I want to think about it and I'll do better if you read it to me."

James nodded, although he had his doubts as to the reason he'd been asked to do the honors, so to speak. "It's from the rancher I worked for up in Missouri. Offered to write the letter on his own hook. I'm never one to turn down a helping hand, so I brought it with me. I'd hoped it might make an impression on someone when I started job hunting. I'd done a good job for him, but it was time to move on. Texas seemed a likely place."

"How long you been looking?" the sheriff asked.

"Not long, a month or so, maybe. I just got into town and put my horse up at the livery stable. I need a decent bed for a night or two, and when the clerk at the hotel told me your deputy had left for greener pastures, I figured it wouldn't hurt to introduce myself to you."

"Well," Brace said lazily, leaning back in his chair, "read it to me. Let me hear what the man has to say. Then why don't you get yourself a room at the hotel for a day or two and I'll stop by at suppertime and we can eat in the dining room there. Their fried chicken is good, and I think they've got roast beef for the special tonight."

James cleared his throat. "Can I just paraphrase the letter?" he asked, embarrassed to read the words that would praise him to the skies.

Brace nodded. "If you like. So long as I know what it says."

James sat up straighter in the chair and began. "First off,

he says that I'm a good man with those under my command. I was his foreman for a couple of years, and we got along pretty well." Glancing down at the letter he held, he flushed a bit.

"He says I'm honest, dependable and a good hand with a gun." With that, Jamie folded the letter and placed it back in the envelope. "I'm not lily-white, Sheriff, and I'm not about to play any games with you." He met the lawman's gaze and hesitated. "I've been a rascal in my time, but my record speaks for my life over the past couple of years."

"What sort of *rascal* are we talking about here?" Brace asked, leaning back in his chair and folding his arms across his chest. "You get in any big trouble while you sowed your wild oats?"

"I hurt some folks. Caused some problems that will probably haunt me till the day I die. But I've done my best to make amends with my family and…"

"And?" Brace nudged his visitor into an explanation.

"And the girl who was hurt by my actions."

"Physically? Were you abusive?" And if the young fella answered the wrong way, he'd be out the door in a heartbeat, Brace decided.

"No. But I left her in the family way and pret' near ruined her life. If my brother hadn't stepped in and cleaned up my mess, I don't know what would have happened." Jamie's face was drawn, aging in moments, Brace thought, as if he bore scars that were still fresh and unhealed.

"There'll be no damn carrying-on from this office. I want you to know that right up front. I don't hold with men taking advantage of womenfolk." Brace spoke his mind with forceful language, and the man across the desk from him nodded in agreement.

"I think we understand each other, Sheriff," James said.

"And now, if it's all right with you, I'll go and get that hotel room." He stood and offered his hand. "I appreciate your time, sir. I want you to know that things in my life have done a turnaround. I've wanted to turn my life in a new direction, and this might be the very thing I need. Working on a ranch was good for me, but I'm ready for something else. This feels like a mighty decent place to hang my hat for a while, and I'm plannin' on settlin' in and makin' a good life here."

Brace Caulfield nodded. "It's a dandy place to live. Lots of good folks hereabouts. In fact," he said, rising from his chair, "here comes one of them right now."

Across the threshold from James stood a tall man, dark haired with piercing blue eyes. "One what, Sheriff?" he asked.

"One of the nice folks from this town," Brace answered with a laugh. "At least I keep telling folks you're a nice fella."

"Well, if you hear of any other nice fellas looking for a job, send them on out to my place. I need a new hired hand."

"Well, you can't have this one, Nick. I'm lookin' him over for the job of deputy."

He turned then to James. "This here is Nicholas Garvey, one of the ranchers hereabouts. If you don't like the offer I make you, maybe he can do better for you."

"I've kinda got my heart set on being a lawman," James said.

"Any special reason?" Nicholas asked.

James stood a bit straighter. "I've got a yen to see justice done. Maybe because I haven't always paid my dues the way I should have, and I need to make up for it. My brother and I buried my pa up in Oklahoma a couple of years ago and it did my heart good when the crook that killed him got sent away for the rest of his life."

"You can't seek revenge on your pa by chasing down the men who misbehave in this town, son," Brace said.

"I don't want revenge. I've already seen the man go off to prison. But I want the chance to be a part of a system that works, where those who hurt others are brought to justice and punished for their crimes. Whether it be a stay in jail or in a federal prison."

"Sounds like your candidate has his head screwed on straight," Nicholas offered, looking James over thoroughly, then smiling at the young man, as if he'd sought imperfections, and failed to find them.

"We'll see," Brace said. "At any rate, I'll meet you for supper at the hotel about six, James. Is that the name your family calls you? James?"

"My brother and sister-in-law have been known to call me Jamie," he said with a grin.

"Sounds like a good name to me. I think I'll pin it on you officially, after we talk tonight. Seems to me I'd better hunt up a deputy's badge for you."

A sense of peace enveloped Jamie. Perhaps his soul searching and wandering days would cease.

Chapter One

Benning, Texas, Spring 1903

"I've been your deputy, working in this office with you for eight years, Sheriff." Jamie leaned against the door frame and managed to roll up his life over the past eight years into a neat bundle. A bundle he no longer wanted to live with.

"I assume you're about to quit," Brace said. "And I don't like it, not one little bit. Unhappy with me? Or the wages? Or just the life of a deputy, in general?"

"None of the choices you've just pulled out of the hat," Jamie returned quickly. "I just don't feel that I'm getting anywhere. I'm a whiz at breaking up fights in the saloons, I'm up to date on all the wanted posters and to tell the truth, I'm sick and tired of standing on the sidelines while you've managed in the past four years to put together a life with the prettiest girl in town, along with you and Sarah adopting her nephew.

"But I'll have to admit, it's been a real education watching you with Sarah and Stephen. Hope I can do as well as you when I get a family of my own."

"I'll have to admit that marriage agrees with me."

"Hope I can say that someday. But for now I've about decided I need to be doing something different with myself."

Brace leaned back in his chair and surveyed his deputy. "To tell the truth, I've been thinking about a proposition I'd like to toss in your direction. See what you think of it."

"Does it include my moving on? Leaving Benning?"

"You don't sound happy about that idea," Brace said. "You haven't put down any roots here, Jamie. You got a problem with living somewhere else?"

"No. But I tend to be a creature of habit." He paused and stood erect, facing the man who had been his mentor and friend. "If you've got something to offer me, let's hear it. I suspect you wouldn't put me on the wrong track, Sheriff."

"Well, to tell the truth, I don't know much myself about the place I'd like to send you. But clear across the state is a piece of property that belongs to my son, Stephen."

"The ranch he inherited from his birth father's family?"

"The very one," Brace said. "There's a man running things on the ranch on a temporary basis, but I'd feel better about the whole thing if I knew more about what was going on behind the letters I get from him. He was the ranch foreman before Stephen's grandfather died three years ago and I've let it go long enough the way it is. The judge ordered us to put a man of my own in place as manager when Sarah and I adopted Stephen legally. It'll give me more control over the ranch, and there'll be a better chance of Stephen taking over a thriving concern when he's old enough."

"Are we talking about me running the ranch?"

"Well, I always did say you catch on quick," Brace said with a chuckle. "Didn't take you long to figure that one out, did it?"

"Let me think about it, Brace. I'll need to know what's expected of me to begin with."

"Just be yourself, get to know the men and make the ranch successful. I'm laying odds you can do that."

"Anything else I should know if I decide to do this?" Jamie felt there was a gap in the information. Something he couldn't put his finger on.

"I've heard that there's a fly in the ointment," Brace admitted. "The daughter of the foreman has been causing some problems among the men. Her daddy is right fond of her, but in one case a couple of the men have come to blows over her, and things are unsettled right now. Sort of a state of armed warfare."

Jamie shook his head. "You're talking about sending me into a full-fledged battle, aren't you?"

"If I didn't think you could handle things, I wouldn't have brought it up or made you an offer. There's a nice, big raise in pay attached, son. Enough to make it worth your while."

"I've kept my nose clean here in Benning, Brace. Learned that dealing with a female is mighty wearing on a man. Especially if it's a woman who already has a string of admirers a mile long and would no doubt like to add another one to her list."

"You can handle it. You've managed to handle yourself pretty well here. Not a woman in sight has complained about you."

"I'm pretty boring these days. Kind of a reformed scamp, Sheriff. I learned a long time ago to behave myself with the ladies."

Brace leaned back in his chair and shot Jamie an inquiring look. "Maybe you really did learn your lesson, son. I haven't pried too much into your past, but I'm sure you've got one worth talking about."

"I'm not much for making a fuss over something I can't erase from my record. I've told you before about my brother and his wife and their two children. They're still in Oklahoma, and we're on good terms," Jamie said. "That's the extent of my family, except for my mother, who lives near Dallas with her sister."

"Well, I've found you to be honest and capable. If you want the job, it's yours."

Three weeks later Jamie arrived at his destination. The ranch looked to be a prosperous one, he decided. He rode up to the sign, hanging over a long lane that obviously led to the house and a series of outbuildings beyond it. The name on the sign was simple: Clark & Sons. It would have to be changed, Jamie thought. The present owner was still related to the Clark family, but Stephen was officially named Caulfield, and as the legal deed holder to the land and buildings on it, even though he was underage—just twelve years old—he deserved to have a say in the name of his property.

Maybe he'd write to Stephen and let him figure out a name; perhaps the boy would want to consult with Brace and Sarah before he made up his mind. On the other hand, it wouldn't hurt to come up with a new sign for the place, something that would reflect a new owner. In the meantime, there were folks to meet and a job to do right here. His horse turned eagerly up the lane and Jamie took note of a smoke house, chicken coop and a large barn. As if the gelding scented hay and oats in his future, he broke into a quick trot.

It had been a long ride from Benning, north of Dallas, but finding the ranch in good condition and catching sight of a herd of healthy-appearing cattle in the verdant pasture beside the lane made Jamie feel he'd come home here near the border between Texas and New Mexico. And with that in mind, he rode up to the house and around it to the back door. A watering trough with a pitcher pump next to it, which would pro-

vide fresh water for his horse, drew his attention, and he rode
in that direction, past a woodshed whose open door revealed
a good supply within.

Removing the bit from his gelding's mouth, he watched
as the horse drank deeply, then led him to a nearby hitching
rail to tie him firmly in place. A ranch hand came from the
barn as Jamie lifted his saddlebags from the animal's back.

"Hi there, mister," the tall, lanky cowhand called out.
"Who you lookin' for?"

"Whoever's in charge," Jamie answered, knowing well
that the foreman's name was Hank Powers.

"That would be Hank," the cowhand said. "He's in the
house. Can I walk your horse for you?"

"Sure thing. He's had a long morning, and he needs to be
cooled before I feed him."

"Yes sir, I can do that. My name's Chet Dawson by the
way." He looked Jamie over with apparent interest. "You
wouldn't be the new man from Benning, would you?"

"The very one," Jamie said. "Were you expecting me?"

"Yeah, Hank told us you were on your way. Welcome to
the ranch."

"Thanks," Jamie answered agreeably, and turned to the
house.

The back door opened and a young woman stood on the
threshold, looking at him with interest. She stepped back as
he approached and he followed her into the kitchen. A man sat
at the table, a full plate of food before him, a fork in his hand.

"Mr. Powers?" Jamie asked, removing his hat and standing just inside the doorway.

"That's me, son," the man answered. "But the name is
Hank. And you're Jamie, unless I miss my guess." After a mo-
ment's pause, he looked up at the young woman beside him.
"This is my daughter, Alexis."

The woman had eyes like none he'd ever seen before, green as grass, with a sparkle built in, Jamie decided. They glittered in the light from the open door as she allowed her gaze to sweep over him. "I understand you've been sheriff for some time, east of here," she said, her voice low, with a tinge of humor touching her words.

"No," Jamie replied honestly. "I've been a deputy, and that's a long way from being a sheriff, ma'am. But I've done the job for eight years."

"Your boss seems to think you qualify for a chance at running this ranch," Hank said, his cool eyes doing a once-over on Jamie, making him feel like a prize pig at the county fair.

"That's what he told me. It was a mighty appealing offer or I wouldn't have left a sure thing in Benning to ride clear across the state to come here."

"Well, welcome," Hank said expansively. "You've just freed me up to handle my own concerns, instead of minding the store here."

"Where do I put my gear?" Jamie asked, feeling a need for coffee and a chair that would receive his tired body. Riding as he had, he'd come to appreciate the comfort of a soft bed and cup of fresh-brewed coffee, neither of which he'd been offered for several days. Sleeping under a tree and drinking the dregs of last night's coffee for his breakfast was a vivid memory as he scented the freshness of the cup delivered to the table before him.

"Just drop your saddlebag on the floor and we'll fix you up with a place to put it once you've had some food," Alexis told him, watching as he pulled the sugar bowl toward him and spooned a heaping teaspoon of sugar into his black coffee.

"No cream?" she asked.

He shook his head as he picked up his cup. "No, this is

fine." And fine it was, dark, thick and sweet, tasting of fragrant coffee beans, freshly ground.

Alexis filled a plate from the skillets on the stove, lifting pancakes from one, sausage from another, then positioned it squarely before Jamie. "I hope you're hungry," she said, placing a fork beside his plate.

He looked up at her, noting the cool flash of silver in her green eyes, contrasting with the warmth of full lips that revealed even white teeth as she spoke. Her hair was golden, drawn up at the back of her head, small wispy curls escaping to frame her face. It was no wonder the men were *ga-ga* over her, he decided. Pretty as a picture, and no doubt more than aware of it. Her features were just short of being considered beautiful, with a small cleft in her chin and a birthmark on her right cheek, just beneath her temple.

Not that either of those defects would put off a determined man, set on seduction. He was no exception to the rule, given his lack of female companionship over the past little while. Longer than that. He'd not been out courting or even walking a young lady home from church or one of the dances held in Benning in months. As he'd promised the sheriff there, he'd kept his hands to himself and not been a hand with the ladies even when the opportunity arose.

For some reason, his energy had gone into his work, women taking a backseat to his job in the sheriff's office. Now he had a whole new set of circumstances staring him in the face, number one being his new job. There wasn't time to be looking at a woman, even one as pretty and appealing as Alexis Powers. But he might just consider the matter. Sometimes a man needed the warmth of a woman and unless he missed his guess, this one was a prime specimen.

He tucked into his plate of food, relishing the light pancakes especially. "Tastes like the pancakes my mama used to make me for breakfast." His approval was apparent, and Alexis offered him two more, balanced on her pancake turner. Jamie nodded his thanks at the offer, and buttered them lavishly, then poured on a generous helping of syrup.

Across the table from him, Hank finished up his own share of the food and leaned back in his chair, as if assessing the young man who'd come to take over the running of the ranch. "What are your plans, Webster?" His query was nicely worded, but his eyes told a different story, flashing fire in Jamie's direction.

"Haven't got any yet," James answered. "I just got here, Hank. Give me a week to settle in and I'll answer your questions."

"Is Brace Caulfield unhappy with my work here? He hasn't given me any grief up until now," Hank said. "I've kept him up to date on everything that goes on."

"He's pleased the ranch is thriving, but he seems to want someone in charge who'll have a vested interest in the ranch. And that's me. I answer directly to Brace, with an eye to presenting a first-class operation to the boy when the time comes for him to take over."

"He's a Clark," Hank said quietly, and yet Jamie caught a hint of bitterness in the words.

"Yeah, he is. And just what do you mean by that?" Jamie asked, on the alert for the man's negative attitude toward Stephen. The boy might have been born a Clark, but Brace and Sarah had given him more than just a new name.

Hank shrugged, a slow movement of his wide shoulders. "Just that old man Clark was pretty much a rascal, and so were the sons. I suspect blood runs true in the family, at least from what I've seen for myself, and I don't look for much in the boy."

"The *boy,* as you call him, is named Stephen and is being

brought up by Brace Caulfield and his wife, Sarah, Stephen's aunt. Even though he came from a father who abused him, he has a good home and will have a top-notch upbringing. I don't think he'll be a disgrace to his folks, and one day he's going to take over this ranch and run it well, contrary to what his heritage suggests might be the case. Sarah's twin was his mother and he's gonna do her proud."

"You ever consider bein' a lawyer?" Hank asked with a grin. "You do a dandy job of defending the boy."

"I suspect he's too honest to be a lawyer," Alexis said quietly, the coffeepot in her hand as she approached the table and the two men sitting there. "More coffee, Mr. Webster?" she asked.

"Thanks, I believe I will," Jamie said, careful not to pay any particular attention to the girl. Woman is more like it, he thought glancing down to where her booted feet stood beside his chair. It was understandable that the men on this ranch were squabbling for the chance to court her. Causing discord among the men was forbidden, though, and he would not stand for it.

"And what do you do with your time, Miss Alexis?" he asked, picking up his cup.

"I cook a bit, ride a lot and in general do whatever needs to be done. I'm more interested in the young foals, but that job is pretty well already taken by men probably more capable than I am. My father won't let me work on the round-up or in the branding pens, but I lend a hand with the orphaned calves when necessary. I'm real handy with a bottle when the mama has lost the battle and a calf is left alone."

"A lot of those for you to tend?" Jamie asked, looking up at her with bland interest. At least he hoped his look didn't hold a shred of the attraction he felt for the girl.

"Usually several in the spring, only two this year. We were lucky." She turned and set the coffeepot back on the stove and hesitated.

"What do you plan on doing with your time, Mr. Webster?"

"Can we make it Jamie, or James?" he asked with a bland smile. "Whichever you like will do."

She turned then, gave him a long look as if she read his thoughts, and her answer was what he had expected. "If you'll be informal enough to call me Alex or Alexis, whichever you like."

"I can do that," Jamie answered quickly. "If it's all right with your pa."

"She's her own woman," Hank said, leaning back in his chair and smiling at his daughter. "I quit tellin' her what to do when she started puttin' her hair up."

Jamie looked at Alexis, whose hair hung in golden splendor around her shoulders and halfway down her back. "And when was that?" he asked.

"Well, most of the time she's all gussied up with that mop of hair on top of her head or hanging in a braid down her back. It's usually only at breakfast time that we see her this-a-way." Hank laughed and shot a tender look at his daughter. "I kinda like breakfast," he said softly.

Alexis left the stove to fend for itself and circled the table to stand next to her father. "He's a bit prejudiced," she told Jamie, bending to plant a kiss on her father's temple.

"I can see why." Jamie swallowed the rest of his coffee and stood, wondering how those lips would taste against his own. "I'm gonna take a look around, if you don't mind," he said to Hank. "Kinda get the feel of things."

"No problem with that. It's all yours now, Webster."

"Not really," Jamie said, contradicting the man. "You'll still have a bundle of work to do, keeping up with all the numbers and giving me tips. Right now I'd like to meet the men who are working close-by."

"I wrote to Caulfield and told him I'd give you my support. I'll be happy to do whatever you have in mind for me."

It was almost too easy, Jamie thought. Too slick a turnover, with a stranger coming in and the foreman stepping back without an argument. And yet, maybe Hank was tired of the hassle involved with dealing with men and a ranch of this size.

"I'll come out with you and we can ride around to where the men are working," Hank said. "You want a different horse, or are you planning to use your own?"

"My gelding is pretty worn-out from crossing Texas in the past few days," Jamie said. "What do you have in the barn?"

"A couple of nice mares and a hot-blooded stallion that'll give you a run for your money. I guess you get to choose any horse you want, boss."

Jamie lifted an eyebrow and hitched up his trousers, feeling his gun as it thumped against his thigh. "I'm not much for being the bossy type, Hank. I hope you know right off the bat that I'm not here to make any sweeping changes or chop any heads off. I'm just doing a job for my boss. And that's the man I answer to in the long run."

"I've already exchanged 'howdies' with Chet," Jamie said. "Just haven't shaken his hand yet."

"Here's your chance then," Hank said as their horses moved to stand beside that of the ranch hand in question.

Jamie stuck out his right hand and Chet did not hesitate, grasping it in a friendly manner. "Yes sir, I've taken a gander at this fella before, Hank. He rides a right pretty horse."

"Pretty horse?" Hank repeated, lifting his eyebrow as if he mocked the phrase.

"You know what I'm sayin'," Chet said with a laugh. "If

it was a mare, I'd call her a beauty. Since he rides a gelding, and a nice-lookin' pinto at that, he's simply pretty."

"Chet's our number one hand around here," Hank said with a grin in Jamie's direction. "He's an old-timer. Been around for more years than I have."

"This is home," Chet said, with a trace of smug satisfaction in his voice. "I was raised here by my pa after my mother died."

"Who else do we have working out here?" Jamie asked, nodding at Chet's words. "I'll warrant there's no one else with your record."

"Nope. But Slim comes right close," Chet told him. "He's been here since he was sixteen or so. A good man with horses. He's out back with the horses right now."

The girl had mentioned horses, he remembered, stating her liking for them. "You're running a big herd of horses, along with your cattle here?" Jamie asked.

Hank nodded. "If it's a bad year for cattle, drought or flood conditions or whatever might happen along to give us problems, we can rely on the horses to take up the slack. We had a big storm a few years ago in February, snowed us in for three days, and all the time we had cows calving out in the back forty. Lost twelve of our heifers and most of their calves. We'd just as soon not see that happen again. Winter storms can be disasters for us."

"Why hadn't you brought the cows in closer to the barn, knowing they were at risk?" Jamie asked, his words a blunt criticism of Hank's actions.

"The storm hit before we were prepared for it. It had been warming up right well for a couple of weeks, and no one looked for snow, least of all me."

"Maybe we'll bring the pregnant cows in close next winter and keep them within sight. I'd hate to see that sort of thing happen again," Jamie said firmly.

"You're right," Hank told him. "In fact, I'm beginning to think you'll be good for the Clark ranch. You're young and you're bound to have fresh ideas."

"That's another thing. We're gonna change the name of the ranch," Jamie told him. "Until I get other instructions from Brace Caulfield, we'll call this place the Double C. I'd like to see a sign put together and hung down at the county road. What do you think?"

"Clark and Caulfield, huh? Sounds all right to me."

"Who can make a sign? A big one on a slab of hardwood," Jamie asked.

Chet spoke up quickly. "That would be Woody, and you get one guess why we call him that." His chuckle was short and he underlined his words. "The man is a whiz with anything to do with building stuff or working with wood. He's been around for years, and the big house has a bunch of his furniture inside. Take a look at the tables in the parlor, Webster," he said, his pride audible, as if he were, in some way, responsible for Woody's reputation.

"I'll do that." Jamie looked around, back toward the barn. "Where is he now?"

"Working on new mangers for the standing stalls," Chet told him. "We went over the barn pretty good, and Woody said they needed to be replaced. And what Woody says, goes, as far as fixin' up the barn is concerned."

"Sounds like a handy fella to have around." Jamie said, thinking he'd like to meet this paragon of woodworking today.

"You'll find out," Chet told him flatly. "We all depend on Woody."

Jamie turned his mount in a tight circle and headed back to the barn. "I'll take a look here before we go any farther afield," he told Hank. The stallion he'd chosen to ride was skittish, but Jamie held him in with a firm hand, and, once he'd dismounted, led him into the barn, seeking the man in question.

The sound of a hammer drew him down the aisle and toward the farthest stall. A big man, easily six inches or so past six feet tall, backed into the aisle ahead of him and turned to face Jamie.

"You must be Woody," Jamie said. "I've been hearing about you."

"Well, don't believe everything you hear," the big man said. "I don't make magic with my saw and hammer. In fact, I just do what I enjoy most, and the boss thinks I'm a wonder child."

"If the interior of this barn is a tribute to your skill, I'd have to agree with him," Jamie said, surveying the well-built stalls. "Can you work as well with the livestock as you do with wood?"

"You better believe it," Woody said. "I was raised on a horse by my pa. Been herding cattle for twenty years or so."

Jamie stuck out his hand. "I think we'll get along just fine, Woody." In a few words, Jamie told the man what he wanted, measuring the length and width of the sign he had in mind with outstretched arms, and Woody only nodded agreeably. "Does that sound like something you can put together in a few days?" Jamie asked.

"Send Miss Alex out to print the letters you want on the sign, so I can chip them out and paint them black, and I'll have it done by tonight."

"Alexis?" Jamie was surprised by the request.

"Yeah, I don't read or write real good and she's always a good one to lend a hand."

"I'll ask her, then."

"Ask me what?" From behind him, the woman's voice spoke a challenge and Jamie turned to her.

"Will you give Woody a hand with a sign he's about to make for the ranch?"

"He knows I will," she said, shooting a wide smile in the ranch hand's direction.

Woody was a bit old for her, but she obviously enjoyed practicing her feminine wiles on any handy male. "I'll leave you to it, then," Jamie said, leading his horse past the girl and out the door. She turned as he passed her by, and he was struck again by her eyes, which seemed as bright as the new leaves on a maple tree in the spring.

"Anybody ever tell you you've got eyes that could tempt a man to lose his head?" he asked her quietly, lest Woody hear him. It was bad enough he was flirting with the girl, but to let someone else be privy to his words was not quite the thing, he thought.

And as if she had heard such a flattering query on a daily basis, Alexis only nodded. "Among other things I've been told," she said, "such as hair like sunshine and a face likely to draw men like flies. I'm not impressed."

He'd never been scorned quite so readily, Jamie thought, and yet it made the pursuit all the sweeter, knowing he had to overcome the girl's distrust of him and the male sex in general. At least that was the message he'd gotten from her remarks.

"I wasn't trying to impress you," he told her with a grin, "merely stating a fact."

"It takes more than a smart remark about my green eyes to make me sit up and take notice of a man. I'm not much on men, and certainly cowhands aren't my first choice as suitors."

"Who said I was aiming to be a suitor? I had more in mind a few minutes in the moonlight or on the back porch, rocking the swing back and forth."

"A few minutes in the moonlight? I don't think so. I'm particular about who I spend my time with, and my nighttime hours are spent in the house."

"Your pa watches over you pretty closely, I'll bet," Jamie said. "I could relieve him of the chore a couple of evenings a week. Maybe I'll approach him and see what he thinks of the idea."

"I think you'd better keep your ideas to yourself, and leave me alone. I'm not in the market for a man."

Jamie tipped his hat and walked on, circling his horse and then springing into the saddle with an easy movement. "We'll see," he said, tipping his hat and offering a small salute in her direction.

Her mouth was drawn into a prim line and he was sorely tempted to pick her up and sling her across his saddle. His mouth twitched as he thought of kissing her into submission. She offered a challenge, and he was never one to turn his back on such a thing. Yet, making his way here with care was important. He couldn't do anything to cause Brace's temper to flare in his direction no matter how tempting the woman was.

This job was made for a man like James Webster, working with cows, horses and a handful of cowhands who were already in place and doing a good job. A woman could not be allowed to gain his attention to the extent that he neglected his duties here.

No matter that she was pretty. No, make that lovely, for her golden hair and tempting form were enough to bring James, or any man, he decided promptly, to attention. Features that might grace a statue formed her face, a trim nose, wide eyes that made his gaze veer back to her again, not to mention her lithe and lissome body that filled out the shirt and trousers she wore in an elegant fashion.

He felt an urge to lay his hands on her, and he turned aside, dousing it firmly. She was marriage material and he wasn't ready yet. The memory of one girl in his past still haunted him. Loris, his first real love, a girl he had hurt, almost beyond repair. A woman he should have married. Now she was wed to his brother, and he could only ruefully regret his actions that had lost him her love.

He'd do well to keep his hands and his hungry eyes off Alexis. She was trouble.

Chapter Two

The stench of burning hair and the scorched flesh beneath it were familiar to Jamie, but still not welcome. He'd worked hard for two months, branding calves, cutting bullocks and herding cattle. But living with the odor of the branding iron doing its work was something he was not particularly fond of.

Yet, the other men were sweating as much as he, were at least as tired as his weary body proclaimed with aches and pains in every possible muscle he owned. And he would not rest while they labored. According to Hank, he had the right to oversee, observe and direct the work, but Jamie had learned from a master in Missouri, and found that the men respected a foreman more if he knew how to work alongside them, and did so without making a fuss over it.

They'd set up camp at the farthest north end of the ranch, sleeping on the ground, working long hours and striving to finish the job in record time. Jamie had gained the friendship of his men, found them to be loyal and honest, and most of all trustworthy. If one of them said he would do a chore, he did it. No dithering, no excuses, just a job well done.

"You tired, cowboy?" Alexis spoke from behind him as he sat close to the campfire. She'd shown up today, bedroll behind her saddle, and Cookie had told him that it was her usual habit to come in at the end of branding and lend a hand.

The men appreciated her slender form flitting around the camp, laughed at her remarks and seemed to perk up, their aching bodies forgotten for a while, as they worshipped at her feet. Figuratively speaking, of course, but it wasn't too far a stretch of the imagination to visualize them surrounding her in such a manner.

Now she had approached him, and Jamie swallowed the sharp retort that hovered on his lips. If the girl thought he was the latest in her list of conquests, she was wrong. He'd managed to stay clear of her, and though she tempted him mightily, he'd forged a path that didn't include dallying with Alexis Powers.

"We're all tired, Alex," he said moodily, staring into the smouldering coals before him. "Branding cattle is a hard job and these men have worked for ten days, nonstop."

"They tell me you're doing more than your share, Jamie." She circled him and stood between his spot on the ground and the dying fire. "I suspect Brace Caulfield knew what he was doing when he sent you here. My father sure hasn't found any fault with you, and that's a rare one. He can always pick a man apart, given a while to watch him operate. You've passed the test, I suspect."

Jamie nodded, looking up at the challenge that glittered in her eyes. "I'm sure I'm pleased about that, Alex. It's always nice to gain appreciation for what you do. I'm no exception."

"Can I sit down by you?" she asked, her voice lowering as though she didn't want to be overheard.

"Sure. The ground's kinda hard, but it beats standing there." He felt a twinge of guilt at his offhanded invitation, but she seemed not to notice his words as anything but welcoming.

With a smooth, almost melting glide, she settled beside him, and he felt himself blinking at her method of movement. She'd gone from standing to sitting cross-legged next to him with one easy bend of legs and body. As if her bones were elastic, her muscles more flexible than was normal. "Graceful" was the word he chose to describe her.

Graceful and lovely. Quite a combination. Certainly enough to tempt a man almost beyond reason. And James Webster was a man. He fought the urge to wrap his arm around her waist and tug her closer. His eyes touched the bridge of her nose, the slope of her cheek and the soft pouting lines of her mouth. Unless he was mightily mistaken, the lady was trying to work her way under his skin.

"You haven't paid much attention to me," she said quietly, leaning forward, her elbows on her knees, her chin cupped in her hands.

"I didn't know that was a part of my job. I'd have thought you were wearing a 'hands off' sign around your neck, if your father's attitude was anything to go by. You're a flirt, Miss Powers, and on top of that I consider you forbidden territory."

She turned her head and her smile was feline, like a cat who spies a mouse and is contemplating its capture. "I make the rules, Mr. Webster. And in case you've forgotten, my name is Alexis."

"I forget very little, ma'am. I'm well aware of your name. And I'm aware that you're about the most tempting little piece of womanhood I've run across in quite some time."

"It doesn't show," she said flatly. "You've gone out of your way to ignore me."

"Trust me. You don't want me to pay any mind to you. I play for keeps."

"For keeps? And what is that supposed to mean?"

"I'm not sixteen years old, ma'am. I'm a full-grown man, with all the right equipment to enjoy myself with a woman. I don't do things halfway. If you hang around me very long, you're likely to find yourself in a heap of trouble."

Alexis laughed, a buoyant sound that pleased him, and tempted him mightily.

"Do I look worried? You won't be the first man to try frightening me. I learned a long time ago that men were only little boys, grown up. The only difference is that you're bigger than I am, stronger and probably able to pick me up with one hand. All of that aside, I'm a woman who knows her own mind, and the fact that I sat down here to talk to you doesn't make me available to you. Not in any other way than that of a friend."

"You think I can pick you up in one hand?" He'd caught that part of her speech, smiled to himself as he gauged her height and weight and decided she was right. If she weighed much over a hundred pounds, he'd be surprised. And her height brought her just to his chin, probably an inch or two over five feet. A womanly little package indeed, with much to offer a man.

"Yeah, I do," she answered, laughing again. "I've seen you roping and rassling calves to the ground, and a couple of good-sized bullocks, too. I'll bet you're a tough customer to cross, James Webster. And I have no intention of taking you on."

"Don't you, now?" he asked softly, looking down at her profile, at the line of her chin, her clasped hands beneath it, at the small dip at the bridge of her nose, not noticeable from the front view, but intriguing from where he was sitting.

She looked at him, a quick flash of green eyes, and sat up straight, her head lifting as if she scented something that appealed to her. "I'm no dummy, James. You've been around, I'll bet. You've probably had women from here to yonder and back, and I'm not about to be added to your list."

"How about adding me to your list, then?" he asked bluntly. "I understand that you've had the men here lined up for a smile from you for a long time now."

"Who on earth told you that?" she asked, seeming indignant at his words.

"My boss. Said that you were the most popular creature on this ranch. Told me that all the hands were vying for your attention."

"And have you seen me leading anyone on?" she asked smartly. "Do I come across as a woman of dubious virtue?"

Jamie grinned at her. "No, I'd say you were very much a virgin, sweetheart." He watched as a dark flush rose to cover her cheeks. "You're smart enough to keep the men at bay, at least until the right one comes along and is willing to pay the price for a spot in your bed."

"Pay the price? What is that supposed to mean?" She looked stunned at his words, and he found himself rethinking the harsh statement he'd made.

"I didn't mean to offend you, Alex. Far from it, in fact. I think you're a smart lady, not likely to fall for a line of blarney from any man. I expect one day you'll marry well, and make your daddy proud of you."

"And the price I'll ask for that is?"

"A license to marry, a good bank account and the promise of a man who will cater to your every whim and follow you around like a faithful hound for the rest of your life."

She turned away, and he swallowed hard. She was worth every bit of that, and he wondered if she had even considered what it would take for a man to come up to her father's requirements for her hand in marriage.

"You don't like me, do you?" she asked.

It was his turn to laugh, and he did so with pleasure. If the woman only knew! "I like you, sweetheart. Well enough to haul you off into the woods and make love to you till morning. But, of course, I'm not gonna do that. I'd be layin' my head on a chopping block if I tried such a stunt."

She turned back to him and her chin was lifted a bit, her eyes flashing green fire in his direction. "And you think I'd have nothing to say about that? You think I'd just go along with you without a protest?"

"If I wanted to cart you off, you wouldn't have a word to say. At least you wouldn't be saying anything. I'd have your mouth sufficiently covered to make sure you didn't sound an alarm, and we'd be in the midst of those trees in seconds." He grinned at her again. "But don't get upset, I'm not plannin' on any such a thing, Alex. When I take you to bed, it'll be all aboveboard and legal."

"Legal?" She seemed stunned and he leaned forward, taking advantage of the moment of indecision on her part, placing his mouth squarely on hers and lifting his hand to the back of her head. The kiss was long, warm and wet, Jamie not averse to exploring her mouth, no matter the men who worked just yards away and were likely to be watching.

She pulled away, and he allowed it, removing his hand from her head to hold her shoulder, lest she leap to her feet and disappear. "What do you mean?" she asked. And then blushed as if his words had finally penetrated her mind. "Legal? Like in marriage?"

"Like in marriage," he said quietly. "I've learned not to leap into the fire ahead of the bucket brigade, sweetheart. I'm not into taking a virgin's prized possession ahead of time. I can wait."

She flushed even deeper, her face rosy, her eyes widening.

"You can wait? You surely can, Mr. Webster. For the rest of your life, as far as I'm concerned. Don't try to kiss me again. I won't have it."

With another smooth, lithe movement, she stood and looked down at him. "I wish you a good night's sleep, Mr. Webster. And unless a rattlesnake should come calling, you'll probably be just fine in your blanket roll." Not looking back, she strolled from his side and made her way to the chuck wagon, where Cookie sat on a bench, drinking a cup of coffee.

He looked up at his visitor and smiled a welcome, apparently asking her if she wanted to join him in toasting the night with a mug of her own. Alexis nodded and sat beside him, watching as he bent to pour another cupful from the pot over the flames. She took it from him, smiling with a dazzling display of white teeth, and then set about charming the old man, laughing at his words, drinking his coffee and knowing full well that James was watching.

He could almost read her mind, he decided. He'd named her rightly. She was a flirt, a woman without fear of being scorned by any man, and it was just his luck to be besotted by her. Even as he watched her, his hands itched to touch her perfect skin, to run his fingers through the length of her golden hair. She'd coiled it up atop her head in a braid, and he fantasized about taking it down, undoing the braid and fluffing it around her shoulders and down her back.

He wanted to kiss her again, and the memory of her soft mouth, of the sweetness of her flesh, was a spur in his hide, a burr beneath his saddle. He could, as ranch foreman, as overseer of the whole place, demand that she leave the camp in the morning, once the sun rose, and make her way back to the ranch house.

For her own protection, it would be the best idea. And yet,

it would take her from his sight, from his hearing. That laugh that rippled on the air would be gone. The green eyes that sent him mixed messages would be miles away, and he would yearn for her presence here, no matter how she aggravated him and played havoc with his life.

The woman was exactly what he'd been looking for, during all the years when he played the field, when his methods had been so heartless, so uncaring to the females he'd loved and left behind. Now, this little girl…no, this woman, he thought, had turned his brain to mush, his manhood to iron and given him a foretaste of a sleepless night, one in which he would mentally seek out her bedroll and crawl in beside her.

He watched her as she rose and left the camp cook, wending her way through the three campfires that burned, each of them warming several men, each of whom owned admiring masculine eyes, all of them aimed in her direction.

When she'd made the half circle that brought her past his position, he called her name, softly, but with enough sound to carry to her listening ears. She halted her progress and looked at him, unmoving.

"Come here, Alex," he said. And wonder of wonders, she did as he'd asked. Although commanded might be a better term, he thought.

"What do you want?" she asked, standing before him.

"I want you to unroll your blanket over here, near mine," he said firmly. "I'm planning to keep an eye on you tonight."

"You're going to look after me? I doubt that."

"You'd better believe it, honey. I don't want your daddy on my tail should anybody cause you any trouble out here."

"These men all know me. They know better than to give me any grief." Her words sounded firm, but he sensed a thread of doubt in her posture, her hands stuffed into her pockets, her eyes shifting around the area surrounding them.

"Even so, Alex, I want you over here. I want to be able to see anything that happens during the night. And in case you're going to protest, I'll tell you right now that I'm a light sleeper. I don't miss much."

"I'll just bet you don't." Stalking to where she'd stowed her bedroll, near the chuck wagon, she brought it back, halting about six feet away from him, then rolled it open and sat down. "Happy now?" she asked.

He deigned to answer, only shooting her a complacent look, guaranteed to make her stew, designed to fuel her fires of anger.

It was late when Jamie sought his bed. The girl who'd rolled up in a blanket near him was breathing evenly, her mouth partially open, soft sounds escaping in the night. "I'll bet she'd be madder than a wet hen if I told her she snores," he muttered to himself.

And decided that was one bit of information he'd do well to keep to himself.

"Coffee's on." It was the universal call of the chuck wagon, welcomed by all within the sound of Cookie's voice. Jamie was no exception. He rolled from his place on the hard ground and made quick work of folding his bedroll, then placing it inside the wagon where he'd stowed his gear.

A head of golden hair, reflecting the sun's earliest beams, lay almost completely covered by a blanket, and the owner was curled within the folds of the drab covering. "Alex. Time to get up," Jamie said quietly. "Breakfast is almost ready."

"Not hungry," she muttered, pulling the corner of the blanket higher to better cover her head.

"You need to eat. Come on now." Jamie walked to her, crouched beside her and tugged at the blanket. A pair of blinking eyes tried to focus on his face, and he laughed with a healthy sense of amusement he hadn't felt in a long time. "You look like a baby owl," he whispered, lest he be over-heard by any nearby men.

"Thanks so much, sir," she said, sitting up amid her rumpled blankets. "I'm sure I'm a sight to behold this morning."

Jamie grinned wolfishly. "You have no idea, ma'am. No idea whatsoever. Let me just say that I wouldn't mind seeing you every morning just this way."

"Fat chance of that," she snarled, her words angry, uttered in a voice that growled them aloud.

Jamie was entertained by her bad temper. He wanted to bend down to her, kiss her out of her bad mood and then tumble her back to the ground and hold her firmly in his embrace. And where had that thought come from?

It was morning, there was work to be done, men to be directed, horses to be saddled and calves to be roped. Hopefully today would finish up the job. They'd been at it for two days already, but it was getting to be cleanup time. Only a few of the calves and young bulls were still unbranded. In a rope corral, they awaited their turn with the branding iron or the clamp that would ensure their placid behavior over the next year, or until they were sold as steers on the market.

Alex rose stiffly, as if her muscles protested the hard ground, and then bent to retrieve her blankets, folding them quickly. She turned to Jamie, her bedroll over her arms before her, her eyes still blinking at the bright sunlight that assailed them from the eastern sky.

"I want you to be careful today," Jamie said quietly. "You're my responsibility, and I don't care how many times you've helped with the branding, it's still a dangerous place for a woman. Don't get hurt, Alex, or your dad will have my neck in a noose."

"You're treating me like a child," she told him.

"I know very well that you're not a child, but I'm trying to make you see the effect you have on the men when you're working with them. They're all aware that you're a woman, full grown, but they'll keep an eye out for you, wanting to protect you from harm. I'll tell you this just once. Don't cause me any trouble or I'll be after you quicker than you can say 'scat.'"

Her eyes widened again as he spoke and then she looked aside. Hell, if he didn't know better, he'd think he'd hurt her feelings.

"I know enough not to get in the way," she said quietly, walking away toward the chuck wagon.

Jamie felt a moment's pause, retracing his words and then her response to them. He'd been harsher than he'd intended. And above all, he wasn't trying to frighten her. Only make her aware of her impact on these men.

On him, if the truth be known.

The men finished up their work by midafternoon, and with the satisfaction of a job well done, they packed up camp and headed back to the barn, a ride of two hours or better. The chuck wagon came last, Alexis riding with Cookie, her horse tied on behind.

Jamie could find no fault with her behavior today, he decided, riding just ahead of the chuck wagon. She'd been the soul of discretion, quiet and subdued, and he wondered if she were angry with him, with his long spiel this morning, when he'd effectively told her he would use his strength against her should she disobey him.

The thought shamed him. He'd never hit a woman in his life, never raised a hand against a female, no matter what the temptation. And he wasn't about to begin now. Especially not with a woman he'd set his sights on. And that thought was enough to bring him to a halt. He'd just decided that marriage was not on his agenda, hadn't he?

And now he was flirting with the idea of tying himself down with Alexis Powers. Somehow the loss of his bachelor freedom seemed not so tragic as it had a while ago.

Hell, he'd changed his mind almost overnight, letting the girl get under his skin, considering the lure of her slender body, her soft, plush mouth that tempted him mightily, and now he was thinking of the dreaded "M" word. *Marriage.*

And wouldn't Connor laugh at him if he could see him now. Connor, his older brother, his idol in childhood days, his friend as an adult. Connor had found his true love almost ten years ago, and after the mess Jamie had caused, Connor had married her and shared two children with her.

And Jamie was still wandering the world, unattached and lonely. Maybe it was time to change things, he thought, the vision of Alex before him. And then she was at his left side, the chuck wagon pulled up even with his horse as he rode at a slow walk.

"Something wrong?" Cookie called, his voice a teasing drawl. "Your horse go lame? Or are you just loafin' along?"

"Just thinking," Jamie said quickly, his eyes not straying to the woman who sat only a few feet away from him. "I'll move along a little faster." With a nudge of his heels, the stallion broke into a trot and Jamie rode ahead. The horse had been champing at the bit for a half hour or so, and now with the reins loose in his rider's hands, he took advantage of Jamie's lax behavior and tossed his head, switching his tail and side-stepping a bit, as if he challenged his rider.

It was enough to bring him back to the present, and Jamie allowed the horse his head, leaning forward to urge the stallion on to greater speed. As if he knew his rider's mind, the sleek ears twitched back, his breathing took on a deep, stentorian sound and he flew like the wind, past those who rode more placidly ahead of him, then across the landscape to where a line of trees proclaimed the presence of a stream of water.

Jamie welcomed the sight. Tired and dirty, he'd spent the past three days without a bath, with aching muscles and a case of lust gnawing at him. The shelter of willows was welcoming, and he drew his horse to a halt almost a mile from where the rest of the riders moved on toward the ranch house and barn. The water was clear, not deep, but certainly abundant enough to get himself clean.

With little hesitation, he tied his mount to a tree branch, then stripped off his clothing and waded into the streambed. Cold and clear, the water welcomed him, and he knelt in the deepest spot, splashing his body lavishly with the clean flow. He doused his head, bending to rub his scalp beneath the surface, then lifting his head and shaking the water from it, allowing it to fly where it would. He wiped his face with his wide palms, and bent to his knees, relishing the cool wash of the stream as it rushed past him, the water seeming clear enough to drink. He dipped his hands into it, scooped up a double handful and lifted it to his mouth.

"I've got a perfectly good canteen filled with well water I'd be willing to share with you."

He shook his head again, certain he was hearing things, that his mind was playing tricks on him. And then he turned and looked into green eyes that mocked him, a laughing face that challenged him. She was sitting not far from the bank of the stream, knees lifted, her hands folded atop them, barely able to keep her mirth subdued.

He looked like a Greek god, Alexis thought, as he rose from the streambed, naked and shimmering in the light, the water sluicing off him as he stepped closer to the bank.

"Did anybody ever tell you that you were nothing but trouble?" he asked, and then his eyes narrowed as she faced him, unafraid. "What are you doing here?"

"Which shall I answer first?" she mused aloud. And then grinned. "I told Cookie I wanted to get on my mare for a while, and he accommodated me." Her mouth seemed to be full of cotton, her breath nonexistent as she searched for words to speak in answer to his first query.

"As far as being 'nothing but trouble,' no, not really," she said finally, hurting that he thought of her in that light, his scornful look making her feel small and insignificant before him. He'd walked from the water and stood just in front of her, unashamed of his nakedness, it seemed, and unwilling to turn aside from her scrutiny.

He was magnificent, black-haired, blue-eyed and, altogether, a giant of a man well over six feet tall. Not that he was built on bulky lines, but she'd noticed him, tall and tapered from shoulders to hips, long legged with taut thighs under denim pants that seemed to have been made for him. He was enough to make a woman's mouth water, she'd thought, her mind a fog.

And now he had shed those trousers before he went into the stream and right before her eyes was the proof of his masculinity, bold and brazen, obviously ready for business.

"Why don't you put your clothes on?" she asked, noting the uneven tenor of her voice.

"I was here first," he told her. "I didn't invite you to invade my bath. But since you have, you'll have to take the consequences."

She felt her heart pick up speed. Whatever he meant by that enigmatic statement was up for grabs. And she wasn't about to ask any questions as to his meaning. Instead, she gathered up her things and rose. Now, as never before, she sensed his power, his strength, the force of his masculine being, and she rued her impetuous behavior.

"I'm sorry. I shouldn't have interrupted you. I'll leave."

He took her arm, not in a tight grip, but firmly enough so that she knew she could not escape him should she try. "Why don't you stay, now that we've become better acquainted?" he asked.

"I'm sure I don't know what you mean," she said quickly.

He laughed and turned her to face him. "Don't you?"

"Yes, well I suppose I do, but I don't agree. The fact that I've seen you naked doesn't make our acquaintance any more welcome to me." She tried to look anywhere but at his body, but the brush of dark hair on his chest tempted her to touch the curls and weave her fingers through the lush length of silky fur he wore. It narrowed into a slender arrow, pointing downward, and she knew without looking just what lay in that direction.

"You're blushing," he said quietly. "Am I to assume you've never seen a naked man before?"

"You'd assume right," she answered, with heat still rising in her face.

"Well, don't let me hinder your first experience," he said softly, his other hand moving to wrap long fingers around her shoulder, then drawing her closer.

"Don't," she said harshly. "I'll get all wet." Then she wondered if it might not be worth it to have his body against her own.

His laughter mocked her. "Does that matter? Don't you want to know what sort of danger you've gotten yourself into?"

"You won't hurt me," she told him, looking up into blue eyes that were amused at her expense.

"Maybe not, but then again, they tell me that a woman's

first time is usually painful," he said softly. His slow enunciation of words, the mellow tone of his voice lulled her a bit, but she rallied quickly. He was laying it on pretty thick, but unless she was mighty mistaken, he wouldn't take any chance of her father chasing after him with a shotgun.

"I'm not afraid of you," she said, wondering at the quiver in her voice.

"Aren't you? Then why are you trembling?"

Her hands had rested against his chest and as she watched, her fingers fought to be still, her body shook as if it were chilled from a summer cold.

She felt her mouth twitch, knew a moment of despair then bent her head, knowing she owed him an apology, hoping it would appease him so that she might leave. "Please let me go, Jamie. I'm sorry I intruded. Just let me—"

Her words were cut off abruptly as he bent to her, one hand forcing her head erect, so that their eyes met. His mouth was hot, and open against hers, and his scent, that of a male who has seen his mate and intends to blend his body with hers, enveloped her.

How did she know? What inner sense allowed her to so easily judge the aroma of an aroused man? But, all her confusion aside, she knew she was in imminent danger, not only from the man who held her, but from herself. For she welcomed his kiss, leaned into his embrace as though it were the answer to her prayers, and now his questing male member was making its intention known against her belly.

Fear of the unknown sped down the length of her spine, and she leaned away from him. "Don't do this to me. Please," she whispered. And felt, to her amazement, his hands fall from her as he stepped back, offering her the freedom she'd begged for.

"Go on. Catch up with the chuck wagon. I'll be right behind you, Alex."

Without a second thought, she darted away, running to

where her horse was tied and mounted quickly. The mare ran like lightning, as if she'd been set free to do as she pleased, and Alexis clung to her like a burr, unable to sit upright, content to hold on with tenuous strength to the dark mane, ignoring the reins that dangled.

Behind her, she heard his shout. "Alex. Get ahold of those reins and slow that horse down before you get dumped." And then his words were lost on the wind that blew past her ears. Smart enough to heed his warning, she soothed the mare, reaching low for the reins, forcing herself to sit erect in the saddle, gaining control over the madcap fashion in which she'd allowed the animal to behave.

The mare snorted, shivered and tossed her head, unwilling to comply with Alexis's command, but trained well enough to obey the reins that held her down to a canter, and finally to a walk.

She felt his presence right behind her, and she touched the mare's barrel with her heels, urging her into a faster pace. Ahead of her was the sanctuary of the cook wagon, where she would be safe from the man who followed her. For all his audacity, he would not infringe on her now, but she felt the need of a buffer, and Cookie would serve well.

Pulling her mare down to a trot beside his perch on the high seat of the chuck wagon, she signaled to Cookie and he drew the vehicle to a crawl. With the skill of a woman used to horses and the ways of a ranch, she brought her right leg over the saddle and stepped up on the wagon. The reins in her hand were easily tied to the seat and her mare trotted alongside without a hitch.

"Well, you sure haven't forgotten how to do that," Cookie said, grinning a gap-toothed smile in her direction.

"I grew up here," Alex said. "I can do most anything the men can do on this ranch."

"Well, I'd say you were a sight better at blindsiding that new foreman than anyone else on the place." He laughed as if he'd observed the shenanigans by the streambed. "I saw you chasing off after him, Alex. You want to watch your step with that one. He's a sharp fella, and he'll give you a run for your money."

"I'm not afraid of him," she said scornfully.

"No," he said slowly, "I don't expect you are. But you'd better respect him. He's no fool and he's not about to put up with your teasing him."

"I didn't tease him," she said, disgruntled at his words.

"No, of course you didn't. And the sun didn't rise this morning, either. Just watch yourself, honey. Your pa don't need to be running after that man with a shotgun, but I think he'd do just that very thing if you make the wrong move. I wouldn't push the fella too far, is what I'm trying to say."

"I'm old enough to take care of myself, Cookie," she said sharply. Her old friend saw too much, was too wise to ignore what he saw and didn't mind expressing his opinion.

"Yep. I've heard that story before, Alexis. Just mind your step now. Let's not have a full-scale war on our hands, with your pa mad as a bull chasin' a red flag."

Chapter Three

"What went on out there?" Hank asked, his eyes sharp as they scanned Jamie's face, catching him right after breakfast when Alexis had taken her leave.

"I'm not sure what you're talking about." And yet he was pretty clear on the gossip the men had carried to Hank this morning. Jamie had been the focus of bad jokes and sidelong glances from the men, and he'd be a fool if he didn't recognize that they were wondering what had gone on, what had brought the chuck wagon and its occupants, and the lone rider that followed, back to the barn more than an hour later than was expected.

"You know damn well what I'm asking you," Hank said. "The men said they saw you riding off toward the stream and when Slim looked back, Alexis was riding hell-bent for leather after you. You were late getting back to the barn, and Cookie's not talking. So I'm asking you. Did you spend time alone with my girl?"

"Why don't you ask her? She was the one who followed me, not the other way around." He took a deep breath and met Hank's dark gaze. "Yeah, I spent a few minutes alone with her, but she's just as pure and virtuous as she was when she rode out to the north forty. I made her unroll her blanket near me the night she spent out there, so I could keep an eye on her, and we talked. Of course, there were half a dozen men within hearing distance, and I smelled like a horse and cow patties, so I doubt I was very appealing to a woman of her caliber. I'd suggest again that you ask her."

"I did." Hank gritted his teeth and then grinned. "She's a scamp, James. Loves to lead men around by the nose, and I think she sees you as a challenge. I want to know why she followed you to the stream."

"I can't answer for her, and I won't try," Jamie said flatly. "But I'm smart enough to keep myself in the clear, Hank. I'm not looking to have you pointing a gun my way. I'm not messing with your girl. At least I'm not trying to get into her bed. I think a woman like Alex is better suited to marriage than a quick roll in the hay."

"Well, that's about as blunt as you can get. You got plans to marry the girl?"

"That's not what I said. I'm not sure she'd go along with the idea anyway." Jamie dropped to the top step and leaned against the corner post of the porch roof.

"Maybe I'll ask her what she thinks of the idea," Hank said with a measuring look. "You ready to settle down yet, Webster?"

"I've got a job to do here. I'm not about to get tangled up with a woman, no matter how appealing she is. Ask me that question again in a couple of years."

"Hey, boss. What do you want done with those yearlings?" Woody approached the porch and posed his query in James's direction.

"I'll be right out. I'd say we ought to put them in the far pasture, keep them separated from the others while we work with them."

"What are your plans?" Hank asked, his interest aroused by James's words.

"Nothing unusual. Just getting them used to a bit and bridle. Leading them around in circles and letting them know what a human can do for them." He rose from the steps and turned to face Hank.

"I found out that horses, especially young ones, are a lot like women. They need a bit of pampering, a lot of coaxing and a steady hand on the bit. It takes several months to turn a yearling into an animal that has learned how to respond to his owner, or trainer. But, the lessons are worth the time it takes. I'd like to use Alexis to help with the job, if you don't mind."

"Not at all," Hank said expansively. "It'll be good for her to have the responsibility, and she loves those babies out there anyway. Are you going to ask her about it, or shall I?"

"I will, soon as I get a chance," James said. He set off after Woody, his mind was already racing ahead to the dozen or so yearlings that awaited him and to weighing the difficulties inherent in this whole plan.

To be asked by the foreman to be in the thick of a training regime, she would recognize that there would be problems with jealousy, with those who had done this task in other years. But James had already decided the final result of using the girl for his program would be worth the risk he took.

Not that he feared the men causing an overt problem, but his own interest in her was the challenge. Being with her on a daily basis would be hard on his patience. The urge to be alone with her, to touch her, was growing by the day.

Hell, by the minute. Working closely with her would be a mixed blessing, he thought as he left Woody and headed to the barn. It would lighten the workload when it came to the training sessions, and at the same time cause him a lot of trouble. Just keeping his hands to himself was problem enough.

She tempted him, as no other woman had. Not even those back in his early days when he was trying his wings. "I was a genuine scalawag," he murmured to himself.

"Who says so?" From behind him, Alex had spoken and he stiffened, halting the movement of his hands, currycomb held upright.

"What are you doing out here?" he asked, even as his heart began a rapid pace.

"Dad said you wanted to talk to me." Lifting limpid eyes to his, her smile one of a cat set on mischief, she waited.

"I did. I do," he said, and then turned from her. He could think better when she wasn't right in front of him.

She tapped his shoulder. "Jamie, are you mad at me? Or is this a bad time for me to talk to you?"

"Neither," he said. "Wait till I finish with this horse."

She moved from behind him, and as if his hearing had grown more sensitive, he heard her progress as she walked to where a bench had been built against the wall. Distinctly, he heard the sound of wood shifting as she sat, knew the sound of her boots on the dirt behind him and with an added sense of smell, caught a whiff of the soap she used.

Damn, the woman was going to drive him crazy. His hands worked automatically as he cleaned his horse, but he cut short the process, working quickly on the stud's mane and then turning him loose in the corral.

Looking back down the long aisle, he felt the heat of her gaze touch him, wished for a moment that the sunshine would light the interior of the barn, the better to see the young woman who waited for him. And then he stalked back to where she sat, stopping in front of her, hands on hips, as if he were fitting this conversation into a tight schedule, and she was but a minor detail on his agenda.

"I'd like to offer you a job," he said briefly. "I spoke to your father and he said to ask you about it."

She tilted her head back, the better to see his face. "If you'd sit down next to me, it might work better, boss. What's your problem?"

He spoke without thinking, his voice harsh. "You, Miss Alexis. You're my problem."

"What have I done?" She sounded truly perplexed and he frowned.

"You're a part of this ranch, and I'll have to work closely with you if we go ahead with this project. The whole problem is, I have a powerful urge to pick you up and take you to the hayloft and spend a couple of hours with you, finding out—"

She held up a hand to halt his words. "That's enough, I think."

He watched as her throat moved, knew she swallowed with difficulty and felt a moment of triumph as he realized he'd shocked her. Maybe given her food for thought. And yet, he'd need to watch his step, lest Hank come after him.

He sat down next to Alexis then, their thighs almost touching, the warmth of her body reaching for him like the sunshine on a summer day. "All right," he said. "Let's start over." He cleared his throat and consciously kept his eyes forward. "I'd like you to work with the yearlings, follow a program I've set up for their training. Three or four hours a day should do it."

She was silent and he allowed himself to toss her a sidelong glance. Maybe she wasn't interested, or perhaps she didn't want to work alongside him.

The look of rapt attention she shot his way changed his mind. "You're kidding. You want *me* to work with the yearlings? You'll really let me have a hand in training them?"

"If you want to," he answered, aware now that it was an idea that appealed to her. Maybe even enough so as to put herself in his vicinity daily, giving him jurisdiction over her movements for the morning hours.

"If I want to?" She sighed the words. "I've already told you, early on, how I feel about spending time with the young horses. It's only a dream job come to life, Jamie. I love those yearlings. Working with them would be a pleasure."

"How about working with me?" he asked. "Does that qualify as a pleasure?"

She eyed him soberly. "I think that all depends on you. Can you keep your hands to yourself?"

He grinned. "Yeah, I think so. At least I'll try."

"You don't sound very sure of that, mister. And I'm not in the market for any hanky-panky with the foreman."

"I don't go in for *hanky-panky*. If I set my sights on you, it won't be for fun. But don't worry, sweetheart. When the time comes, you'll know it, up front. I don't play games when I'm dead serious, and I have a notion you'd require a little more attention than a new job or a horse I'd like to own."

Alexis's eyes flashed fire at him. "I'm not sure I like being compared to a horse."

She'd picked apart his statement. He might have known she would. And his natural good humor came to the forefront. "You need a firm hand, just like a frisky mare, sweetheart, but other than that, I can't see that you resemble a horse. Except that you're long-legged and slim, and you move with a sort of elegance."

As if he'd spoken words that were unplanned, he rose and looked toward the bench where she still sat. "Now, I suspect you'll think I've called you a mare, instead of a woman," he said, his smile aimed in her direction.

She shook her head. "I'm not sure what I think. I'm still

trying to digest the 'elegance' remark. No one's ever called me elegant before. I think I kinda like it."

"Yeah," he said, the word drawled slowly, as if it stuck to his tongue. "I like it, too, ma'am. I surely do."

The silhouette of a man filled the back door as Hank Powers strode across the threshold. "What's going on?" he asked heartily.

"I just got a new job," Alexis answered. "The foreman wants me to help him work with the yearlings. Is that all right with you, Dad?"

"He's the boss," Hank said. "And if you want the job, it looks to me like it's yours, Alex."

She stood quickly and went to where he stood, reaching up to kiss his cheek. "Thanks, Dad. You know this is something I'd really like to do." She paused and her voice dropped to a lower tone. "Did you have anything to do with it?" she asked, as if she were suddenly suspicious.

Hank shook his head. "Nope. Jamie told me he wanted you and asked if I objected. I told him to ask you himself." He curled one arm around his daughter's waist. "I'm glad he did, since it seems to make you happy." His gaze swept to James. "Just don't let her try to do anything she's not capable of. Though I don't know what that would be. My girl is pretty well-equipped to handle herself around here. So long as the work isn't too heavy for her, I'll rest easy."

"My main concern is keeping her away from anyone who might give her a hard time, given her tendency to flirt a bit," James said. "A couple of your men are pretty set on courting her, you know."

"She can handle that," Hank said quickly. "At least, she has, so far. The men know she's only friendly, not flirting with them."

James shrugged. "Whatever you say. I'll keep an eye out,

anyway." He looked at Alexis, whose smile was brilliant, now that the training had been approved officially. "You ready to start?" he asked.

"Whenever you say, boss." She almost shivered with anticipation, he thought.

"Now's as good a time as any." He motioned toward the back barn door and she followed his silent order, leaving her father with another brief kiss on his cheek in farewell. James watched as she walked ahead of him, and felt Hank's gaze as if it were a hot branding iron. With a sudden movement, he turned to face the man.

"You got a problem with me, Hank?"

As if he swallowed his objections, Hank was silent for a moment, then shook his head. "I always worry about my girl, Jamie. She's all I've got left in this world that really means anything to me. Just don't hurt her."

"I'm not in the habit of giving women a hard time," James returned sharply. "I won't be making an exception where Alexis is concerned."

Hank's face grew stern. "Just consider yourself warned," he said harshly. "She's got a soft spot for you."

James couldn't have stopped the grin that twisted his lips any more than he could have halted a runaway train. "I'll bear that in mind," he said, forcing a sober expression to rest on his face, hiding the last semblance of his smile. With long strides, he followed Alexis, who had already crossed the corral and opened the gate into the pasture.

"Wait for me," he called, and was rewarded by her quick wave as she passed through the opening, holding the gate for his approach.

"I wasn't going anywhere without you," she told him, tilting her head to one side as he neared. "What was my father saying to you?"

"Just warning me about hurting you. I think he's afraid I have ideas about you."

"What sort of ideas? I'm sure not afraid of you." She sounded exasperated, he thought, and looked even more so. "He tries to make me into a shrinking violet, Jamie. I'm a woman, capable of making my own choices, and he won't get that through his head."

James grinned down at her as they walked farther into the pasture, heading for half a dozen yearlings standing beneath a tree. "Don't fault him for being protective, Alex. I'd be even worse if you were my daughter. And trust me, I'm very happy that you're not. I'll admit my feelings toward you are not fatherly." He sobered as he watched her expression turn watchful.

"I'll repeat it, Alexis. I was a scalawag. There was no other word for me, and I suspect your father recognizes that."

She smiled then, as if she thought he was joking with her, and then laughed aloud, the sound of her amusement ringing like the wind chimes on the back porch. He didn't attempt to hide his reaction, his arm reaching to rest across her shoulders as he drew her to a halt next to him, his action restrained, resisting the temptation she offered.

"Chet tells me you're very good with the horses, and I'll admit I've noticed myself that you seem to have a special touch. But I don't know what your experience is, and I've got some set ideas of my own. I don't want to go any closer," he explained. "I'm gonna rope that black colt on the right, and he'll spook if we sneak up on him."

"All right," she said softly, watching as he uncoiled his lariat and let it lie in a circle at his feet. With a quick motion he had it spinning, and in another moment it was sailing through the air, only to settle gently over the head of the colt in question. The horse jerked against the rope and James held it fast, drawing the animal toward him slowly.

At the same time he walked forward, Alexis close by his side, and his voice took on a crooning quality as he talked to the graceful, black creature he wooed. "You're a beautiful piece of horseflesh, boy. Just come on over here and I'll scratch your ears for you."

"You're very good at this," Alexis murmured quietly as the colt eyed the pair of them and then, as if drawn by an invisible cord, walked haltingly toward them.

James reached out his hand, letting the horse smell his palm, then turned it to rub with affection beneath the horse's chin. His fingernails scratched gently there and then traveled up to a spot between the colt's ears. His voice spoke soft words of encouragement as he stroked the dark head, a never-ceasing river of sounds that seemed to quiet the animal, putting him into a sort of trance.

It worked every time, James thought triumphantly. Gaining the animal's trust was the most important part of the whole procedure, and letting him know you wouldn't harm him was a big part of it. The old theory of the rider being the master was harsh and often damaged a young horse beyond repair.

James thought of his father, how the man had treated his animals. A better teacher could not have been found, he decided, recalling his early days when his father had instructed him in the care of his livestock. The same rules applied to any creature. Kindness went a long way to forming a good relationship.

His glance fell on the woman at his side. *Maybe that was the secret with women, too.*

Alexis reached slowly for the colt, her hand rubbing his neck, her head beside his, her words soft, luring him closer.

And he obliged, leaning into her a bit, then tossing his head and snuffling at her shoulder, as if he imprinted her scent in his memory. She laughed, tossing her head in a like motion, her long hair flying, only to settle in a pale cloud over her shoulders again.

She was a beauty, James thought. Her face was animated with pleasure and her body almost vibrating with the joy of handling the colt. He gave her the end of his lariat and motioned with his hand that she should lead the colt in a circle.

Without hesitation, she obeyed, allowing only a short bit of rope between herself and the horse. And then, as if she had watched him work the same procedure, she let the rope slip through her fingers a bit, until a greater length separated her from the animal she led, till the colt was circling her at her silent command, prancing around her, tossing his head and kicking up his heels as if he would ignore the fact that he was connected to her by a rope.

"Pick up your speed," Jamie said, his voice a low undertone, but audible to her.

She drew the colt in closer and increased his tempo by pacing him herself, tugging the rope to urge him into a trot. He obeyed and she called out to him, encouraging him as his hooves scattered small bits of pebbles and grass behind him.

James was struck with the woman's skill and her beauty, the quick movements of her hands and the way she'd so readily taken to the colt. Between the two of them, they presented a picture of graceful movement he could only admire. And then, as if he felt warmed by another's gaze, James looked back at the barn.

Hank stood in the doorway, his hands in his pockets, a smile on his lips and pride on his features. With a grin, he sent James a silent salute, and then turned to go back in the barn, leaving the two to their privacy.

"You have a name for this one yet?" James asked quietly.

Alexis looked surprised as she glanced his way, and then her attention returned to the colt, as if she were embarrassed. "Who told you about that?"

"Your father. He said you can't help but name every living thing on the ranch. In fact, he said they've used the names you've chosen more often than not."

She rubbed her forehead against the colt's jaw. "He's Black Thunder, out of Black Lightning. And don't you dare laugh at me. Naming the animals is something I like to do."

"I wouldn't think of it," James said soberly, although his heart sang with the pleasure this woman brought to his days. "Black Thunder sounds like a name suitable for a colt who's going to make a name for himself one of these days."

"His formation? Or his disposition?" she asked, drawing up the lead line and walking to where James stood, the horse at her shoulder.

"Both. He'll breed true, I'll warrant. He's built like a champion, and if he keeps that sweet temper of his on a leash, he'll make a good addition to the ranch's breeding program. Nothing worse than a mean stud on the place. They're hell to breed. The mares don't like them."

"*Mean* is a nasty word, no matter who it's applied to," Alex said sharply. "That goes for men as well as animals."

"You sound like you've been acquainted with a few." And if she had, what would he do about it?

"I've seen a few in action," she admitted quietly. "Had a couple of bruises in my time."

"What did your father do about that?"

She shot him a look of defiance. "Nothing. I didn't tell him about it. I told you already, I can take care of myself."

"Who?" he asked harshly. And was rewarded by a look of surprise.

"No one you know," she said, ending the conversation neatly.

"If anyone on the ranch—"

"No one here would give me a bad time," she said, interrupting his threat. "Now forget it, Jamie. It's not worth talking about."

"It is when your safety is involved. I won't have you molested by anyone."

"Not even you?" Her grin was quick, her eyes flashing a challenge.

"Not even me. I'll never molest you, Alex. I might coax you a little, even try a bit of seduction, but I'll never cause you pain."

"You'll never leave bruises?" she asked innocently.

"I didn't say that," he told her. "Sometimes a little—" He halted suddenly, thinking better of what he'd almost said. "Never mind. Forget I suggested such a thing."

She looked curious. "I think I'd like to hear about it one day. Don't forget where we were when I ask you to continue with this."

"I think you'd better let that colt off the lariat and let me rope you another student, ma'am," he told her. "You're about to get in over your head."

"I'm almost twenty years old, Jamie. Don't treat me like a child."

"I don't intend to," he said. "But I'm almost thirty, so just don't tempt me, sweetheart."

He thought she smiled as she turned away, loosening the lariat to take it off the colt's neck. She handed it back to him, watched the colt as he kicked his heels as if he celebrated his freedom, and then raced away across the pasture.

The rope settled over the head of a dark-legged filly, a true blood bay, and with a series of soft entreaties and a steady hand on his rope, he coaxed her closer, walking toward the filly as he spent his litany of praise on her. She sniffed at his hand, apparently judged him acceptable, and followed him to where Alexis stood waiting.

"She's a beauty," he told the woman who had eyes only for the filly. "I don't think she'll give you any trouble. She seems eager to please if you handle her right."

"I'll do my best," she said, tossing him a look of scorn, as if his words had cast doubt on her skills. "This is more fun than work, anyway," she told him, her face glowing. She tossed her head as she walked with the filly to an open spot, away from the trees and the man who stood beneath their branches.

The ritual of training he'd instigated with the colt was repeated, and in twenty minutes time, Alexis brought the prancing animal to him, her smile one of triumph as she awaited his response to her silent challenge.

"You catch on quick, ma'am. Sure you haven't done this before?" he asked her. "Got a name for this one?"

"Of course I've done this before," she answered quickly. "But I just called it playing with the horses, teaching them what they need to know. Then finally getting them used to a saddle and having weight on their back. Dad says I'm better than most men he's seen working with the three-year-olds. And as to naming them, it doesn't take long to size up an animal, see beyond their physical attributes to what's inside." She reached beneath the filly's head, her arm almost circling the graceful neck. "This one is Pretty Girl. She knows she's pretty, and she carries herself like a woman with confidence."

"Well," James said softly. "You've sized her up right well, ma'am. Pretty Girl it is. I'll tell your father this afternoon." He watched as she released the filly from the rope and gave the cavorting yearling a final rub between her ears.

They worked with the other four horses in the next hour or so, and James sorted out the names she had decided on for each of them in his mind. She was uncanny, he decided, finding an element in each animal that was reflected in the name she chose for it. No wonder Hank had said she was gifted at the skill of pronouncing the right name for each horse on the place.

The largest of the group was a tall colt, a chestnut giant who was almost guaranteed to be a fine stud one day. He'd given Alexis a bit of trouble, daring her with his greater strength to keep him under control, and she'd faced up to him without hesitation, speaking sharply when he would have protested her hands on him, drawing him in when he would have had his own way.

"What are we going to call this fella?" James asked as they watched the gleaming colt race across the pasture, once the rope was taken from his neck.

"Red Mick," she said without hesitation.

"Now, I wouldn't have called him that," James said, wondering at her choice.

"He's red, for one thing."

James nodded his agreement.

"And he's full of himself. Reminds me of a man I once knew."

"Well, I can't argue that one," James said. "Doesn't sound like you thought much of the man."

"Not much. He'd probably have made a good gelding, if I'd had my way. The man thought he was a real lady killer…but I didn't."

James laughed, loudly and long. The woman was priceless. "He must have really given you a hard time, sweetheart."

"Not as bad a time as I gave him. He thought he could put his hands on me and I fought him. He had an aching crotch for a while, and Dad fired him without asking me any questions. He knew we'd been out by the pasture fence the night before and when he saw Mick in the morning, limping and unwilling to get in his saddle, he figured things out real quick. I'll give Mick credit. He didn't argue, not for a minute. I think he figured he'd gotten off easy."

"Sounds like he did," James said, thinking what *his* reaction would have been, had he been in Hank's shoes that day.

"He also sent three men after him, just to be certain Mick left the county," she said, shooting James a look that spoke of knowledge better left unsaid.

"I'll bet he wasn't a pretty sight when he hit the other side of town," James said. "I suspect your daddy was madder than a hornet. The man ever show up here again?"

She shook her head. "That was almost two years ago. Haven't seen hide nor hair of him."

"If you ever do, I want to know about it," James told her, his words harsh and commanding. "Some men learn the hard way, sweetheart. I don't want to take any chances with your safety."

She watched as he rolled his lariat up into a loop and held it at his side. "Am I safe with you, Jamie?" As if her own words embarrassed her, she refused to meet his gaze, her cheeks flushed, her mouth looking soft and vulnerable.

"As safe as you want to be, Alexis," he answered. "You won't have to aim any low blows at me."

They walked together back to the barn, and then turned as one for a last look at the yearlings who'd taken up residence under the trees. Their heads were bent to the ground, their tails swished lazily as they brushed flies away, and one of the young colts picked up his head and looked their way, as if he challenged their vigilance.

"He's telling you he has things under control out there,"

Alexis said with a laugh. "That's Red Mick, the leader of the whole bunch, whether they like it or not."

"The fillies don't seem to mind," James observed, as one of the dark, graceful animals touched noses with the young stud they discussed.

"They're foolish creatures, not even suspecting what's ahead for them. When they're all tied up waiting for his attention in a couple of years, they'll not be so docile."

"That's a female for you," James teased. "Always ready to give a man a hard time."

They turned from the door and walked down the aisle to the tack room, where James hung his lariat and stripped off his gloves. Dropping them on the small area he used for minor paperwork, he turned to Alexis, who had followed him through the door, into the small room.

"You're in trouble, coming in here with me," he said quietly.

"Am I?" She faced him without a trace of fear, only anticipation lighting her eyes.

"You know what you're doing?" he asked.

"Do you?" And then she smiled. "Yeah, I'd say you probably do, James Webster."

Gripping her arm lightly, he bent to her, drawing her close, melding her soft curves against his own muscular length. She was amenable to his touch, fitting her body to his without hesitation, moving a bit as if she would mold herself closer.

"Watch out, sweetheart. Too much wiggling will get you in trouble," he warned her, his voice low and husky.

"Show me," she murmured, lifting her face to his, inviting his kiss.

He obliged her, taking his time as he covered her lips with his, brushing the soft pliant flesh and then begging entry with coaxing probes of his tongue. She obliged, a sense of surprise apparent, and he hesitated, as if he would not take advantage of her. And then she sighed and he lost his better judgment, finding her sweet and inviting, seeking out the hidden places that formed her mouth.

His kiss was long, heated and damp, and he feared he had frightened her with the intensity of his desire. But apparently not so, for she clung to him, her arms encircling his neck, her face tucked into the bend of his shoulder, as if she invited his caresses.

His mouth touched her cheek, her closed eyelids and the line of her brow where small curls formed and the heat of the day brought a faint line of perspiration to dwell. She smelled of hay and horse, an aroma not unpleasant to him. Yet, beneath her skin was the scent of woman, that elusive, faint essence of female allure that drew men to their fate.

And he was no different than any other man, he decided. Alexis was exactly what he'd traveled so many miles to find. Courting her was the next step. Convincing her father of his worth would be a task James would have to work at, if he ever planned to win the woman he held in his arms.

"Jamie?" She tipped her head back and eyed him quizzically. "What are you thinking about? Your forehead is all wrinkled and you look like something has you all riled up."

"Just you," he said, allowing a smile to take residence on his lips. "I'm trying to behave myself. How did you say it? Keep my hands to myself. You make it pretty hard, ma'am." And then he laughed aloud as he recognized the truth of his statement, and drew back from her lest she be frightened or insulted by the blatant nudge of his manhood against her.

"You don't frighten me," she said boldly. "And I kinda like your hands right where they are, Jamie."

He felt the line of her back beneath his fingertips, the flaring of her hips, the narrowing of her waist, and as he slid his palms upward, knew the fullness of her breasts against his chest as he measured her width, his fingertips touching at the center of her back.

She was silent, unmoving, as if any bit of protest from her might halt his meandering. And so it might. For he was in uncharted territory here, he realized.

His hands slipped to her ribs, then forward just a bit, cradling the weight of her breasts against his thumbs. It was all he could do not to clasp the softness, but he thought better of it, and wisely left it for another time. For there would be another time.

Of that he was certain.

Chapter Four

Bringing trouble down on himself was not Jamie's intent, and so he'd backed off in his pursuit of Alexis over the following two months. She was a joy to watch, a natural. Her patience with the yearlings was beyond what James had hoped for. She pampered them, coaxed them through their paces and treated them as if they were her children, petting, hugging and talking to them in an almost nonstop litany of praise as they performed to her commands.

She was a born horsewoman, with an innate sense of rightness when it came to dealing with her charges, no matter their moods or behavior. He gladly gave Alexis her due as their trainer. She'd accepted his program without argument, had gone along with his ideas and was the talk of the ranch hands. If they secretly admired James's control over her, they did not let it be known. If they were jealous of his long hours in her company, they kept it secret. And yet, he was the subject of pointed looks from the men who worked for him, but who still took his orders without question.

If Hank suspected there was anything going on in the training sessions that was directly opposed to his daughter's care and safety, he kept it to himself, only questioning James about the success of the yearlings' training. To Hank, James was openly willing to praise Alexis for her work.

And work she did. For several hours each day, she did as James instructed her, brushing, currying and in all ways tending the yearlings. They came to know her well, recognizing her scent as she approached the pasture, running with coltish grace to where she awaited them, always with a carrot or bit of apple for each of them.

And they performed well for her, gave her what she demanded of them, and were soon ready to go on to the next phase of their training. Alexis was light, probably not weighing much more than a hundred pounds, James figured. She was not tall, but petite and slender, agile and quick in her movements.

She leaned against the horses, bent low to stroke their bellies, picked up their feet, one after another, preparing them for the handling they would receive as mature animals. They had to learn to accept being shod in another year or so. Men would brush them, lead them, handle them, expect much of them in the future. It was Alexis's job to see to it that they were not shy around others, that they would accept another's hands on them.

She possessed a rare sense of communication with the animals, and with that in mind, he thought to utilize her in his work with the three-year-olds.

"Would you like to give me a hand, Alex?" he asked her. They were at the breakfast table, a meal cooked and served by the cook, a buxom lady named Ellen, brought out from town to fill the job Alexis no longer had the time nor inclination to do.

"Doing what?" she asked, buttering her toast and then reaching for the jam jar.

"Getting the three-year-olds used to a saddle and rider."

Hank spoke up quickly. "I don't want my girl dumped by an ornery horse. That's a man's job."

Darting a warning look at Alexis, James grinned at Hank. "Don't you think Alex can do as well as any of the men on the place?"

"In some ways," Hank allowed, eyeing Alexis warily, as if he recognized that his quick refusal had caused her to bristle.

He was right. She was stewing quietly, but her temper was close to the boiling point as she listened to the two men discussing her. Jamie had given her more responsibility than she'd expected, allowing her a free hand with the yearlings for almost two months. With a mental pat on the back, she judged she had done a job that no one could find fault with.

The ranch was the proud possessor of a dozen or so yearlings, all easily handled, all trained to walk, trot and lope at the end of a rope, on command. They carried a blanket and sometimes a twenty-five pound weight on their backs, and would become accustomed to that before the poundage was increased.

"Why don't I have the chance to answer your question, Jamie?" she asked, as the conversation came to a halt.

"You can say whatever you like, so far as I'm concerned," he told her.

"You're a woman, Alexis," her father reminded her. "You can't be expected to do a man's work."

"And who says that only men can train horses? I think I've done all right so far. I'd like to have a chance at the three-year-olds. If Jamie thinks I can handle it, that's good enough for me."

"Have you been coaxing him into asking about this?" her father asked roughly.

"I'm not underhanded," she told him, her anger coming to the forefront. "If I want something, I can approach you without Jamie's permission. So to answer your question, no, I've not been *coaxing* him into anything."

She looked at the man across the table, whose handsome features were partially buried in his hand, as if he hid a smile from her view.

Hank blustered a bit. "The first time you get tossed off a horse, you're done, Alex," he said. "I won't have you killed just to prove a point."

She aimed a questioning look at him. "And what point is that?"

"You know what I'm saying. Jamie and I agree that you have a natural ability, you're a born trainer. You have a gift not given to many people in this world, a natural affinity for horses. But you can't win them all. There's bound to be a horse that won't respond to you, and that one could kill you. You don't have the physical strength to handle a determined stud."

"At least give me a chance, Dad. I won't do anything Jamie thinks isn't safe. Will that make you feel better?"

"So long as you don't try to persuade him otherwise," Hank told her firmly.

"She won't get around me," James said, and Alexis ducked her head, hiding the look of triumph she felt washing over her countenance.

Assuming an affable smile, she faced her father again. "He's tough, Dad. If he makes a statement, you can bet he'll do as he says."

Hank shot her a level look, his brow furrowed in a frown. "I know you too well, Alexis. You can be mighty persuasive when you want to."

James looked her way, an imperceptible twist of his head

warning her to desist before she said too much, and then spoke forthrightly in Hank's direction. "She won't put me in a bind, sir. I know her tricks."

Alex fought the rush of heat that appeared at his words. "I haven't any bag of tricks, Jamie. I play fair. I'd think you'd know that by now."

"You're a woman," he said, as if that were the final word on the subject. And to add emphasis to his statement, he rose from the table and picked up his cup, swallowing the last of his coffee. "I'll go by whatever you decide, Hank. Let me know."

"Don't go yet," Hank said quickly. "I'm willing to give it a chance. Just keep an eye out."

"I won't expect too much from her," James told him, and then motioned at Alex. "Let's go, ma'am. We've got work to do."

With mixed emotions, Alexis followed him out the door, waving at her father as she crossed the threshold, forming her lips into a quick "thank you" in his direction. Stepping double-time, she caught up with James and strode beside him. This man was very good at irritating her, his lifted eyebrow speaking volumes. And then his single word verified her thoughts.

"Satisfied?" he asked, looking down at her.

"Not quite, but almost," she said, lifting her chin in a gesture of defiance. "Once I get on top of one of those beauties, I'll be happy."

"Don't push it," James said gruffly.

"I won't. Just know that you're going to have the best trained bunch of horses in the county. I'll ride them all before I'm done."

"Pride goeth—"

"I know the rest of it," she said sharply. "And it isn't pride that drives me. I know what I can do, and so do you, or you wouldn't have pushed my father for this."

James grinned at her, a sudden switch of mood that threw her off balance. "All right, sweetheart. Strut your stuff. We'll start with the pinto mare. She's not as big as some of the others."

It was a long day. They broke for dinner at noon and then went back to the corral, where several of the hands happened to meander past, their eyes watchful as Alexis grew familiar with each horse she handled.

"Who's been in charge of these?" James asked. "Who worked with them before I got here?"

"Slim, mostly," Alexis told him. "He's about the best on the place."

James shook his head, a silent rebuttal of her words. "No, sweetheart. That's where you're wrong. You're the best on the place."

Her heart soared with the words of praise. So easily he could brush aside her barriers and set her heart beating double-time. Between his Irish blue eyes and the shock of black hair that begged for her touch, he was a man she was finding it hard to resist. In fact, she wondered some days and nights why she bothered. She was past the age of girlhood, she was a mature woman, and if she chose to know James Webster on a deeper level, it was no one's business but her own. But not for the world would she let him know how readily he affected her.

He paused beside her and touched her elbow, his gaze seeming to look past the facade of nonchalance she offered. "I'm going to turn you into the top trainer in the county," he told her. "And it won't take much on my part to do it. You're already well on your way, Alex."

"Got a charley-horse?" James asked. Breakfast was a thing of the past, and he'd waited impatiently for Alexis to join him.

Now he watched her walk toward him across the yard, and when she neared, he shot her a quick grin. "I'll bet it kept you up last night, didn't it?"

"Does it show?" Alexis walked as if she had a decided cramp in her calf, and he could almost envision himself scooping her up from the ground if it should give way beneath her.

"You betcha it shows," he said with a chuckle. "I noticed when you came down for breakfast that you were favoring it. Kinda goes with the territory, sweetheart. Come on in the barn and I'll massage it for you."

She lifted a brow and hesitated. "I'm not sure that's a good idea, boss."

"Strictly a professional gesture," he told her, motioning to the door of the tack room. She entered, James behind her, and when she sat on a chair, he squatted in front of her. His hands worked her boot off and then slid up her calf, his fingers seeking out the muscle that had tightened even more when she sat down.

"While you keep walking on it, it'll behave. But sit down and it tightens up and pulls from your heel. Nasty business." His fingers were digging deeply into the clenched muscle, working out the knot, even as he kept an eye on her face.

She winced, jerked once as he touched on the core of the spasm and he muttered a quick word of apology. Unless he missed his guess, she was struggling against tears, and the thought of her pain made him angry.

"Are you sure this is a good idea?" he asked. "You don't have to work so hard at this, you know."

"I don't work any harder than you do. I don't expect to be pampered. I'm here to do a job. And if I can't do it well, you'll have Slim all over you like greased lightning. He's got a short nose as it is, what with my doing the job he's thought of as his for a long time."

"I know all that," he said, sighing in exasperation as he felt the muscle softening a bit. His hands fit around her calf and he applied pressure where he knew it hurt the worst. He'd had his share in the past years. Charley-horses were part of the job. Especially when beginning a new phase of training or when a man was new to the job. In this case, a woman was involved, and James felt responsible for her pain.

"Forget about Slim. If you can't do the job well, he can fill in. But for now, you're doing just fine and Slim has enough to keep him busy." He looked down at her leg and his mouth flattened over his teeth.

"If you were a man, I'd have you out of those britches so I could handle this better," he told her. And then, almost as an afterthought, he tossed her a quick grin. "But, to tell the truth, I'm awfully glad you're not a man, sweetheart."

She bit her lip and was silent, her eyes shiny, perhaps with tears she hoarded to herself, he thought. And then she bent toward him and her mouth touched his forehead. "I'm glad I'm not a man, Jamie. Men are nice people for the most part, but in this case, I'd rather be what I am."

"Tempting? A green-eyed witch? A hip-twitching female?" He offered her choices, and she shot him a smug look, blinking back the moisture she had not allowed to fall. Her mouth formed a smile and he thought triumph dwelled there, the exultation of a woman who has gained her man's attention.

"You noticed? Especially the hip-twitching part?"

"How could I help it? You've got the sweetest little fanny I've ever spent any time watching, ma'am."

She ducked her head, as if suddenly unsure of herself. "I think I should be embarrassed, Jamie. At least a bit put out with you, talking to me this way."

"I'm only stating facts, Alex. There isn't a man breathing

who wouldn't watch you if he had a chance. You're as easy on the eyes as any female I've ever known."

"Thank you, sir. At least I think that was a compliment."

"Bend a little closer and I guarantee you'll know it was," he told her, reaching to encircle her waist with his hands, tugging her forward so that she lost her balance and fell against him. He caught her deftly, held her firmly and touched her mouth with his. As kisses went, it wasn't the best he'd ever aimed at a woman, but the power of their lips meeting in such a fashion shot through him.

"Jamie, you're supposed to be taking care of my leg, not kissing me," she said quietly, her breath sweet against his lips.

"I'd rather kiss you," he told her, rising and drawing her up from the chair. "Your leg feel better now?" he asked.

"Much," she told him. "Let me get my boot back on, will you?"

"I'll put it on for you. In just a minute."

She watched him, her cheeks rosy, her eyes glowing as she waited. Her mouth was pink and lush, luring him with its softness, promising pleasure should he accept the silent offering before him.

"You're a beauty, Miss Alexis. A man could get lost in your eyes, and lose his head over your lips. You feel like heaven in my arms," he murmured, wondering at his own fluent compliments. And then he bent to touch her ear with the tip of his tongue, and used his greater strength to ease her against himself, fitting her securely there, even as he acknowledged the thrust of his male member seeking shelter in the notch of her thighs.

"I think this is getting out of hand," she said, her palms firm against his chest. "I won't be treated like a mare in a stall, Jamie."

"And I won't do that to you," he answered. "When I make

love to you, it won't be in the tack room where anybody could come wandering by. I'll find a private place where we can be alone, where no one will disturb us."

"*When* you make love to me?" she asked tartly. "What makes you think it's a foregone conclusion?"

"Isn't it?" he asked, smiling at her, knowing his grin was arrogant. His mouth was twisted wryly and she was getting angrier by the second.

"I don't think so."

Her answer was what he had expected, and he wasn't long disappointed.

"I have no intention of performing any intimacies with you, Mr. Webster. I can't afford to give away what my husband will claim as his own on the day I marry."

"I'd say that all depends on who your husband turns out to be," he told her, his arms tightening around her, one hand lifting her chin, the better to position her for his kiss. No matter that she silently protested, turning her head away, pushing at him with futile strength.

He was by far the more powerful, his need was great and his aim was true. His mouth took hers with sure, certain touches, his lips forming to hers, the movement of his tongue urging her to open to him. If he was arrogant, so be it, he thought, sensing her ambivalence as she initially fought his arms and finally surrendered to his strength.

Her mouth opened and he lifted from her a bit. "You taste like honey," he whispered, "so sweet, I could eat you with a spoon." And then he altered his words. "On second thought, I don't think I need a utensil. My mouth will do just fine on its own."

She laughed, a chuckle emerging as she gasped for a breath.

"This is serious stuff," he told her. "Don't be laughing at me."

"I didn't know that kissing could be fun," she told him, her lips brushing against his as she spoke. "I mean, I know it's supposed to be enjoyable, but—"

"And how many men have you kissed to gain that opinion?" he asked, lifting his head and eyeing her with open appreciation.

"A few," she said, as if she would not elaborate further.

"And were they fun to kiss? Did they make you laugh?"

She looked thoughtful, he decided, as if she must search her recollections for those remembered caresses received from other men. "No one makes me laugh the way you do, Jamie," she confessed. "I've never known anyone like you. And several of the kisses that were forced on me made me gag. Not much fun there." She took a deep breath and her look was troubled, as if she knew she had revealed more than was wise. "Now that I've made you happy, help me put my boots on, mister."

His head tilted backward as he thought of her revelation. "I think we'll talk about your experience with kissing later on, sweetheart. As easily as you respond to me, I find it hard to believe that anyone would turn you off so totally. Unless it was a man who was out to give you grief." And with that bit of thought, he decided it would be as well if he dropped the matter for now.

"How come you've got a woman doing my job, boss?" Slim stood before him, just inside the barn door, his face stony with anger. Under control, but still apparent.

"She's good at what she does," James said bluntly, "but she's not strong enough physically to handle some of the work the men do. So I gave her a job she *can* handle, one she's capable of. That frees you up for other things."

James gave Slim his undivided attention, knowing that his

own face was registering his displeasure at the man's questioning. "On top of that, it was a decision made by Hank and I together, and since we're the ones running this operation, I can't see that anyone should have any problem with it. Do I make myself clear?"

"Yeah. I get the drift of things," Slim said, his tone taunting.

"Well, if you're suggesting that Alexis got the job by persuading me in any way, shape or form, you're dead wrong, Slim. There's nothing going on there, and if there ever is, it won't have anything to do with the running of this ranch."

He couldn't make it any plainer than that, James decided. And if the man wanted to get things in an uproar, he could have at it. But Slim walked away without another word, and James watched him with a frown. The man could cause trouble, split the loyalty of the hands in the bunkhouse, maybe even turn them against Alexis or himself. He'd have to keep a watchful eye on things.

"I knew this would happen," Alexis said quietly from behind him.

He turned to face her, surprised by her presence. "Where did you come from?"

"I was in the tack room and overheard Slim talking to you. He's jealous, isn't he?"

"Now, that, Alexis, is an understatement if I ever heard one."

"Do you want to change your mind about me working with you?"

James dug in, planting his feet firmly, squaring his shoulders and thrusting his hands deeply into his front pockets. "I don't bow down to a bit of opposition, ma'am. If Slim wants to run the show, he'll have to find another ranch to work at. He won't tell his boss what to do here. We can replace him if we have to, but that isn't my first choice. Right now, we could use another hand to take up the slack. And I don't fancy looking for two good men. Though the Double C is probably one of the best places around here."

"Which reminds me," Alexis said, smiling brightly. "I saw the new sign out by the county road. Looks really smart, Mr. Webster. Woody did a nice job on it. I'll bet the young man who owns this place will be pleased." She buried her hands in her own pockets, imitating his gesture, and her smile warmed as she watched him.

"Any chance of the boy coming out here to see the place?" she asked. "I've wondered if he might be interested in looking us over."

"He no doubt is," James said with a chuckle. "Stephen is all boy, with a horse and a dog of his own, and a couple of the best folks you've ever met as his parents. His daddy is the sheriff in Benning, and I worked for him for a lot of years. He married a pretty lady named Sarah, and Stephen is her nephew.

"You already know what a nasty fella his blood father was, and all the brothers were cut from the same cloth if you ask me," James continued. "I don't know how Stephen turned out so well, but—no, as a matter of fact, I do know. He's had the influence of his parents and grandparents in his life. They're all good folks."

"It sounds to me like you took a real shine to the boy," Alexis said.

"Couldn't help it. He's prime stock. And I wouldn't be surprised to see him here within a couple of years. He's real curious about this place."

"It's gonna be tough for him to fill your boots when he gets a little older, Jamie. And I sure hope he doesn't run into any of the clan hereabouts when he arrives. Most all of the menfolk are a bad bunch. In fact, the Clarks have a nasty reputation. Have had for years, I understand."

"How many of them are there?"

"A couple of families, cousins, I think. They were fond of the old man, though I never could figure out why. He was a rascal, my pa always said, and I agree with him on that. Mean is more the word I'd chose to describe him. I didn't know him for long, or very well, but I can't say he's been missed much around here."

"Did your father come in when the old man died?" James asked.

"Before that, when he was pretty sick already. He wrote back and forth to Brace Caulfield before Caulfield kept Dad on here. I think he was sounding him out, trying to get to know him better before he let him run the place. Then the lawyer stopped by and told Dad that he'd advised Sheriff Caulfield to hire his own man and send him here. He told Dad it would give the sheriff a better hold here. I was madder than a wet hen when he gave his opinion, but Dad seemed to understand. That was a while before you arrived."

"And how do you feel about me now?" James asked. "You've had a good long time to look me over and see me operate. What do you think?"

"You know what I think," she said, her cheeks turning a lovely shade of pink, her eyes sparkling with green fire. "You're the best thing that's happened here since Dad and I arrived. The men respect you, Dad thinks you're good at your job and I—"

She broke off suddenly and James grinned, moving his hands from his pockets to grasp her elbows, drawing her a bit closer. "And you what?" he asked softly. "How do you feel about me, Alexis?"

She shook her head and tried to move her arms from his

grasp. It didn't work, for he only shifted his hands upward to her shoulders. "I think you're too close for comfort, Jamie. We're out in the middle of the barn where anyone could see us, and you've got your hands all over me."

"Whoa, there, lady. I've got them on your shoulders, and that's a far cry from being where they'd like to be. As far as anyone seeing us, I really don't give a good gol-durn."

She laughed. "That wasn't the word I'd have thought you'd use," she said.

"My mama raised me to be respectful of ladies, and not use bad language around the fairer sex." He grinned, enjoying the quick smile she gave him, the shimmer of her eyes and the curls that framed her face. And that brought up another thing he'd considered before. "Don't ever cut your hair, Alexis," he said quietly. "It's so pretty, the way it waves and curls." His hand left her shoulder to brush at the small wisps that fell against her forehead and cheeks. "It makes you seem kin to a princess in a storybook." He felt a bit foolish at his own words, but finished determinedly in a low, hushed voice. "It looks like spun gold when you stand in the sun."

Her brows raised at his words. "You're quite the eloquent man, Jamie. No one's ever talked to me the way you do. I guess the best I ever got was when one of the men told me I had a nice headful of hair." She laughed at that memory and her eyes crinkled a bit, tempting him nearer.

"I don't want the men telling you anything," James said, hearing the harsh note in his own voice and wondering at it.

"You're jealous," she said firmly, and yet her voice lifted in surprise. "I can't believe you're jealous."

"You'd better believe it, lady. If anyone tells you how pretty you are and looks you over, it better be me. I'm staking a claim, in case you haven't noticed."

"Oh? And have you talked to my father about this?" she asked. "You sound a little like a dog with a bone, Jamie. I'm not sure I like that."

"I'd say I sound like a man with his eye on a woman, Alexis. A woman he plans on having for his own. That's what staking a claim means. One day you'll be mine."

"Really?" She stiffened beneath his touch and stepped backward. He allowed it, sensing her anger and not wanting to rile her further. "When I decide to let you stake a claim on me, I'll let you know, mister. Till then, keep your hands to yourself."

"I'll give you a long lead line, Alexis. But when I pull you closer, you'll come, and when I decide my waiting is over, you'll know it." He stepped closer to her and lifted one long finger to touch her chin, raising it for his pleasure. "I don't make threats, sweetheart, only promises."

He bent and his mouth touched hers, briefly, but with a trace of possessiveness that made her flush again. And then, as if he'd changed his mind, and needed more than the brief caress he'd offered, he caught her off balance and hauled her into his embrace. He bent to kiss her again, a hot, wet laving of her mouth that did not sit well with her, if her hands pushing against his chest were any indication.

"Let me go," she insisted, her voice trembling, her lips damp and a bit swollen.

He touched the upper lip with his index finger and rubbed it dry. "Did I hurt you?"

She shook her head. "No, and I won't give you a chance to. But I bruise easy. I make it a practice not to let any man hurt me, boss. I learned that the hard way."

"Well, I won't be so rough the next time I kiss you. I acted before I thought and I apologize. I'm afraid you're mad at me with good reason."

"There won't be a next time," she said curtly, pushing his hand away from her mouth.

James looked long and hard at the rosy lips, swollen from his attentions and again tempting him to taste the sweetness of their owner. "Don't count on that," he said, his voice a low growl. With easy movements, he stepped closer to her, and his arms were gentle as he clasped her in his embrace. His mouth was gentle now against hers, his tongue a tool of healing as it traced the swollen line of her lip, and he offered a warmth and tenderness he'd withheld before.

She stiffened against him, and then with a sigh that might have signified surrender, she leaned into him, perhaps enticed by his kiss, he thought. At any rate, he recognized the submission to his greater strength implicit in her movements, for she seemed to glory in the firm embrace that enclosed her. Her arms circled his neck and she pressed her head against his shoulder, turning her face upward to his. His mouth touched her closed eyelids, the soft skin of her cheek and again the temptation of her mouth. But he was gentle, careful not to do as his body demanded of him.

For now, this was enough. For today, he would be a gentleman. And as he released her and watched her walk away, he smiled at the confusion that colored her face.

The girl didn't know, didn't have a clue, he thought.

Chapter Five

Mick Jenson entered the saloon and took a quick look around, breathing a sigh of relief as he saw no one he recognized. Except for the barkeeper.

"What are you doin' around here, Jenson?" the white-aproned man asked, wiping the moisture from the polished walnut wood before him.

"Maybe looking for a job," Mick answered quietly.

"Doesn't sound like a wise idea to me," the bartender said with a laugh. "You're not exactly a favorite with the folks hereabouts. I suppose you came in lookin' for a drink," he said with little humor. "What'll you have?"

"Whiskey," the cowhand said briefly, then turned to look again at the scant number of men who inhabited the saloon in the middle of the afternoon. "What's new in town?" he asked, in what appeared to be a subtle query for information.

"Not much. Lula doesn't work here anymore. Got a rancher to marry her and moved on. I heard she's playin' mother to his kids and gonna have one of her own pretty soon." Sliding a glass of whiskey before his customer, the man continued.

"Oh, and there's a new place in town, a fella from up north says he's gonna sell horseless carriages. Sounds like a scam to me, but I reckon you never know."

Mick leaned with casual ease on one elbow, lifting his drink to his lips. "Anything goin' on out at the Clark place?"

"You got a one-way ticket out of town a year or so ago from a couple of men out there. Doesn't seem like you'd be lookin' to be hired on again. I doubt the new boss would welcome you like a prodigal son."

"New boss? What happened to Hank Powers?" Mick asked.

"He's still there, but when the old man died, the place was left to his first grandson, and there's a fella there running things for the boy."

Mick tossed back the rest of his whiskey and shoved the glass toward the man behind the bar. "Fill it up again."

"You haven't paid for the first one yet," the barman told him harshly. "Let's see your money."

Mick dug in his pocket and found a gold piece. "I reckon this'll buy all the booze I can drink in the next hour."

Without protest, the bartender poured another shot of whiskey in the glass and put the bottle back against the wall. "Just as a friendly gesture, I'd suggest you stay well away from the Double C these days, Jenson."

"If I want a job there, I'll get it," Mick said with a triumphant laugh.

"Just a friendly warning," the bartender said quietly. "You'd do better to stay away from the place. If I remember right, it was trouble with Hank's girl that got you shipped out of there once before."

"Yeah, and somebody's gonna pay for that mess, too." Lifting his shot glass, Mick slammed it down on the gleaming walnut slab and growled his order. "Fill it up."

With a shrug of studied nonchalance, the bartender did as directed and then took the gold piece from the bar and made change from beneath, placing the coins before Mick.

"Here you go, Jenson. But, if I was you, I'd take it easy on the hard stuff. You'll end up drunker than a skunk, and out like a light before suppertime."

"I can handle it," Mick said with a sneer. "I got plans to make, and I think better with a little rotgut in my belly."

Chet Dawson stomped up the steps to the back porch and rapped twice on the screened door. From the kitchen table, Hank answered with a call of welcome.

"Come on in, Chet. What's up?" He motioned to a chair. "Have a cup of coffee. Ellen here just made a fresh pan of cinnamon rolls. Have one."

"Let me wash up first," Chet said with a sidelong look at the new cook. "I'm kinda partial to sweet rolls. Don't mind if I have one, ma'am."

Without reply, Ellen poured a cup of coffee and cut Chet a generous portion, placing it on the table in front of the chair he would occupy. He scrubbed his hands quickly at the sink and returned to the table. "Looks good," he said, spreading butter lavishly.

"You got some sort of problem?" Hank asked. "It's not like you to come to the house so early on."

"I don't have a problem, but you just might, Hank." Chet took a bite of his roll and a swig of coffee, then wiped his mouth with the back of his hand.

"What's up?" James asked, watching the man closely. And if it had Alexis's name attached, he'd handle it, he decided.

Chet tossed him a quelling look and then at Hank's glare, seemed to change his tactics. With a quick grin, he stated the facts he'd heard as the gospel truth from two of the ranch hands.

"A couple of the boys were in the saloon last night, the Red Rose, you know, where Gracie works."

Hank waved his hand impatiently. "Every man in the county knows where Gracie works, Chet. What did the boys hear that was so important."

"Mick Jenson's in town."

"Jenson's back?" Hank stood to his feet, his chair hitting the floor behind him.

"Are you sure?" James asked quietly, picking up Hank's chair and pressing him back down in it, one hand on the man's shoulder.

"The barkeeper told the men that we'd better keep a watch out. Said Mick was layin' plans."

"What sort of plans?" James asked.

Chet looked at him, a frown wrinkling his forehead. "Must be you haven't heard about Mick and Alexis. It wasn't a pretty story."

"I've heard," James said shortly, earning a quick glance from Hank.

"What did Mick have to say to the bartender?" Hank asked.

"Just that he was lookin' for a job, and he's got plans to make."

"Sounds like trouble to me," Hank said. "Pass the word that if any man on the place sees him, I want to know about it."

"What does he look like?" James asked.

Chet finished his coffee and leaned back in his chair. "Kinda big fella, tall and husky. Dark hair and a heavy beard. Big hands with a lot of hair on the backs. Thinks he's a real hand with the ladies."

"Does Alexis know about this?" James asked.

"She does now." From the hallway, Alexis answered the question for herself. "Don't worry about it, Dad," she said confidently. "I know enough to stay out of Mick's way. I'll carry a gun if I have to."

"And what would you do with it?" Hank asked. "I can't see you shooting a man, Alex. You're too soft-hearted for that."

"If I see Mick hereabouts, I won't hesitate," she told her father. "He's bad, all the way through."

"I don't want you up on charges if you kill him," Hank said sternly.

"You think the sheriff would take her in?" Chet asked. "Sounds kinda doubtful to me. Not with Mick's past history on record."

"I'd rather not have a man's death haunting her," Hank said stubbornly.

"I agree with that," James said. "But I don't think it's a bad idea for her to carry a gun for her own protection. I just don't think she needs to shoot the man unless he tries to give her trouble."

"Why don't the two of you just let me take care of myself?" Alexis stood, hands on hips, feet apart, her cheeks flushed with anger.

"You're a woman," Hank said shortly.

"I've heard that before," Alexis said, tilting her chin and facing her father without fear of his anger.

"It's still as true as it was the last time he told you that," James added. "A woman doesn't stand a chance against a mad man. And from what I'm hearing, Mick Jenson qualifies."

"He'll bleed just like anyone else." Alexis was as stubborn as her father, James decided, hiding his smile. She was a piece of work, all right. Hardheaded as the day was long.

With a flip of her long braid, she left the kitchen, having had the last word, and Hank shot James a look of sympathy. "I'm glad you're the one gonna be handling her today, son. She's fit to be tied."

"I can handle her," James said, hoping he was right on that count, and wondering what the day would hold.

When he reached the corral, he found out, for Alexis had one of the three-year-old mares saddled.

"You haven't got her to the point of holding your weight yet," James said firmly.

"That's just your opinion," Alexis said, her back to him as she adjusted the stirrups.

"And my opinion is what counts here. She isn't ready for this."

"I've fiddled around with her for a week. I think she'll let me on without any trouble."

"I thought you had a future as a trainer, but if you're gonna go off half-cocked just because you had an argument with your father, you're already a failure at the job, Alexis. We aren't going to argue about this."

"Damn right we're not." She exploded, turning to face him with a quick twist of her body. "This horse is ready to ride, and I'm going to ride her."

"If you get tossed, your father won't let you out here again."

"He's not the boss here anymore."

"I'll stand behind him on this one," James told her firmly.

She tossed him a look of arrogance. "Then I'll have to be certain I stay on, won't I?" With soft words to the horse she'd saddled, she led the animal toward the opposite side of the corral. James watched as she alternately petted and spoke to the horse, running her hands over the mare's neck and head, whispering praise in the velvet-textured ears. She darted a triumphant look at Jamie, as if she dared him to intervene, and it was all he could do not to interfere. Only the look of total confidence in the woman's eyes halted his natural inclination to keep her from harm.

With care, moving slowly, she moved to the horse's left side, tugging at the stirrup, letting the mare feel her weight against it. The pinto side-stepped, her ears back, and Alexis moved forward again, standing at her head, speaking softly, her hands never leaving the animal's body.

Again, she approached the mare's left side, and in a quick movement slipped her foot into the stirrup and swung into the saddle. The mare shivered, a visible movement, and Alexis bent low over her neck, speaking softly. Then, as if demon-possessed, the horse scraped against the corral fence, trying to dislodge the weight on her back.

Her head went down and James knew he was too far away to snatch at the bridle, not near enough to pull the horse from her position. Even as he moved toward her, the mare left the ground, all four feet tucked up beneath her as she twisted her body to dislodge the woman who clung to the saddle.

"Get back," Alexis called out to James. "Let me handle her."

"Son of a gun," James snarled. "Get off that mare, Alex. Hold her down and let me help you."

"No." Her hands were full with the bucking horse beneath her, and wisely, James backed off. If he distracted her further, she could very well hit the ground, and that was the one thing he dreaded having happen. So he watched.

The mare bucked again, side-stepped and twisted beneath Alexis, and the woman clung to the saddle like a burr. By the time two or three minutes had passed, the corral fence was lined with the men who had been working near the barn, all of them silent as they watched, two of them already sitting on the fence, as if they waited for Alexis to hit the ground and were prepared to move to her side to protect her from the horse.

And then the mare settled down, shivering and tossing her head, her tail swishing, her hooves shifting as she stood spraddle-legged in the center of the corral. "Good girl." Alexis bent to pat the mare's neck and in a quick move, slid from the saddle, only to lead the horse to where James stood, holding the bridle in one hand, brushing back her windblown hair with the other.

"She'll be fine the next time," she told James, and then as if she'd only now noticed the men who'd lined the fence, she grinned. "The show's over, fellas. Get back to work."

As one, they clapped and cheered, and Alexis blushed at their praise. Then with a quick look at James, she led the mare to the gate and after exchanging her bridle for a halter, and loosening the cinch and sliding her saddle off, she reached for a rough towel hanging on the gate and rubbed over the animal's back and neck. With another quick word of praise, she released her into the pasture.

James stood without moving, watching the woman, angry with her, even as he could not help but admire the skill she'd displayed. And then he moved, following her into the barn. His hands were rough as he turned her to face him.

"I'll have bruises tomorrow," she said, frowning down at his grip on her arms.

"Ask me if I care. You're lucky you didn't take a spill out there. You could have broken a leg, or even worse." His mouth twisted with an emotion akin to fear, and he gripped her tightly, then shook her, taking her off guard.

"Don't push it, boss," she said, her voice trembling.

"Well, you've pushed me far enough for one day. I'm tempted to turn you over my knee, little girl."

"I'm not a little girl. I'm a grown woman. And I knew what I was doing out there," she said with a trace of arrogance that angered him even more.

"I know you're a grown woman, but you acted like a stubborn child, riding that mare and refusing help."

"I didn't need any help." She lifted her chin and threw another look of chilled disdain his way.

"That does it," he said, turning her toward the tack room, shoving her inside and closing the door behind them, turning her toward it with a quick shove, catching her off guard. His fingers pressed into her flesh, his body was a wall of stone as he pushed her up against the door, and then he bent his head, taking her mouth without care, with none of the tenderness he'd been wont to spend on her flesh.

His anger was manifest in the harshness he dealt her, and her own was apparent in her failure to fight him. She hung in his grasp, her jaw set, her mouth taut and her eyes wide as he pressed his lips against hers. And then she lifted her knee in a quick movement. It was only his suspicious mind that saved him from serious pain, as he twisted away from her, taking the glancing blow against his thigh.

"That won't work with me," he grunted, shaking her in his grasp. And then he turned, hauling her with him to the cot against the far wall. He lifted her and then with a thump, deposited her there and loomed over her.

"You'll break the cot this way," she said, her voice trembling, but fury shining from green eyes that were dark and forbidding.

"Who the hell cares?" He felt reckless, swept by the desire he'd allowed to be set free in his body. His fingers were nimble on the buttons of her shirt and he parted them, exposing a thin, white vest beneath. Pearl buttons held it closed and he exhibited his prowess quickly, the tiny fastenings obedient to his touch.

Her flesh was mere inches from his hands, the pale skin tempting his fingers to lower to the surface, where blue veins were formed beneath the surface. He lowered his head, his mouth breathing heated air against her, and then his tongue touched the upper rise of her right breast and he tasted the sweetness there.

"Jamie, you're angry with me. Don't do this," she whispered. "Please, don't."

He lifted his head to look in her eyes. "I'm not going to hurt you, Alex. This isn't the time or place for us. But you've got me in a twist, and it's either this or I'll say things I'd be sorry for later. I'm gonna kiss you a bit, taste your skin, sample your flesh a little."

"I don't want you to," she protested, wiggling beneath him.

"You'd better lie quietly. Too much wiggling and I may change my mind."

Her cheeks were rosy, her eyes shining with anger and her lips still damp from his kiss. He thought her the loveliest woman he'd ever seen. An image of Alexis in his bed, hair undone and loose upon his pillow, entered his mind and he swallowed the temptation it extended in his direction. The time would come. But not today, and not in the tack room.

Opening her vest wider, he gazed upon the perfect globes of her bosom and bent to touch one puckered crest, feeling her shiver of fear even as he forbid himself the taste of it in his mouth. Instead, he bent low and kissed her skin, lifting her breast, exposing the tender underside to his touch, then tracing the firm flesh with fervent kisses that seemed to hold her immobile.

She was quiet then, but for the harshness of her breathing. On an indrawn sigh, she murmured his name, and that only a whisper. Her hands reached to clasp his head, fingers forming runnels through his hair, then holding him firmly against herself, as if she would keep his eager lips against her flesh.

"I thought you would…" She caught her breath, as if unable to continue.

"You thought I'd hurt you? Take more from you than this?" he asked roughly.

Her nod was unsure, and then she quickly shook her head. "No, I think I knew better, Jamie. You've only given me warmth and pleasure."

Her words were a spur to his desire, but he quelled the harsh grip of passion and set it aside. "I have to quit," he muttered darkly, picking up his head to fasten his gaze on her face. "If I don't stop now, it'll be too late, Alex. Tell me to stop."

She laughed, releasing his head and dropping her hands to where her vest and shirt gaped open. "Stop, Jamie." And then she laughed again. "Is that what you wanted?"

He shook his head. "No. But it's what I needed to hear. I want you, Alex. I have a powerful need to mate with you. But my willpower is mighty thin right now."

She pushed at him and rose from the cot, buttoning the topmost button on her shirt. "I probably wouldn't have stopped you, Jamie," she confessed in a low voice.

"I know," he said, reaching for her and holding her close. His mouth was on her hair, moving to her temple where he spent a dozen kisses. "You were a big temptation, Alex, but I'd rather wait."

She curled against him and he rocked her a bit, holding her fast. "Please don't take any chances, will you?"

"I'm not foolish, Jamie. And whether you mean with Mick in the vicinity or on the horses, it doesn't matter. I'm too smart to risk myself."

"I think you understood all right," he told her. "I meant in both cases, especially where Mick Jenson is concerned. He's an unknown to me, and I don't know just what he's capable of, but I fear his size and temperament could be too much for you to handle. The horses aren't as much a problem as he is.

I'm pretty sure you can handle any of them, so long as you're careful. But from what Chet said, Jenson is a big fella. You wouldn't stand a chance against him. He'll be looking for you to attack him if he gets a chance at you."

"I know that. And I will be careful. I don't trust him, not one little bit. I think he may be out to get me."

"If he touches you, I'll kill him," James said harshly. "You can bet on it."

"Can I assume your intentions toward my daughter are honorable?" Hank stood with one foot on the corral fence and questioned James with a bluntness that seemed perfectly logical to James. If Alexis were his daughter, he'd probably be holding a shotgun about now.

Knowing that Hank had seen them coming out of the tack room yesterday had been preying on James's mind all night. Now, in the light of day, with Alexis atop one of the horses, one she'd quieted and coaxed into trotting around the corral, he faced her father. "You can assume that," he said quietly. "I love Alexis, sir. I want to marry her."

"What does she say about that?" Hank asked.

"I haven't asked her yet."

Hank's eyebrow rose. "Don't you think it's about time? After the time you spent with her in the tack room yesterday, I'd say you were walking on the wild side. I came pretty close to calling you on it when I saw the pair of you."

"Alexis didn't see you," James told him. "If she had, I'd have cleared the air then and there. As it is, I'd rather wait and talk to her when I get her alone."

"Just make sure you spend the time talking," Hank said, his brows lowered, his face taut with emotion. "I won't have my girl taken advantage of, Jamie. You'll marry her before you bed her if I have anything to say about it."

"You haven't," James said. And then he held up his hand as Hank moved toward him. "Hold on, Hank. What I'm saying is that I have a brand-new set of rules I'm playing by when it comes to Alexis. Marriage comes first for a woman like her, and I have no intention of jumping the gun." He grinned at the disbelief on Hank's face, the man looking as if he were stunned by James's words. "She'll be a virgin on her wedding day. And that's a promise."

Hank stuck out his hand and James grasped it, shaking it firmly. "Are we seeing things the same way now?" He waited for an answering nod from Hank before he released his hand. "Now if you don't mind, sir, I'd like to spend some time with your daughter. Wave goodbye to her and walk away. This is personal business I'm about to transact."

Hank laughed and waved at Alexis, who nodded and glanced from James to her father and back again, as if she were trying to figure them out. "Let me know if you succeed, son," Hank said, walking into the back of the barn and down the aisle to the yard, and then toward the house.

Alexis rode the gelding she was on to where James watched and bent toward him. "What's going on? Was Dad upset?"

"Not so's you could notice," James said. "How about putting that horse away for now. I need to talk to you."

"All right. Open the gate for me, would you?" With an easy movement, she turned the horse in a half circle and rode to the pasture gate, sliding from the gelding's back and loosening his cinch.

James reached to take the saddle, leaving Alexis to trade bridle for halter, and then they watched as the gelding loped across the pasture to join the dozen or so horses that cropped the grass beneath a grove of trees.

"They're smart, staying out of the sun," Alexis said, turning toward the barn, bridle in hand. James followed her, carrying her saddle, heaving it over the sawhorse where his own rested. She went on to the tack room to hang up the bridle and he followed her.

She turned to him and pushed at his chest ineffectually. "I'm not going to spend another hour in here with you today, Jamie. I almost got in trouble yesterday."

"Just a few minutes, Alex. And we don't have to stay in here. We can do as well in the barn or out in back."

She looked curious, her cat's eyes slanted as they surveyed him. "What is it?" she asked. "What do you want?"

He grinned, not touching her, but standing close enough to feel her breath as she turned her head up toward him. "You, Alexis. I want you."

She grinned. "You've made that pretty clear already. I got the message yesterday. What else is new?"

"I want you on a permanent basis," he said soberly. "All joking aside, sweetheart, I'm asking you to marry me, be my wife, tie the knot. However you want me to say it, I will. So long as your answer is yes."

"Marry you?" She looked stunned, and he was surprised.

"I thought you'd figured out already that I was dead serious about you, honey. I thought you'd be expecting me to want to set a date. I'm an impatient man when it comes to some things and right now that means you. I want to marry you, Alex."

"To get me in bed?" she asked, a pout forming. "I didn't think you'd go to all the trouble of a wedding to succeed at that. Not that I'd go along with it, but I was sure you'd try."

"I've already told you I'd wait." His jaw was firm, as if he'd suffered an insult.

She was silent for a moment, her gaze softening as she searched his face, as though some message might be there in the complex formation of eyes, mouth and brow. "You really mean it, don't you?" she whispered.

"Let's go about this starting from the first question you asked. No, I'm not marrying you just to get you in my bed." He hesitated and grinned. "Well, hell, yes. I want you there, so there's that, too," he said. "But mostly because I want to spend my life with you. We'll have a good time together. We get along, except for when we're fighting, and that doesn't happen very often. And then there's the fire that comes to life between us when we touch, when I hold you close. That in itself is almost enough reason for me to marry you. But more important than that is the fact that I like you. I really like you, girl. That doesn't sound very romantic, I know, but it's true. I've been in love with you for a while, but liking you is almost more important to me."

She stood before him, seemingly transfixed by his speech. For that was surely what it was. He'd listed all the reasons for his proposal and now he waited to hear her answer. It was not long in coming.

"I like you, too, Jamie. I have from the first day you got here, when you told me my pancakes tasted like your mama's. That was quite a compliment, coming from a man who obviously was well fed as a child."

"You think I'm fat?" he asked, looking down at his trim waist.

"Far from it. But you looked healthy to me the first time I saw you, and only a man who's been well fed his whole life has the color you have and the overall look of good health." She reached out a hand and touched his shirtfront. "You're not fat, Jamie. In fact, you're about as well built as any man I've ever seen. I like your broad shoulders and your narrow hips and the muscles in your—"

"Muscles in my what?" he asked, grinning foolishly.

"Never mind," she told him, blushing as she realized what she'd almost said aloud. *In your legs. And your arms. Across your back.* The man had muscles everywhere a man was supposed to have them. Jamie had his share and more.

And now, she'd just told him she would marry him, and unless she was mighty mistaken, he was ready to set a date.

"When, Alex?" he asked, verifying her suspicion.

"As soon as you like," she said quickly. "My father will want to give a party for the neighbors and the townspeople. We can't get away without that."

The wave of his arm was expansive. "No problem, sweetheart. He can invite anyone he likes, so long as you and I are both there, along with the preacher."

"You want to get married here? Not in church?" she asked.

"Wherever you like," he said. "It's your party, honey. I'll just be here to ride off in the sunset with you."

"Where will we go?" she asked, wide-eyed.

He laughed. "I'll figure something out. Maybe the hotel in town."

"No. Everyone will be watching for us the next day. I'd be embarrassed."

"Well, then we'll ride to Perryville. It's only ten miles away. They've got a big hotel there, I suspect. The stage stops there, so they're probably well equipped for travelers."

"They have," she said agreeably. "Bigger than the one in town. With a nice restaurant."

"Well, that's settled," he said with a sigh that sounded like relief to her. "Now, let's go and tell your father."

"Will he be surprised?" she asked, intent on his face. He looked a bit guilty, she thought, as if he had already talked this whole thing over with Hank Powers.

"Not really," James said. "He wanted to know if my intentions were honorable."

"When did he ask you that?" She sounded huffy, and then she laughed. "Never mind. I know when. While I was riding the gelding, wasn't it?"

"Yeah," he drawled. "He saw us coming out of the tack room yesterday and I think he was going to warn me away from you if I didn't have marriage on the mind. I assured him that I was on the verge of making a proposal and he backed off."

"He saw us?" She was shocked, thinking of what her father must have felt, watching the two of them exiting the tack room, her with her hair all ruffled and her shirt probably half-untucked from her trousers.

"He saw us. But he's not mad. I told him I hadn't asked you yet."

"You did?" she asked. "Why didn't you tell me?"

"'Cause I knew you'd get upset over it. Just like you are right now."

She looked at him, tempted to exhibit her anger more physically. "I'm not upset, James Webster. I'm damn mad. From now on, you tell me anything that goes on, you hear? I don't like being kept in the dark."

"Yes, ma'am," he said meekly. "I surely will." And then he grinned, a cocky smile of triumph. "So, you're gonna marry me. How about that."

With a flexing of muscles, he reached for her, picked her up and swung her in a circle, then made his way through the barn, across the yard and up on the back porch.

"Hank. You in there?" he shouted.

"Jamie. Stop yelling. The men will all hear you."

"I've got something to shout about," he said, bending his head to plant a damp kiss on her mouth, just as the screened door swung open and Hank appeared on the threshold.

"And what's that?" Hank asked, hiding his smile unsuccessfully.

"She's gonna marry me, Pop. Maybe next week or the Saturday after."

"Pop?" Hank's mouth dropped open. And then he recovered quickly. "Make it the week after, so I can plan a party."

"What did I tell you?" Alexis crowed. "I knew what he'd say."

"You're not really going to call me Pop, are you?" Hank asked the man who had his arms full of woman.

"I've kinda gotten used to Hank," James said. "Will that do?"

"That'll do. Now, put that girl down and let me shake your hand, son. I owe you big-time for taking her off my hands."

Chapter Six

They'd eaten their supper, James quiet, as if his mind were filled with plans. Alexis spoke with her father about plans for the party, seemingly ignoring Jamie's silence. And then, once the meal was finished, she led him to the back porch, seating herself on one end of the swing.

The chains squeaked as Jamie's foot touched the floor of the porch, stirring the swing into motion with his right foot, moving in an easy rhythm. Beside him, Alexis turned her face up to his, her thoughts awash with his very presence. Her mind grasped a moment of passion, replaying it slowly again in her mind, recognizing her own pleasure and finally acknowledging the depth of his need for her.

He'd said he truly liked her, and offered it partially as a basis for marriage, but her honest heart recognized that more than just having her in his life, he wanted her in his bed. To be the object of his desire, to know his passion was directed at her was exciting in the extreme, giving a satisfying boost to her woman's ego and joy to her heart.

To be wanted was one thing. Heavenly days, half the men who had ever worked on the ranch had wanted her, a carnal lust for a woman's body their driving purpose. But being needed—now there was a matter that could endear a man to her. To know that Jamie truly felt excitement and passion at the thought of spending his life with her was indeed most gratifying.

The best part of which was that she felt a like need for him, for the strength of his body and spirit, the protection of his presence, the hope for a family of her own. But above and beyond that was the love she knew bloomed within her, the manifestation of her attraction to him and all that he promised.

And so she sat with him, this man who vowed to be her future, whose word could be trusted. A man who had been honest and aboveboard since the day she first met him. And now the reason for his need to speak with her must surely have to do with their lives beyond the wedding. A conversation she was eager to pursue.

"I can't believe Dad went to bed and left us out here alone," she said with a muffled laugh. James's arm tugged her closer to his side and she leaned her head back on his shoulder, enjoying the quiet of the night, the darkness that surrounded them.

"I reckon he knew we had things to talk about," he said quietly. "At least I need to talk about something," he said soberly. "I've got a couple of things to tell you and I can't put it off until after we're married. It wouldn't be right, Alexis. You have a right to know more about me before you say your vows."

She jerked and sat upright. "I think you're frightening me, Jamie. What on earth is in your past that would make a difference in the way I feel about you?"

"That's what we're going to talk about. It happened a long time ago, but I was old enough to know better and I've carried the guilt around with me for years."

Alexis inhaled deeply and then prepared herself to listen, realizing this conversation was not concerning bright plans for their years to come. "Go ahead. Tell me."

He cleared his throat, looking out at the night, there where the moonlight silvered the barn and spread a trail across the yard. It wasn't easy to begin, for he knew he was putting his future on the line.

"When I was a boy, back in Oklahoma, I lived on the farm with my mom and dad and my brother, Connor," he began slowly. "Dad always gave Connor more respect than he did me, but I was the privileged one. And between my parents, they spoiled me rotten. I was my mama's favored child, and I got so I expected everything to fall in my lap. Including the girl Connor was engaged to."

A dark wave of envy swept through Alexis. She'd known that Jamie was no angel, but the thought that he might have caused trouble over a woman was pretty important stuff in a family. Perhaps there was more to the years of his past than she had suspected.

"Who was she? What did you do?" Her voice was low, neutral and pitched just above a whisper.

"I persuaded her to dance with me at a party while Connor was out of town on a buying trip, and then I took her outdoors and kissed her. It was hard staying away from her after that, and she liked me, too. We met secretly a few times and one day we ended up in her daddy's barn."

He looked at Alexis then and his voice faltered. There was no backing down now, he decided, knowing that his plans for marriage to this woman were in danger of blowing up in his face. His teeth were gritted and his jaw ached from the pressure, but he continued. "I made love to her, Alexis. I made love to my brother's intended. She was wearing his ring, and I betrayed Connor."

Alexis felt quick tears fill her eyes. "You were a dirty rat, Jamie. I'm ashamed of you, and I don't even know your brother or the girl." She trembled beside him and he held her arm when she would have risen from the swing.

"Wait, Alexis. The worst is yet to come. When Loris told me almost two months later that she was going to have my child, I skipped town and accepted a job in Missouri. I left money with Connor for her, and rode away."

Alexis sat on the edge of the swing now, perched as if she might run at any moment. "I can't imagine you doing a thing like that," she said sadly. "You must have been a different man then."

"I was a spoiled kid, not a man at all," he admitted. "I didn't even think twice about leaving Loris, didn't even consider what her parents would do."

"And what did they do?"

"Kicked her out. It was January, and snowing the night she left home. She was on foot, carrying only a blanket and a few things in a valise. It was a miracle that she didn't curl up by the side of the road and freeze to death. Anyway, Connor set off to find her the next day and before long, he was taking care of her, staying with her at an abandoned farm. He used the money I'd left and when he went into town he paid the back taxes on the place, and assumed ownership in her name. And then he married her."

"Where is your child?" Alexis asked, her mind trying to imagine the small boy or girl who lived in Oklahoma. A child with Jamie's blue eyes and black hair.

His grief vibrated in the words he spoke. "The baby died. They buried him in the orchard. It was almost too much for Loris to bear, especially when my mother got into the picture and tried to have Loris run out of town. She caused a lot of trouble for Connor, even had a plan to kill Loris." He breathed deeply. "I can't tell you how miserable she was and how much grief my brother suffered over the whole mess. And then my father was killed." He bent his head and she thought she'd never seen a man so stricken by his own confession.

"What happened to Connor and Loris?"

"What I wished for, once my eyes were open. They've had two children. They're living on the farm and things are going well for them. No thanks to me."

"Your mother blamed the girl, didn't she?" Alexis could just imagine the woman's anguish when she saw her favored son making such a botch of things. Of course, it had to be someone else's fault. And since Loris was handy, she was given the blame for the brothers' estrangement.

"Yeah, she blamed Loris and if she'd had her way, Connor and I would be enemies now instead of brothers."

"What do you want me to say, Jamie? Should I be angry with you over something that happened a long time ago? Should I call off our wedding because you behaved like a child instead of a man?" *Because you aren't the man I'd thought you were?*

"I don't know what I expect of you," he said harshly. "I had to tell you, Alexis. I've changed, and I'm not saying that to persuade you into this marriage. I hurt a lot of people, a couple of them almost beyond measure."

"Have they forgiven you?" She waited for his answer, knowing that much depended on it.

"Yeah. Much to my surprise. We parted on good terms. Loris wanted nothing more than for Connor and I to be friends, the way we were growing up together. It took a while, but now I can look at her and see her as a sister. You need to know that, so when the time comes that we see them, you won't be thinking I have any feelings for her, other than as a member of my family, and Connor's wife. I've put all the rotten things I did into a neat bundle and pushed them into the past, and I rarely think about those days.

"I just knew I couldn't marry you without you being aware of what happened. I wanted you to understand that my behavior was that of a low-life rascal. I did wrong, and I've lived to regret it. I've cried a lot of tears over the trouble I caused. If you can accept me as I am, I'll be forever grateful." He bent to her, his mouth touching her forehead in a brief, tender caress, as if he feared she would rebuff him.

"I want to marry you, Alexis. More than anything in the world, I want you for my wife. But I need to know that you can forgive me and overlook my past. I'll be the first to admit that I'm asking a lot of you. Maybe too much."

She tipped her head back and found her own tears near the surface. That James could have hurt his brother so, not to mention the young woman he'd seduced and forsaken…it was almost too much to absorb, the pain of his actions too cruel to be those of the man who faced her now.

"I was right," he said bitterly. "I'm asking too much of you. I'm not good enough for you, Alexis. You deserve a man with a decent past, not one who has caused pain and hard feelings in his family, the way I have."

And for a moment she stared at him, at the dark hair and blue eyes that had so attracted her to him. As they had lured on a woman in his past. Was he right? Could he be the husband she yearned for? Or was she asking for trouble, jumping into this?

And then she shook herself mentally. She could not pretend to be judge and jury over his future. She could only accept him, forgive the young man he had been and be thankful that his life had changed.

She lifted her hands to his face, touching the skin of his temples and jaws, holding him firmly, persuading him to draw near. Her kiss was gentle, asking nothing of him, only giving him the sweetness of her mouth. And as if he'd been gifted with something most precious, he smiled down at her, his arms circling her as he lifted her to sit on his lap.

"I didn't know I'd find someone like you, Alex. It's like discovering gold at the end of the rainbow." His fingers rose to her back where her braid hung almost to her waist. He slipped the ribbon from it and spent long moments untangling it from the imprisoning plait she'd formed early on in the day. "You have beautiful hair, sweetheart. I've a yen to see it loose tonight."

Again the joy of knowing she could so easily please him struck her, and her voice was teasing as she spoke. "You know better, Jamie," she said. "It's not considered proper for you to take a woman's hair down."

"You're not just any woman," he told her, his breath warm in her ear. "You're going to be my wife, and I *have* the right."

"Not till we're married," she said, yet knowing she would not deny him this. "That's when you learn all my secrets."

"How many do you have?" he asked, his hands stilling, his breath deepening.

She hesitated and he grasped her shoulder and leaned her back, the better to see her face, aware that she teased him. "I'll almost guarantee you have nothing to hide from me, Alexis. You're too open and easy to read to be hiding any lovers in your past." He smiled, a faint movement of his mouth as if his trust in her was implicit.

Then he sighed, a dramatic sound that made her smile. "All right, tell me. Is there anything important I need to know?"

She shook her head. "Probably not, given the confession you've made. I've kissed a couple of men and walked in the moonlight with three or four, but I'm a virgin, Jamie. No one has ever touched me but you."

"I haven't—"

"Yes, you have," she said, denying his words. "You opened my shirt and vest and I let you. I've never done that with another man."

He buried his face in her shoulder, turned his head and kissed her throat. "Damn, you had me worried there for a minute, sweetheart, with hinting about a lurid past."

"Hardly. I can't claim any experience, Jamie. I hope you won't be disappointed in me. I'm a greenhorn at the whole game of loving."

He laughed. "That's about the nicest thing anyone's ever told me," he said. "A man likes to hear that from his bride. Didn't you know that? It means no one else has ever had what you're going to give me, and trust me, baby, no one else will ever have a chance at you. Not while I'm alive." His fingers had completed their task and her hair hung loose, waves and curls freed from bondage.

"You'll be alive for at least the next fifty years or so, Jamie. And after that I'll be too old to care."

"Ah, no. That's where you're wrong, sweetheart. We'll never get too old to care. Love isn't just for the youngsters, you know. Wait and see. One of these days I'll remind you of this conversation and you'll admit I'm right."

She was silent, with no rebuttal to offer, only the hope that it would be as he had said. And in the moonlight, he cherished her, his hands buried in the wealth of gold he'd set loose, his mouth and hands assuring her of his love.

"I spoke to the preacher in town today," James said. It was the next evening and they were sitting around the supper table, Ellen having put the bowls and platters in place. She sat down beside Hank and waited as he bowed his head and uttered a brief blessing.

The next words out of his mouth were directed at James. "What did you tell him?"

"I asked him to come out here next Saturday and tie the knot between Alexis and me. He agreed. He'll be here around two o'clock." He turned to look at Alexis. "Is that all right?"

She nodded. "I've got things all set up for three, and when I invited folks I told them to be here shortly after two, so as to give us time to gather out by the orchard. I thought we could get married there, beneath the trees."

James gave her a look that brought color to her cheeks. "As long as you and I are there and the preacher shows up, that's all that matters, sweetheart."

"Now there," said Ellen smartly, "is a man besotted by his bride."

"And that's the truth," James agreed. He shot a glance at Hank, gaining his attention. "I'll work at getting things in order before we leave. There shouldn't be much for you to do with us being gone for just a couple of days. Just have Slim work with the horses. I don't want them out of the habit of daily exercise. And Alexis won't be here for…" he looked at her with a wide smile "…a couple of days and nights."

"And I suppose you're keeping your destination a secret, aren't you?" Hank asked.

"You betcha," James answered quickly. "I'm no dummy. I don't want any shivaree going on. Being dragged off to who knows where in the middle of the night isn't my idea of fun."

"Well, I'm sure we can handle things for a few days without the pair of you," Hank said. "Ellen and I will keep the home fires burning and I'll play at being the boss."

"Sometimes I wonder why Brace Caulfield sent me here," James said. "You were doing a fine job, and I'd be between a rock and a hard place some days, even now, if you weren't here."

"I can see why he wanted you here, Jamie. You're a born leader. You get along well with the men, and they respect you. I was unknown to the sheriff, and he felt better having someone in charge that he knew firsthand."

"Well, Alexis," Ellen said, bringing three pairs of eyes to rest on her. "What would you like me to do for the wedding. Besides cooking, I mean?"

"Probably that will be enough for you to tackle," Alexis said. "Dad will no doubt roast a pig or put a steer in a fire pit, but you'll have the rest of it to fix."

"Maybe we'll have both," Hank said. "I only have one daughter, and she's only gonna be married once, so we'll go all out for it. How many folks you figure will be here?"

"Close to a hundred, I think. If the townspeople show up, plus our neighbors, it'll be quite a bunch," Alexis said.

"I'll have the boys put together some sawhorses," James said. "We can lay planks on them to make tables for the food."

"The biggest job you've got is getting Alexis out of here without half the young men from town following you," Hank said. "They'll be hot to trot, ready to chase you down and trying to find out where you're going."

"They don't have a chance," James told him. "I have it all planned."

As weddings went, it was a dandy, Alexis thought dreamily, looking out from her bedroom window as the wagons and buggies gathered in the side yard below. Friends and neighbors brought food, the ladies having notified Ellen of their contributions days earlier, and now they carried bowls and crocks into the ranch kitchen, their voices rising in conversation as they prepared the feast to come.

At the appointed time, Alexis walked down the staircase on her father's arm, through the door and into the orchard, where Jamie awaited her. Chet and Ellen stood with him, prepared to witness the marriage. The minister stood behind a makeshift altar, its surface laden with flowers, and before him was the arch Woody had prepared. She stood in its shelter, finally facing the man she would wed, her father speaking the words that would give her into the hands of James Webster.

And then came the low, intense tones of the pastor who officiated. "Dearly beloved…" The familiar passages spoke to her heart, for the first time their meaning was rich and relevant to her. And when Jamie's dark, strong voice spoke his vows into her hearing, she secreted them in her heart, knowing she would never forget these moments.

"…to love…to honor…and to obey." The words came easily to her, even the edict that her will would no longer be her own, but that of the man she'd chosen to wed. In her heart of hearts was the knowledge that Jamie would not cast orders in her direction, that his main concern would be for her welfare, and that he would in all things place her first and foremost.

"You may kiss your bride," the pastor intoned, and she was securely clasped in the arms of her husband, kissed circumspectly, but well. Behind them, the crowd of onlookers burst into laughter and applause as the newlyweds turned to face them. And then they were swamped by well-wishers, by those who had been friends for all the years of her life, those who wanted the best for her that life had to offer.

The best in this case was the person of James Webster, and happily she claimed him as her own. His hand grasping her arm spoke of possession, a word she had heretofore derided as unbecoming, threatening to a woman's being. Now the thought of being possessed by this man was exactly what she had spent her life seeking.

Mrs. James Webster. She rolled the words silently on her tongue and acknowledged them to be most satisfactory.

The feast was sumptuous, the food varied and delicious, the neighboring ladies proud of their skills in the kitchen. Jamie fed her bites of ham and chicken, and in between times flirted with the little girls who gathered around them, their eyes wide with admiration for the tall man who had claimed Alexis. His knowledge of children was natural, it seemed. For she knew he had not had any younger brothers or sisters, only been a part of Brace Caulfield's family and a close friend to their son, Stephen.

As the wedding cake was presented, she held the knife, Jamie's own fingers pressing against hers, and the cake was cut, to the cheers and laughter of the crowd. Slices were passed out and the tall, three layered creation duly admired by all. Alexis barely tasted the light boiled icing, sharing her own generous piece with Jamie, feeding him with her fork and delighting in his happiness.

For his eyes were lit with a delight that pleased her, his mouth curved in a smile that brought happiness to her heart, and his hand was touching her, his fingers warm against her back, his palm curving to fit the flare of her hip.

"How will we leave?" she asked him quietly as they danced, the moon and stars now providing light for those who had moved their dancing into the yard.

With an amused smile, he bent to her. "I told you I had it figured out. Trust me."

The barn was clean, the large center aisle swept and scrubbed for dancing, and dance they did. Twirled in the arms of most every neighbor, even the young boys who barely came to her shoulder, Alexis was the center of attention. And yet her own eyes were only on the man who was her husband. Leading her to the floor, he began the familiar steps of a waltz as the instruments played. Square dancing followed for several hours until the instruments began another slow melody seemingly made for lovers.

And finally it was the last dance and she was held in his arms, her gown flowing about her legs, their steps in harmony as if they had planned for just such a performance in front of the watching crowd. For it was as he'd said earlier.

"The first and the last dances are mine," he'd informed her after the fiddle had been tuned up, and the piano carted out of the house for the occasion. Claimed by the local school-teacher, who gave lessons on the side to many of the young girls in town, it played a joyous background to the dancing that was a big part of such celebrations.

So it was that they made their escape without anyone being the wiser. James had hidden the buggy beyond the orchard, tied the mare to a tree and left them out of sight of the guests. Occupied with the dancing and the abundance of food, the barn and surrounding grassy spots were peopled by those who sat or danced or rested on quilts beneath the trees.

In the twilight, their disappearance went smoothly, James and Alexis going into the house, where Alexis changed into a new dress, bought especially for the occasion. It was not as full and lacy as her wedding dress, but was cut on narrower lines, made of silk organza, with an overskirt that made her look regal.

At least that was what James said when he caught sight of her standing before a long mirror in her bedroom. He'd rapped on the door, and then entered, catching her unaware. She turned to him, startled. And then smiled as his eyes gleamed with a desire he did not attempt to hide from her. "You're beautiful," he said. "You look like a princess in a fairy tale."

"And you treat me like a lady." She preened, twirling in a circle, her skirt flaring around her legs. "Am I honeymoon material?" she asked. And his answering grin, complete with uplifted eyebrow, answered her question, leaving no doubt as to his opinion of his bride.

He lifted her valise, into which she'd placed a clean set of clothing for him and a spare shirt. Her own things took up the majority of the space, but there was still room for his shaving brush and mug and straight razor to be included.

"You're going to shave?" she asked, watching as he opened the bag and put in his last-minute additions.

"I don't want to leave whisker burns on your…" He paused and flicked her a glance of promise. "You'll find out," he said, his voice low and husky with a wealth of emotion he made no attempt to hide.

She came to him then, lifted her face and kissed him with an urgency he hadn't expected. "Please be patient with me, Jamie," she said. "I don't know much about all this marriage stuff."

"I'll bet you're a fast learner," he told her, his laughter ringing out. "And I promise to be a patient bridegroom."

They left from the front door of the house, finding the porch empty, with all the guests still out in back and scattered through the orchard. With stealthy moves, they made their way across the field of hay on the opposite side of the lane and into the furthest part of the orchard. Behind them, laughter exploded in the night air, a fiddle played for a host of dancers and no one took notice of the furtive escape of the bride and groom.

James lifted her into the buggy and then untied the horse and led the mare through the trees, toward the road. Once beyond the range of hearing, he climbed into the buggy and lifted the reins. The mare trotted down the road willingly, tossing her head, as if she welcomed the chance to kick up her heels and run off her excess energy.

The ride was long, almost two hours, but they spent it deep in conversation, going over the training of the horses, the running of the ranch and finally Alexis told James details of her childhood and the loss of her mother when she was very young. He'd noticed that her attachment to Ellen had formed quickly, and now began to understand that her feminine heart needed the care and guidance of an older woman.

"Did you get the bride speech from Ellen?" he asked, shooting Alexis a knowing grin.

She obliged by ducking her head as if she hid a blush and then laughed softly. "She gave me some pointers, but then she said experience was the best teacher, anyway."

"I suspect she's right. I just don't want you all worried. You don't have to do anything or be anything but yourself, honey. Just let me love you, and we'll do just fine."

The town of Perryville was aglow on the horizon, and James felt the mare's surge of speed, as if she scented hay and oats at the livery stable. The owner of that establishment had told James to leave his horse and buggy in front of the hotel and he would take it in hand early in the morning, keeping the mare until they should leave to return home.

The hitching rail before the hotel only held one other vehicle, and James tied his horse up quickly, then turned to lift Alexis from the buggy. The valise in one hand, his other arm around her waist, he approached the big, glass-paneled door.

"Can you turn the knob?" he asked, and Alexis obliged, opening the door, and then stepping inside, where she paused to look around the lobby. Carpeted with a thick maroon rug, it gave off an aura of prosperity, the heavy desk across one wall matching the wood trim on the overstuffed chairs scattered against the walls.

She waited at the foot of the staircase for James, watching as he signed the book with a flourish and then bent to pick

up their valise. With a satisfied smile, he joined her and together, they walked up the steps to the hallway on the second
floor.

"Room 208," James said in an undertone, leading her down
the corridor to where their accommodations awaited. With a
key given to him by the clerk, he opened the door and waited
for her to enter. The light from the street below lit the room
enough to allow them sight of the bed and dresser.

A lamp on the bedside table stood waiting, and James
found a box of matches there and lit the wick. The light flared,
illuminating the corners, and focusing attention on the wide
bed. At least Alexis seemed preoccupied with the presence of
the bed, its surface covered by a white coverlet, piled with pillows and possessing a high headboard, the polished wood
gleaming richly against the wall.

"Do I need to leave so you can get undressed?" he asked
her, dropping the valise and approaching her with care. Not
for the world would he frighten her or give her reason to turn
from him. And to that end, he looked toward the corner where
a dry sink stood, a basin and pitcher waiting for their ablu-
tions.

"I'll brush my teeth first and wash up a little," he said, giving her a few moments of privacy. "Are you sure you're all
right with me being here?"

She shook her head, her eyes wide, her mouth quivering a
bit. "Stay here and help me, Jamie. I want to start this marriage off right."

"You don't mind my seeing—"

She held up her hand, halting his query. "No, I don't mind
what you see. It will all be yours anyway."

He grinned. "Now, that's the kind of stuff I like to hear,"
he told her. "Turn around, sweetheart, and let me help you
with your dress."

Without hesitation, she turned with her back to him, and he undid the buttons that closed her dress. "How did you get this thing done up back at the ranch?" he asked.

"Ellen came in the house behind us, and helped me. She knew I'd have a problem with it. And then she left before you got to my room."

"Smart lady, that Ellen," he murmured, sliding the garment from Alexis's shoulders. It fell to the floor and she stepped from the circle formed around her feet, bending to lift the dress and fold it over carefully.

"I'll wear it tomorrow," she said, almost to herself. "Maybe we can walk around town and look at the stores."

"Whatever you want, sweetheart. This is your wedding trip, and I want you to be happy."

"I'm with you, Jamie," she said simply. "That's enough to make me happy."

His mood was expansive, his hands gentle as he turned her to face him. "Let's get these petticoats off next," he said, loosening the tapes at her waist and allowing the fullness of yards of fabric to fall to the floor. She was left wearing a lacy chemise and he put out one finger to trace the line of lace that edged the top of the dainty garment.

"This sure is pretty," he said, his words taking on a tone of warmth that gave away his thoughts. "But I think I'd like it better if we took it off. You can have it back in the morning."

She stiffened a bit in his hands and looked down at herself. "I'll be naked," she said, the words bringing a smile to James's mouth.

"So you will." He bent to pick up her petticoats and she stepped away, freeing them from her feet. "Why don't you sit down first, sweetheart? Right here on the edge of the bed, and I'll take off your shoes and stockings. But first, let me get my boots off." He tugged at them quickly, standing them side by side next to the chair where her clothing lay.

As if his removal of her stockings and shoes were more than she had bargained for, Alexis nodded dubiously, but did as he asked, sitting stiffly upright at the edge of the mattress, her chemise pulled down to cover her thighs as much as possible, her knee-high silk stockings pale against her legs.

James knelt before her, rubbing his fingers distractedly over the lacy garters she wore, as if fascinated by the tiny flowers embroidered on them, and then he lowered them, the stockings following in their wake. She lifted her feet and he tossed the wispy bits of silk to a chair, then tugged at the chemise she wore.

"Jamie?" Her whisper was soft, pleading perhaps, he decided, and he rested his hands at her waist, bending toward her, his gaze questioning her. "Please. Turn out the lamp," she asked. "Just this once, I feel…"

"I think I know how you feel," he said, understanding alive in his voice. "You're a bride who's about to become a wife, Alexis, and you're a bit anxious about the whole thing." He kissed her, reaching to place his lips above the lacy chemise, inhaling the sweet scent of her skin. "But, I've waited a long time for this, and I want the light on for just a while longer.

"The problem is that I don't know how long I can wait for you, sweetheart. I'm feeling like a randy boy, aching to hold you and needing your warmth in my arms. And I don't want to frighten you."

"I'm not frightened, Jamie," she assured him. "A bit anxious, I guess, but I'm ready to be your wife." She pulled at the hem of her chemise, and together, they drew it over her head, exposing her to his view. He gazed at her body, at the round, firm breasts he'd seen but once before. Now, their bounty was his to caress and own, and he bent to kiss each of them with damp touches that made her shiver.

His hands were dark against her skin as he felt the narrow width of her waist and then the fullness of her hips. He slid his palms down to the firm curves of her thighs, and bent closer to her, his lips soft against the pale flesh of her belly, his chin feeling the touch of golden curls as he caught the aroma of her feminine arousal.

Straightening, he rose and stripped from his clothing, aware of her attention focused on him, the lamp's glow reflecting a sparkling green fire from her eyes. His drawers were pulled down with his trousers and he slid from his stockings at the same time.

He was unashamedly aroused, his male member prominent and he thought she seemed stunned by the sight. Her eyes widened and her mouth opened as if she would speak, and then she ventured a look into his face, her own a rosy pink.

"I've never seen anything like that before," she explained. "I think it just surprised me."

"You felt it against you, that day in the tack room," he said.

"It didn't seem that large," she told him, and then blushed again, as if stunned by her own words.

"This is what you do to me. It's just a part of me that reacts to you, a part that is aching right now to find its place in your body." Looking down at her, he smiled as if he would reassure her of his concern and care of her and then bent, urging her to move to the center of the bed.

She pulled the coverlet back, then the sheets, easing her way beneath them to where plump pillows awaited her head. "I forgot to take my hair down," she said, sitting up abruptly and removing pins from the braid that circled her crown.

"Let me," he said, taking the bone hairpins from her hands and placing them on the bedside table. Sitting down beside her, he undid the braid, running his fingers through the length of silky hair, admiring the golden highlights that gleamed richly in his hands. "I like your hair," he said softly. "It was the first thing I noticed about you that day when I arrived. That and your green eyes. They flare at me sometimes like lightning flashing, and I especially like it when they grow warm and settle on my face with that look you get once in a while."

"What look?" she asked, looking as if she'd like to laugh aloud at his eloquence.

"You know what look," he said, pouting just a bit. "When you wrinkle your eyes and smile and make me feel like a man."

"I don't think you need any help to make you feel like a man. You're already about as arrogant and stubborn as any man I've ever seen in my life."

"And you're about as pretty and strong-willed as any woman who ever walked the face of the earth," he returned, rolling onto the mattress and tumbling her to her back, looming over her, one hand propped on the mattress on either side of her head.

She pursed her lips. "I'm not strong-willed. That's just another word for stubborn, and I'm only quietly determined. There's a difference."

"Really?" His brow tilted as he heard her words of explanation, and then he laughed aloud. "Quietly determined, huh? That's a new one."

And then he kissed her, a quick taking of her mouth that began as a teasing gesture, and then escalated into an expression of the passion that possessed him. Her lowered himself almost atop her, feeling the soft plush lines of her breasts against his chest, reining in his desire lest he frighten her with the power of his need.

She responded to his kiss, opening to him, answering his love play with caresses he relished, her hands moving freely over his shoulders and back, touching each muscle, each square inch of skin, exploring this man she'd married, as if she had been given leave to investigate him in a new and glorious way. And so she was.

He was heavy, his arms firm and strong, his back narrowing at his hips, then becoming slim, his bottom flat and yet rounded in her palms. She felt the taut lines of powerful sinews and the restrained strength he controlled with tender care, lest she be overpowered by his greater size. And felt a rush of thanksgiving that she had captured this man for her own. That he loved her enough to marry her and give her his name.

His mouth was hot against her skin, his breath warm and scented with the peppermint tooth powder he'd used, and she was pleased that he cared enough for her to come to her as clean and fresh as a man could be. His lips curled around the hard peaks of her breasts and he tugged them, suckling first one, then the other.

Like a flowing current, his touch there lit fires of yearning in the feminine parts of her body she had patently ignored for most of her life, only caring for herself as needed. Perhaps it was the thought of what would one day take place there that had kept her mind from exploring her own femininity, but now she was trembling, aware of each fold and crevice between her thighs.

Jamie lifted his head and looked down at her. "Do I need to blow out the lamp now?" he asked. "Or will you let me leave it on a bit longer?"

She swallowed with an effort. "You can leave it on, Jamie. I know you want to."

"I want you to be comfortable, sweet." His words were firm, and she knew if she said the word, he would rise and the light would illuminate her body no longer.

With a slow shake of her head, she conveyed the message

of her acquiescence, and could not help but smile at the look
of satisfaction and yearning she saw in his eyes.

With gentle fingers, he explored her body, leaving no place
untouched, his hands soothing and careful, as if she were
made of fine porcelain, and he the man who would acquire
her as his own. She felt treasured, cherished and filled to the
brim with the pleasure he brought her. If she quivered at his
touch, it was only because no one had explored her femininity in such a way before. If she whispered her surprise in wondering tones, it was because she'd never known the thrill of
a man's power over the secret places in her body.

And if she cried soundlessly when he joined them as one,
feeling the sharp pain as her maidenhead gave way to his
entry, it was but a release of tears that signified her joy at this
final act that would forever make them husband and wife.

For it was not pain that brought her tears to the surface,
but the tenderness of his taking, the care he dealt her body,
the soft touches of fingers that cherished her soft flesh and
brought her to a fulfillment she had not imagined.

Jamie rolled with her, still enclosed within her body, his
arms around her in an embrace that warmed her spirit and
nourished her soul. "I'm really your wife now, aren't I?" she
asked, wonder alive in each syllable she spoke.

"Yes, sweetheart. You're my wife. You've made me hap-
pier than I deserve to be." His words were slow, wooing her,
giving her the assurance that his feelings for her were sincere,
that his arms would protect her from any perils to come their
way. "I love you, Alexis, with all that I am. I'm yours for as
long as you can stand to have me around."

She giggled and poked him with her index finger. He
jerked and laughed beneath his breath. "I didn't know you
were ticklish," she said, pleased to have discovered a fresh
hold over him. "And so far as keeping you around, you'd bet-

ter not ever try to get away, James Webster. I married you for life, and I'm not about to change my mind about that."

"For which I'll be eternally grateful," he murmured, holding her close, even as she felt his body relax in sleep.

Chapter Seven

The next morning they slept late, then walked through town. "Perryville is larger than I'd thought," Alexis said, holding Jamie's arm in a tenacious grip. They'd dawdled down one side of the main street, looking into store windows, admiring hats in the millinery shop, Jamie agog at the horseless carriages in Perryville's first auto agency.

His plea to go for a ride in one fell on deaf ears, as Alexis merely shook her head and dug in her heels. "If we were meant to ride in one of those noisy things, we'd come equipped with goggles and suffocating clothing already a part of our anatomy," she said firmly. "If you want to go for a jaunt, be my guest, Jamie. But don't expect me to ride in one of those foolish contraptions. They'll never take the place of a horse and buggy, you mark my words."

He grinned. "Maybe not, but they sure look like fun."

"Too much to learn, just to get them out of the barn," she muttered. "Turn a crank, pull a lever, do this and do that, and maybe, just *maybe* you'll get where you're going. No, thank you. I'll stick to my mare and get there before you do."

He hugged her close and laughed at her nonsense. "Whatever you say, sweetheart. Just remember that in ten years, when we're driving one of those *contraptions* to town, and I remind you of today. You'll eat your words, all served up on your goggles."

She glared at him. "It'll never happen. And if it does, you can drive away on your own, Jamie."

"Uh-uh, sweetheart. From now on, it's the two of us, all the way. Where you go, there I'll be. And when I take a notion to haul buggy to town, you'll be with me. No more him and her stuff. From now on it's *us*. And don't you forget it."

"Which reminds me," she said, shooting him a look of challenge. "Which bedroom are we going to use? Yours or mine?"

"Whichever you like, sweet. So long as we're both in it. Whichever is larger, I guess, and that would be yours. You got room for my three pair of pants and four shirts in there?"

"You can even have your own drawer in my dresser," she offered, grasping his hand and leading him to the next store. It was large, with benches out front for the men who sat and watched the world go by. A sign above the door designated it as the Emporium, and Alexis nudged Jamie toward the double doors.

"What do you need in here?" he asked. "You already look pretty well put together to me."

"It's not for me, love," she said sweetly. "I want to buy you some clothes. Four shirts is not enough for any man, and I won't have a husband who has to wait for the laundry to be done and the clothes ironed before he can put on a clean shirt. You need enough clothes to last all week."

"You got any money?" he teased, well knowing that his own pocket was ample to buy anything she pointed at. He'd not spent his money for weeks, only set it aside each time a letter from Brace arrived. Now he carried some in a money

belt, another portion of his wages in his pocket and still had
a tidy sum in his room back at the ranch.

"I'm well-heeled," she said smugly. "My father has always
paid me an embarrassing amount for doing the housework and
cooking and even with Ellen there, he said I still needed to
be on the payroll, due to my work with the horses."

"Well, I didn't know when I left him in charge of the
cash flow he was going to indulge you this way," James
said, feigning anger. It was no use. She could see through
him with no trouble at all, and he was amused at her dis-
dainful look.

"I earn every penny I get, mister. You don't scare me, not
one little bit. And if I want to spend my money on new clothes
for you, I will. Not another word, you hear?"

They marched in unison up to the counter where a man
waited, his white apron in place, his moustache lush and
curled at the ends, and his big hands looking capable of lifting down any number of boxes for them to sort through.

"We'd like to see some shirts for my husband," Alexis said
sweetly, and darted a look of warning at James.

"What size are you looking for, ma'am?" the gentleman
asked.

James grinned. The little fox didn't know his size, that was
for sure.

"Extra-large," Alexis said quickly. "With extra-long sleeves."

He bent to her and his whisper was directed at her left ear.
"How did you find that out?"

"Guess who's been doing the washing?"

"You looked, you little minx."

"I needed to find out all I could about you, just in case I
decided you were the man I wanted."

"Just in case?"

Her mouth opened to reply, and then closed abruptly as the

storekeeper brought two glass bins to the counter and began lifting shirts from their depths. "Take a look at these," he said nicely. "There's more where they came from."

"I like this for work," Alexis said quickly, picking up a light blue chambray, and then another in tan. "What do you think?" she asked Jamie.

"I've already got a blue shirt. But I guess I could use two if you say so."

She laughed scornfully. "You need more than just two new ones, Jamie. You haven't anything to wear to church."

"Are we goin'?" he asked, lifting an eyebrow at her.

"You better believe it. Starting Sunday next. You'll need a good pair of trousers and a dress shirt and a tie. And you can't wear your boots. You'll need a new pair of shoes."

"Now that's where I draw the line. I wear boots. I've worn them for thirty years and I'm not about to walk around in a pair of sissified leather oxfords."

"How about a pair of river boots from the catalogue?" the storekeeper asked eagerly. "Let me show you a picture." Without further prompting, he brought a fat book from beneath the counter and opened it with little fuss to a page where boots reigned supreme.

"Now here's a nice boot," he said, pointing at a picture of a hand-tooled leather boot, with the same type of heel James was used to wearing. "It's only two dollars and ninety-nine cents a pair," the storekeeper said. "Quite a bargain, and very little for shipping."

"We won't be in town long enough to order a pair right now," James said. "Maybe we can stop in the general store at home and place an order there."

The storekeeper looked a bit disappointed at the loss of a substantial sale, but bore up bravely. "Well, maybe you'd like a pair of the ones I keep in stock," he said cheerfully.

"Let's take a look," James said, only too aware of Alexis's frown.

"Do you need more boots?" she asked in an undertone as the aproned gentleman led them to a counter on the opposite side of the store.

"Yeah, if you want me to look pretty when we go to church," James said, tossing a smug look her way.

With a subdued grumble, she paused by the counter as the man in charge placed three pair of leather boots on the gleaming display case. Sporting the same sort of hand-tooling on the leather, they looked exceedingly masculine, and very expensive.

"I can let you have this pair for just two-fifty," the gentleman said, his eyes eager as if he sniffed a sale just over the horizon.

"If they fit, you've just made a sale," James said, looking around to seek out a chair.

"Use that bench over there," he was told. "Just shuck your boots off and put these on. They look to be the right size," he judged, leaning over the counter to take a look at James's footwear.

"I wear a twelve," James warned him.

"Well, that's exactly the size of this pair," the man said, selecting a pair of black boots, by far the most elaborate of the three he'd shown them.

James sat down and tugged his own footwear off, then replaced it with the one he'd already decided to purchase. A quick look at Alexis told him her opinion, a smile creasing her cheeks as she nodded her approval.

"We'll take this pair," James said, replacing his own boot and standing. "And whatever else my wife chooses."

Given a free hand, Alexis marched back across the store to the counter where shirts were piled in three stacks. She sorted through them all, checking on sizes and holding up several to better judge their quality and workmanship.

"I think these two will do for Sundays," she said finally, placing the white, percale items she'd chosen on the counter. "And we'll need collars and cuffs, too."

"Collars are ten cents apiece and cuffs are fourteen cents a pair," the storekeeper said obligingly.

"We'll take four collars and four pair of cuffs," Alexis said, and then turned to James. "We'll need a pair of nice trousers, too. Don't you think?"

Relieved that he was to be given the privilege of choosing his own pants, James nodded and held up three different pairs to his waist, deciding on the fabric and then allowing the man to measure his waist and inseam to insure the right fit.

"I think that should do it," Alexis said, her index finger touching her chin as she debated the merits of several ties the storekeeper had brought out for her approval. "Just this one tie, please."

"Not on your life," James said. "We'll see a couple of new dresses for my wife, too. Something pretty and bright-colored, with flowers or lace or fancy ruffles on the bottom."

"I think I have just the thing for you," the man said, turning to slide another glass box from the shelf behind him. "You're not very big, ma'am, and I believe these will fit." He held up a white voile dress with tiny blue flowers scattered over the fabric, and then another dress in pale green, striped in white with lace on the collar and cuffs.

"I like them both," James said firmly. He looked down at Alexis. "What do you think, sweetheart?"

She looked flabbergasted at his generosity. "Two new dresses?" she asked. "Surely one would do. I already have several at home."

"Two new dresses," James said firmly, "and some shirts for working with the horses. Yours are pretty worn."

"All right," she said, agreeing quickly. "I'd like a blue flannel, probably a boy's size large, and a chambray double-breasted."

James thought she flushed again as she recited the style of shirt she wanted, knowing that her feminine side shrank from saying the words aloud. He grinned down at her and as if she read his thoughts, she jabbed her elbow in his ribs.

"Unless my wife would like a pair of shoes or boots, that will be all for now," James said.

As Alexis strolled across the store to investigate a counter where bolts of fabric rested and ribbons were rolled on wooden spindles, James leaned over the counter and spoke in a low tone. The man behind the counter nodded, smiling with glee, perhaps thinking of the profit he would make from today's sale, and reached for another glass box, lifting a sheer, lacy shift from its depths. He held it up, one eye on Alexis, lest she turn and see him, and Jamie nodded, then pointed at the next garment in the box.

"Let me see that one, too," he said in a low voice. And with a nod and glimmer of pleasure in his eyes, he chose them both, watching as the man wrapped them carefully in a separate piece of paper and added them to the growing pile on the counter.

They left the store, piled high with purchases, James determined they should return to the hotel to deposit their things before they went any farther.

Climbing the long staircase, he teased her unmercifully, hinting at a surprise he had for her, refusing to give any details, only telling her that he wanted her to undress as soon as they entered their room so that he could see her dressed properly.

Alexis shook her head at his foolishness, scoffing at his demands. And then found that he was not joking, that his mind was made up. She should be out of her clothing in record time, and since Jamie was determined to help her accomplish the deed, it was a done deal. Before many minutes had passed she was standing before him, dressed only in her shift and her stockings.

He'd locked the door upon entering, tossing their purchases on the bed, and now he bent to unwrap one of the parcels, drawing forth a smaller package from within. "Now, I want you to try this on," he said firmly. "I've been waiting for ten full minutes to see you in this thing, and I'm an impatient man, love."

With a flourish, he held up the second shift he'd chosen, and allowed the sunlight from the windows to shine through its sheer fabric.

"I can't possibly wear that thing," Alexis said firmly. "It's indecent. You'll have to take it back, Jamie."

"Not on your life, honey," he said, approaching her, shift in hand. "Now just lift up your arms and we'll get yours off and this one on before you know it."

She backed away and he followed, until she was pressed against the wall, with his body pinning her there. She tilted her head, a major undertaking, since she was firmly enclosed by him, even her head touching the flowered wallpaper.

"I'm not going to take off my shift in broad daylight," she said, alarm lifting her voice to a higher range.

James stopped, shift in hand, one arm enclosing her in an embrace. "Am I frightening you, Alex? That's not what I meant to do. I just want to see you in this."

He felt her heart beating against his chest, noted the frantic look in her eyes and relented, stepping back from her. "I've gone too fast for you, haven't I? You're not ready for such foolishness yet."

"Foolishness?" she asked. "Being naked in front of you isn't foolishness, Jamie. It's a part of being married. I just hadn't thought about it before."

"If I close my eyes, will you slip out of that shift and into this one? I promise not to peek."

She laughed. "What a liar you turned out to be. I know very well you'll peek."

He assumed a look of pain, as if she had bruised his feelings. "You really think I'd lie to you?"

She nodded. "When it comes to not peeking at me when I'm naked, yes. I know you, Jamie, and even though I'll do as you ask, I'll almost guarantee that your eyes will be open."

He stepped back, the shift held toward her, his other hand covering his eyes. "See, Alexis. I'm not peeking." And then he laughed, unable to keep back the pleasure he took in their sparring. "But I'm gonna."

She lifted the shift over her head and tossed it over him, effectively covering his face, and then snatched the new one from his hand and carefully slid into it. It felt like a bit of cobweb against her skin, the material clinging to her, ending at her thighs, where an inch of lace was gathered.

"Is it silk, Jamie?" she asked, her awe apparent in the breathless words she spoke.

"Genuine silk," he said, tossing her old garment aside as he held her at arm's length and viewed the perfection of her slender form. Dark circles were barely seen beneath the sheer fabric, there where her breasts formed the silk into a covering for the beauty beneath. He scanned her length, viewing the slender hips and then the length of legs that were exposed to him. Strong and well muscled, she possessed curved calves, rounded thighs and slender feet, her skin soft to the touch, he remembered, her flesh pliant and yet firm.

It was more than he could resist, this picture of womanhood before him, the knowledge that she was his, all his, and the rest of the world was going past without touching them here in this room. She was a temptation he did not attempt to resist. His hands moved to her hair, pulling the pins from place, allowing it to fall about her shoulders and down her back in a cascade that delighted him.

With a quick movement he bent and gathered her up in his arms and strode to the bed, holding her close as he looked into her eyes. "Is this all right?" he asked. "You're not too sore from last night?"

She smiled, a feminine signal he could not misread, and then her face took on a look of sheer pleasure, as if she were beginning to realize the power she held over this man she'd married. "I'm not too sore," she said. "I'm not sore at all. Not right now, anyway, and if you're careful, I doubt I'll complain much."

He placed her on the bed, feasting on the look of her, the creamy texture of her skin, the eyes that had softened, luring him closer. His hands had readied her for him, and he thought of the pins he'd left scattered on the floor across the room. Now the waves and curls lay in a mass of gold, circling her head, tempting his fingers to explore its strands.

He fought the dark side of himself, the demon that drove him to possess her, the primitive need to conquer, and then realized that she was his already. That her arms were lifting to enclose him, her mouth was forming to his, her kiss warm and damp and all he had ever dreamed of. There would be no conquering here. Only a joyful union of two bodies and souls that sought for true love in the depths of their physical joining.

And found it. Found the pleasure of pleasing, each of them giving of themselves, patience coming to the forefront with the melding of their bodies, a sense of joyous anticipation accompanying the melding of their souls.

He could find no words to speak, could only hold her close, his hands touching the places he'd yearned to own, his mouth caressing the softness he had craved and his inner self rejoicing at the blending of two people here in this bed. She was his wife. His barrier against all the problems to come, his champion in all of his battles, the love he had sought for so long.

"I love you, Alex," he murmured, not willing to part from their closeness yet. Unable to free her from his hold. And she seemed to be of the same mind, her arms tight around him, her fingertips roaming the muscles and tendons of his back, her mouth kissing wherever she could reach.

"I love you, too," she whispered, lifting to reach his mouth again, her own demanding, as if she could not yet be sated by his loving. And he found, to his surprise, that he, too, was more than ready to please her, to please himself.

"Can we stay here for a while?" he asked her, lifting over her, the better to see the slender body he'd so recently claimed. Her new shift was on the floor, and he'd been careful not to tear it or shred the lace, knowing the pleasure it would bring to him on future nights when they were back at the ranch in their own room.

She lay before him without a trace of fear or trembling, allowing him his husband's privilege of viewing her body, watching him with a smile of pure satisfaction. "I think staying right here is a good idea," she said. "We'll work up an appetite for supper this way." Her mouth pursed a bit and then she gave him an arch look of promise. "You are taking me somewhere special to eat tonight, aren't you?"

"Maybe I'll go downstairs and bring some food back up. We can eat right here."

"Not on your life, fella," she said with a grin. "I have two new dresses and I'm planning on wearing one of them to supper tonight. You'll take me to the restaurant downstairs or that nice place we saw down the street."

"Whatever you say, sweet. I can't refuse you anything right now." He rolled to his back and propped his hands behind his head. "I don't think anyone has ever had such a wonderful wedding trip as this. I hate to think of going back home."

"We're not going today, are we?" she asked, full well knowing the answer.

"Not on your life. We have two more days here. I told your father we'd be gone at least three days."

"He almost cried when he gave me away at the wedding," she said, sobering as she recalled the moment when Hank had placed her hand in Jamie's and then stepped back, signifying his claim on her was ended and he'd given the responsibility for her care and keeping into the hands of another.

"I don't blame him. When it comes time for our first daughter to marry, I'll no doubt feel the same way."

"Our *first* daughter?" she asked. "Just how many are you planning on?"

"I thought we'd begin with both boys and girls, a couple of each. Then maybe we'll want more. It all depends on how much room we have to put them in."

"There are seven bedrooms in that house. And I'm not going to attempt to fill all of them. I think four is enough."

"Whatever you say, love. After all, you'll be the one to do all the hard work. Just so long as you give me a son. First or last, I don't care. I love girls, especially this one," he said, laughing as he bent to nuzzle in her neck, "and I'd like a whole slew of daughters. But I would like a son."

"I'll see to it," she said smugly. "Just be nice to me and I'll see what I can do for you."

"I thought I'd been pretty nice already," he said, teasing

her again, tasting the sweetness of her breasts with lips that tantalized and tempted.

"I'll give you two days to stop," she said softly. "In fact, how about fifty years?"

"That sounds more like it," he murmured. "Fifty years ought to just about do it."

If the hired hands shot him sidelong looks of envy, and if Hank looked at his daughter as if searching out signs of abuse, it was to be expected, James thought. And surely even Hank, indulgent father that he was, could see from the get-go that Alexis was glowing. She'd never looked so pleased with herself, even the first time she'd gotten on the three-year-old pinto mare. There was a glow about her, a triumphant gleam in her eyes and a smug look of satisfaction on her smiling face.

Ellen seemed, of all of them, the one to understand the bride's elation at crossing the bridge from girl to woman. With a sly wink and a hug around his waist, she approached James and whispered in his ear, "She seems happy, James, my boy. And I know who to thank for it. You've put a spring in her step and a look of happiness on her face. Bless you, young man."

That was high praise, James decided, given that Ellen was set in her ways, old enough to write volumes about men and their faults, and certainly the closest thing to a mother Alexis was liable to have for the next little while. He grinned his thanks at the cook and felt a flush creep over his cheeks.

"She's easy to love," he said, as if that were the final word. And then sat down at the table as the woman in question entered the kitchen. She passed behind his chair, halting long enough to drop a quick kiss on his cheek and placing her hand on his shoulder in a proprietary way before she took her own chair.

"Sleep well?" Ellen asked, her back to Alexis, her tone normal as she asked the daily question of the girl.

"Not really," Alexis said sweetly, "but that's all right. I'll catch up tonight."

"You hope," Ellen said smartly, turning to dish up eggs on Alexis's plate. "With this scalawag around, you may never get a good night's sleep again."

"Tell me I didn't hear what I thought I just heard." From behind him, James heard the rough voice of Hank as he made his way to the table.

At the stove, Ellen was red-faced, fumbling with the skillet, making an inordinate amount of noise as she ignored his words. And James was having a difficult time hiding his laughter from everyone. Alexis kicked him beneath the table and then set to with a will, making short work of her fried eggs. A slice of bread was buttered and a spoonful of strawberry jam spread on its surface before she looked up at her father.

"What's on the list for today, Dad?" she asked, effectively schooling her expression to one of innocence and sobriety.

"Those horses aren't performing well for anyone else," he said. "You'd better plan on a long session out there today." He looked at James then. "And you've got a length of fence down on the north forty. I sent out two men early this morning, but you may want to ride out and have a look yourself."

"Thanks, Hank. I appreciate you taking care of it," James said, thinking of how he could talk Alexis into riding with him.

"Why don't I go out with you?" she asked him, neatly solving his problem. "I can spend the whole afternoon working with the three-year-olds, can't I?"

"That sounds like you have it all figured out," James told her, shooting her a look that showed his pleasure in her plan.

"Well, we've got that settled," Hank said. "You got a letter yesterday, Jamie. Chet brought it home from town for you. It's on your desk."

James nodded his thanks, and excused himself from the table. "Let me know when you're ready to go, Alex," he said, touching her hair as he walked past her chair.

"About half an hour," she called to him as he walked into the hallway and down to where a small room held two desks and chairs and the files needed to run the ranch. Even though James had made it clear that Hank was in charge of all financial records and had a free hand with the men and the running of the operation, Hank had gladly moved his own desk over to make room for James's weeks ago. The men shared the office without problems.

He sat down at his desk, glanced at the stack of papers in front of him and wondered idly if Hank would notice if he moved them all to the other desk. Unable to be so unwilling to do his share, James decided instead to spend the evening here, sorting through things and doing this part of his job, distasteful as it was.

Now he searched out the letter, and found it just beneath the top sheaf of papers, listing the newborn calves and foals for his approval. He tossed those doing with business aside to be read later and settled back in his chair to read the word from Benning, the place he'd called home for so long.

It was from Sarah, Brace's wife, and James grinned as he read the salutation. *Dear Jamie, (or are you too dignified to still answer to that?)*

"Never," he murmured beneath his breath. After all, it was what Alexis called him and he gloried in the soft syllables as she spoke it in the night hours, her arms enclosing him, her lips offering their bounty to his own.

He shook his head, dismissing Alexis for the moment, and

went back to the letter. Sarah was talkative, telling him of Stephen, of how he'd grown proficient at riding, was thinking about learning to use a lasso and how much the boy had grown in the months of the summer just past.

James looked out the window. He hadn't even paid attention to the changing of seasons, to the turning leaves and the chill air of autumn. So involved in his courtship of Alexis, he'd allowed the weeks to go by without paying much mind to the longer nights and shorter days. Only the thought of marriage to Alexis had possessed him, and now he took a deep breath, and read on, freshly aware that it had been months since he'd left Benning.

Sarah wrote that they had thought of traveling across the state to visit James, that Stephen wanted to see the ranch his grandfather had left him and Brace said he could take time from his job for a week or so. Would it be all right for them to come?

James grinned widely, looking out the window, envisioning Brace walking beside him, saddling a horse by the barn and riding with him across the fields. And then he backed up a bit. He'd have to find a mount for Stephen, too, and include the boy in their exploration. Surely Stephen would be excited at seeing his property close up.

And Sarah. Just the thought of her meeting Alexis was enough to set his heart beating faster. Seeing the two of them together would be wonderful, a pleasure to behold, and on top of it all they would bring the twins with them, he was certain. He and Alex would have to fit out a room for them to stay in with the girls. And another for Stephen.

His mind worked a mile a minute as he made plans. And then, with a rush that sent his chair rolling back to the wall, he rose and headed for the kitchen, his letter in one hand. Looking for Alexis, he stopped dead in the doorway. She was nowhere to be seen.

"She's gone up to change clothes," Ellen volunteered. "She told you a half hour, James." And as he turned toward the stairway, Ellen called after him. "If you're planning on going to town anytime this morning, you'd do well to stay down here and leave her alone to get ready."

James smothered a chuckle. The woman had him pegged, that was for sure. Going to their room would be a big mistake right now, and Ellen had nicely put him in his place. He solved the problem by shouting Alexis's name up the stairway.

She opened the bedroom door and answered. "I told you a half hour and I'm way ahead of schedule. I'm almost ready, James. Just hike out to the barn and saddle our horses. You're not doing any good at all standing down there, hollering at me." With a bang, the bedroom door slammed shut, and James laughed aloud.

"She's a sassy one," Hank said from the kitchen. "You might as well do what she told you, son. She usually manages to have the last word."

"So I've already found out," James said, trying to look put upon, and not succeeding. Ellen's grin told him he was transparent, and Hank's parting words were about what he expected.

"I think she's got you broke in pretty good, son. You'll be dancing to her tune if you're not careful."

And did that bother him? James halted on the porch and wondered at his acquiescence to Alexis's words. She could be a bossy little sass box, that was for sure, but he wasn't sure he'd want her any other way. She suited him just fine. And with that in mind, he walked to the barn and took care of saddles and bridles. By the time she came out a mere ten minutes later, he was about ready to ride.

But first, he needed to set her straight about one thing. He left the two horses tied to a sawhorse and went to her, aware that his eyes were even now sending her a message of frustration. She backed up a step and put up a hand to halt his progress.

"What's wrong, Jamie?" she asked, and then burst into a litany he was in no mood to hear. "I wasn't serious when I told you what to do. But I'd already told you a half hour and you were shouting at me and it made me…upset, I suppose," she said, the last words uttered in a mild manner.

"I wasn't shouting at you. I called your name." And that was the truth.

"I know. But you were being impatient with me, and I didn't like it."

"Well, get used to it, baby, 'cause I don't have a long lead line on my temper. When I call your name, you can answer without biting my head off, can't you?"

She stepped toward him, her eyes flashing, her hands propped on her hips and her face showing the anger she'd tried to control. "Are we fighting? Because if we are, I can really make a fuss, and you won't like it, Mr. Webster."

He grabbed her shoulders and pulled her almost off her feet, so harshly did he move her toward him. She stumbled, clutching at him for balance and then he held her securely, her arms trapped between them, unable to move until he should allow it.

"Let me tell you, sweetheart. We're not fighting yet, but if you want to, I'll oblige you. But I warn you, Mrs. Webster, I'm a dirty fighter, and I don't pull my punches."

"You'd punch me?" Her eyes widened.

"Hell, no, I wouldn't punch you. That was just a figure of speech, but you can bet your bottom dollar I'd get my pound of flesh in some way or another. Do you want to test me out right now? Or are you ready to call a truce?"

"Your pound of flesh? What on earth does that mean?" And then as he shot her a look that reminded her of the stud sniffing at a mare, she understood his threat. And knew that if they had some privacy and time alone, she'd take him up on his words. She'd like to see how Jamie followed through on his claim.

"You know damn well what it means, baby," he murmured, bending to kiss her, a dark, avid blending of their lips that sent lightning sizzling through her body. She'd seen a tree go up in flames when a summer storm had shot just such a bolt through it, and now she understood what the tree had felt as its branches burned. As if magic had touched it with a flaming wand. As if she had been burned by the fire that raged within Jamie now.

She felt it surround her, knew the touch of his passion in the hands that ran with deft thoroughness over her, touching where he would, leaving her with no defense, only the need to be taken by him with the fury of desire he seemed unable to control.

"The tack room," she whispered, unable to speak aloud.

"You mean it?" His brow cocked and his mouth thinned, his eyes blazing as if the fire would leap from them to sear her soul.

"I mean it." She waited, compliant and willing to do whatever he needed of her.

In two minutes she'd found out, for he'd carried her to the tack room, bolted the door behind them and had her out of her clothing, and was stripping from his own.

"This won't be sweet and gentle," he warned her.

"I know." And she did know, knew that now she would see and feel the animal that lurked inside Jamie, the dark side of his being that would take her as a marauder. Yet she felt no fear, for he was innately gentle, a man who had vowed his love to her, and though she might wear a bruise or two, she would welcome this display of his passion.

He was right. It was neither sweet nor gentle. Rather, it was hot and quick, a blending that shot power through her body, turned her from an innocent girl—for she had been loved carefully and tenderly until now—into a woman who knew the depths of a man's passion, knew the desire he could not contain or control.

There was warmth and a trace of tenderness in his touch as he lifted from her, and perhaps a bit of concern and fear in his eyes, she thought. But the arrogant sweep of his lashes as he stood and viewed her naked form plainly labeled her as belonging to him. And then he knelt by the cot and kissed her. It was a far cry from the wet, biting, sucking kisses he'd spent on her just minutes before. And his words told her she had gauged his fear well.

"Did I hurt you?" He sounded contrite, she thought, as if he worried she would not forgive him for his actions. "Are you ready to get out your gun and shoot me?"

She looked up at him soberly. "Am I hurt? Of course not, Jamie. You didn't marry a shrinking violet. I'm a woman, and I'm capable of holding my own with you. I wasn't sure just what you had in mind, but let me tell you, mister, that anytime you get upset with me, you can have your pound of flesh, if that's what you want to call it."

Chapter Eight

Christmas Eve 1903

They would arrive within minutes. Alexis was sure of it. And she was ready for them, for all of them, even though her heart beat faster as she thought of what they might think of her. She was a rancher's daughter, and Jamie was…Jamie was a man among men. But best of all, he was hers, and that alone should give her the courage she desperately needed right now.

The tree was up, the candles ready to light, the ornaments hung and the garlands fell in great loops from the branches. She'd worked hours on them, as she did every year. Hank had said once, years past, that she put an awful lot of toil into something that would only last for two weeks. But she didn't care. If the ranch hands didn't mind getting the pine branches for her, she surely didn't mind the job of twining them together and forming the long ropes that decorated the house. And on Christmas Eve, when the men who were here for the holidays came into the house for the celebration, she knew they felt a sense of pride when they saw the results of their contribution to the decorations.

FREE BOOKS OFFER

To get you started, we'll send you
2 FREE books and a FREE gift

- -

There's no catch, everything is **FREE**

Accepting your 2 **FREE** books and **FREE** mystery gift
places you under no obligation to buy anything.

Be part of the Mills & Boon® Book Club™ and receive your favourite
Series books up to 2 months before they are in the shops and delivered
straight to your door. Plus, enjoy a wide range of **EXCLUSIVE** benefits!

- Best new women's fiction – delivered right to
  your door with FREE P&P

- Avoid disappointment – get your books up to
  2 months before they are in the shops

- No contract – no obligation to buy

We hope that after receiving your free books you'll
want to remain a member. But the choice is yours.
So why not give us a go? You'll be glad you did!

Visit millsandboon.co.uk to stay up to date
with offers and to sign-up for our newsletter

2 **FREE** books
and a
FREE gift

H0DIA

Mrs/Miss/Ms/Mr   Initials

BLOCK CAPITALS PLEASE

Surname

Address

Postcode

Email

MILLS & BOON®

The Mills & Boon® Book Club™ – Here's how it works:

Accepting your free books places you under no obligation to buy anything. You may keep the books and gift and return the despatch note marked "cancel". If we do not hear from you, about a month later we'll send you 4 brand new books priced at £3.79* each. That is the complete price – there is no extra charge for post and packaging. You may cancel at any time, otherwise we will send you 4 stories a month which you may purchase or return to us – the choice is yours.

*Terms and prices subject to change without notice.

MILLS & BOON®
Book Club

FREE BOOK OFFER
FREEPOST NAT 10298
RICHMOND
TW9 1BR

NO STAMP
NECESSARY
IF POSTED IN
THE U.K. OR N.I.

She'd helped Ellen bake cookies, had frosted and then sprinkled nuts and bits of sugar candy on them, decorating what seemed like a million of them. Now at least four dozen hung from the branches of the magnificent tree, catching the light from the kerosene lamp overhead. The canes and ribbon candy were strung on pieces of red yarn and placed on the ends of many of the branches, and those branches that didn't hold candy were decorated with small metal candle holders, with white candles ready for the match, once the company arrived and ate their supper.

She'd had little company over the years. Perhaps that was why she now was so imbued with excitement and a twinge of fear at the prospect of Jamie's family coming as well as Brace, Sarah, the twins and Stephen. What if they didn't like her? she asked herself for the tenth time. And Jamie's words resounded in her mind.

They'll love you. You're my wife.

He'd assured her just yesterday, "Sarah is about bustin' her buttons to get here. And Brace has Stephen all wound up, wanting to see his ranch firsthand."

"What about Loris?" she'd asked, fearful that Jamie might still hold a bit of love in his heart for the girl who had borne his child. And buried it.

"She's my sister now," Jamie had said firmly. "I want you to stop worrying about everything." He'd seemed to have a sudden thought and he'd turned to her abruptly. "You didn't tell your father or Ellen—"

She shook her head, knowing without hearing the words spoken just what he feared. "I wouldn't do that, Jamie. You told me in confidence, and I'd never repeat it. Not to anyone."

"I thought not," he'd answered softly, his love glowing in his eyes.

Ellen had supper about ready. All that was required were

a number of chairs to be filled around the table plus a long bench for the children at the far side.

At eight years of age, Connor's daughter, Rose would be old enough to sit up and eat with the adults, she thought. And perhaps the little boy, Jacob, would be able to sit on a pillow, beside his sister, enabling him to reach the table. He was six years old, Jamie had said. And then there were Brace and Sarah's twins, and Stephen. Her heart sang with the thought of meeting all of Jamie's family, of knowing the two women he cared for.

The yearning to carry Jamie's child beneath her heart struck her suddenly. She hadn't thought of it much until lately, only that it would keep her from riding for a while. But now it filled her mind, and she rejoiced silently, touching the flat surface of her tummy, aware that it contained, even now, the tiny being who would call her "Mama."

With the coming of four youngsters, Jamie's nephew and niece and Brace and Sarah's twin girls, the idea of children around the house seemed to make Christmas more fun. Stephen was older, still a child, but yet hovering on the verge of manhood. And seeing his property for the first time would be an occasion for him to cherish.

A shopping trip a week ago had been fruitful, and they'd come home loaded with their purchases. She thought of the gifts she'd wrapped for the children, the boots Jamie had bought for his brother, with another pair almost identical to them for Brace, and the new capes he'd chosen for Loris and Sarah from the catalog. Alexis had been without a clue as to what to give them, until she thought of hand-tooling a bridle for Connor and a second for Brace. And then she'd thought of Stephen and had spent long hours on a bridle for the boy, knowing that he was a very special child, the very light of Brace's eye. Several hours had then been spent making leather purses for Loris and Sarah.

From that, she went on to take up her knitting needles, long since relegated to the attic, and boned up on knitting mittens.

Now they were wrapped, thanks to Ellen's expert help when Alexis had become stuck, her needle having pulled from the almost completed red mitten she was working on. But, inexperienced or not, Alexis had persevered, binding them off and chaining a string with her crochet hook for each pair. It would go up one sleeve, across their small shoulders and down the other sleeve, keeping the four pairs of mittens from getting lost.

She'd earned a grin from James when she picked out ten cents worth of hard candy for each of the children, a red bouncing ball and a bag full of marbles for Jacob. Then came Rose's gift, and Alexis tried to imagine what the little girl would like. When she saw a matching mirror and brush set, she couldn't resist them and picked them up, darting a glance at James to catch his look of approval. For the twins, she chose baby dolls, identical but for the blue and pink blankets they were wrapped in.

She'd wrapped them all with care and now the packages were under the Christmas tree, including the things she'd gotten for Ellen and her father. And for James, who would find a gift on Christmas morning, plus another that would please him most to be delivered about seven months in the future.

She stood in the parlor, looking around to be certain that everything was ready for their guests, delighting in the beautiful tree the men had found and delivered to her this week. As if they recognized her delight, they'd bustled about, making a tree stand and finally setting it up in the parlor before they went out to find her evergreen boughs for the garlands.

Her thoughts rushed back to James, as she heard his voice in the back of the house. If he had any suspicions about her condition, he was keeping it to himself, but Alexis was almost positive she was indeed carrying a child. She'd caught Ellen looking at her askance several mornings lately, and had put on a show of eating breakfast, even though the food had lost its appeal. Ellen probably had a good idea of what was going on, but bless her heart, she hadn't said a word.

"I saw a surrey coming up the road a minute ago, and I'll bet it'll turn into our lane. It's probably Connor and Loris," James said, calling again for his wife. "Alexis, are you in the parlor?"

She came through the hallway. "I was, but I'm here now. Did I hear you say you thought they were almost here?" She scampered to the window and looked out into the afternoon sunlight, noting that evening was not far off, and they would need to light a lantern in order to see their Christmas Eve supper.

She was almost trembling, so great was her anticipation, and when Jamie touched her shoulder, she turned quickly and buried her face in his chest.

"Here, here," he whispered. "What's wrong, sweetheart?"

She lifted eyes that almost overflowed with tears, and her words were trembling as they left her mouth. "What if they don't like me?" She watched Jamie's face as he mulled over her words for a moment, and then he smiled at her, shaking his head.

"Sweetheart, they'll love you. Anyone in their right mind would love you, and trust me, Connor and Loris qualify. They'll be so pleased that I found a wonderful wife. Just you wait and see."

As if he would offer all the comfort at his disposal, he bent and kissed her, patting her back and whispering words of praise in her ear—telling her how pretty she was, how talented, and most of all how much he loved her.

"I'm being foolish," she said after a minute, wiping her eyes and searching out her hankie in her apron pocket.

"Maybe so," he said. "But I think I understand how you feel. This is all unknown to you, and you want so badly to have them think well of you that it's managed to upset you. I won't have it, Alex. I just won't have it. You're my wife, the woman I love and my family will take to you like ducks to the pond in the meadow."

She laughed at his words, thinking that Jamie always knew the right thing to say.

And then they both lifted their faces and spoke simultaneously.

"They're here." Those magic words that announced the arrival of Jamie's family, the words that turned him into an eager young man, surely too young to be a responsible married gentleman. He opened the door and stepped out onto the porch, snagging Loris from the high seat of their conveyance, and kissing her cheek soundly. Setting her aside he reached for the two children who watched from the second seat. They were beautiful, Alexis decided, their cheeks rosy from the chill in the air, their clothing stylish and obviously new.

Connor, a man with dark hair and built like his brother, climbed down by himself, rounded to where Jamie stood and wrapped him in an embrace that brought their emotions close to the surface. "Hey there, brother," Jamie said, his fist punching Connor's shoulder as he released him. Like two peas in a pod, they grinned at each other.

"We've missed you," Loris said, sliding her arm into that of her husband. "Now meet your niece and nephew, why don't you?" She gripped Jacob by the arm and motioned at Rose, a small child with dark hair and an engaging smile, bringing them to stand in front of James.

"This is your uncle, children, and unless I miss my guess, that's your new aunt on the porch." She lifted a hand and waved. "Hey there, Alexis. It's good to finally see you in person. Jamie's letters leave a bit to be desired. He only rattles on about Alexis, and we didn't know if he, himself, was alive or dead. Or we wouldn't have known if he hadn't written. Connor and I are so happy to meet you."

Her words were spoken as she walked to the porch, the two children fast on her trail, and when she climbed the steps, she reached for Alexis, arms wide, her face glowing with happiness. They hugged, exchanging whispers and laughing as do women when they discover a new friend.

Then it was Jacob and Rose's turn for hugs, and Alexis gladly obliged. "Come on inside," she said after a minute or two. "You have to meet Ellen, our cook, and of course my father."

The kitchen was warm, the scent of fresh bread, cinnamon rolls and a simmering kettle of chicken soup making their mouths water.

"I'm hungry, Mama," Jacob said, and Connor cast him a look that begged his silence.

"He has his father's manners," Loris said, blithely ignoring Connor's attempt at discipline. "Fortunately, Rose is like her mama."

Rose preened, brushing down her pinafore and pushing her hair back behind her ears. "Mama is teaching me how to be a lady," she confided quietly. "I don't think Jacob will ever make it."

"I'm gonna be a gentleman. Papa told me so," Jacob said, ready for a battle.

"Well, I'm sure you're both ideal children," Alexis said, laughing at Loris's face as their mother frowned, sending dubious looks at both the children.

"If you folks are gonna eat anytime soon, I'll dish up," Ellen said from the stove. "No sense in letting good food go to waste, I always say."

"Let me just wash the children's hands and faces," Loris said, searching out the sink against the back wall.

"I'll get you a cloth," Alexis said. "And there's hot water in the reservoir on the stove."

"It's just like mine at home," Loris said with delight. "It won't take me long to find my way around here, Alexis. I feel at home already."

"Has anyone called the men in yet?" Hank asked, looking out toward the bunkhouse, and then turning back to the room of people.

Ellen swung to face him. "Call the men in? I thought they'd be going home for a day or so."

"Dang! I forgot to tell you. We always have the boys eat with us on Christmas Eve and then spend the evening in the parlor with the family. Some of them don't have families, and a couple will be leaving tomorrow for a holiday at home. But for tonight, they're part of our family."

"Well, that's no problem," Ellen said cheerfully. "I've got enough food here for a small army. Somebody go ring the bell. And where's the rest of the company, anyway?"

James stepped onto the porch, Connor behind him and in moments the bell was clanging loud enough to be heard from the far side of the pasture. The two men grinned at each other, as if pleased with the joint effort, and found themselves in the midst of an impulsive embrace, their hands slapping a message of brotherly love on each other's backs. From the kitchen, their wives watched and shared a look of mutual understanding, Loris wiping away surreptitiously at her tears.

And then the two women came together in a like embrace and their tears flowed, as if peace had come to unite the whole family. "I'm so glad we made the trip," Loris said, sniffling her last into the handkerchief she'd found in her pocket.

Lone Star Bride

"James has missed his brother," Alexis said. "And you, too, Loris. He's been carrying around a whole stack of memories that stuck in his craw and put up imaginary walls between himself and Connor. I'm so glad they've managed to recognize the love they've shared for years." She looked over at Ellen. "This is a celebration, Ellen. We have a lot to be thankful for."

"I kinda gathered that," Ellen said with a grin. "Maybe I should have cooked a special dinner for the occasion. Chicken soup just don't seem like a celebration meal to me."

"It suits us just fine," Loris said. "The children love soup, and I know it will hit the spot." She looked to where Rose and Jacob watched the adults, both of them looking wary, as if events were worrying them. Perhaps seeing their mother in tears was difficult for them to understand.

As though she sensed their distress, Loris went to them, hugging them as they sat together on the bench, bending low to enclose them in her arms and leaving them with noisy kisses on their rosy cheeks. "I'd say we need to get this food on the table," she said. "Those men will be in here before we know it." She went to the cupboard to find bowls and plates, and halted, her hands touching the stack of bowls. "How many men are we talking about?"

"There'll be four more coming in to eat," Alexis said. "Slim, Chet, Woody and Joey. Ellen generally sends them out a kettleful of whatever she makes for the rest of us for supper at night, and at dinnertime they either come in the house, or I tote a basket out to wherever they're working."

Loris picked up four more bowls and returned to the table, rearranging the settings to include the extras, Alexis behind her with silverware. "We'll need to slice some of that fresh bread, too," she said, "and get out small plates." She looked over the table and then went to the pantry.

"How about a bowl of applesauce?" she called out, aiming her words at Ellen.

"Sounds pretty good to me," the cook answered, and Loris agreed with a nod as the two children bounced on the bench.

"We like applesauce," Rose said joyfully. "We get apples from Grandma's house and make some every year to keep in the pantry."

"Well we'll have bread and fresh cinnamon rolls with it, and eat a real Christmas dinner tomorrow," Ellen told her. "I'll roast a couple of chickens and make a pan of dressing and scout around for some vegetables to go with it. Thought I'd put together some pumpkin pies in the morning. We had a good crop this year."

Rose bounced again on the bench, poking her brother playfully. "Ain't you glad we came to visit Aunt Alexis and Uncle Jamie?" she asked, her face rosy with delight.

Jacob tossed her a superior look that so well mimicked Jamie's own, Alexis laughed aloud. "You look just like your uncle that way," she said, rounding the table to where Jacob sat and bending to squeeze him in a warm embrace.

"He gets it from his father," Loris told her. "Must be a family thing."

"Arrogance is Jamie's besetting sin," Alexis said. "He always thinks he's right." She laughed, as if she'd pleased herself with the statement. "And he usually is, now that I think about it."

"Well, for heaven's sake, don't let him hear you say that," Loris told her.

"Don't let me hear what?" From the doorway, Jamie shot a look that included both women, and they laughed simultaneously at the frown he wore.

"See what I mean?" Alexis said, almost choking on the words.

"Arrogant," Loris agreed.

And then they were interrupted by the entry of the four hired men who had washed at the horse trough. "Could'a come in here and used warm water," Ellen said, turning to watch as Chet approached the stove.

"Your soup will warm us up just fine," he said, peering over her shoulder into the kettle she stirred with a final flourish. If he seemed a bit taken with the cook, it was no surprise to Alexis, for she'd noted his attention being spent on Ellen before. And perhaps there was something there that would bear watching, she decided.

They settled around the table, Joey joking and quizzing the children about their trip and the home they had left behind for the holiday. Rose gazed at the young ranch hand with an expression akin to worship, Alexis thought, and even Jacob seemed to have found a hero to look up to. With a promise of a long ride on his horse tomorrow afternoon, Joey had forever impressed himself on the child, and Jacob slid to the end of the bench to be as close to Joey's chair as he could get.

They ate well, waiting first for Hank to bless the food and express thanksgiving for the safe travel of the guests, and then tucking into the simple meal with a will. Clearing the table and washing up the dishes was a community effort, with all pitching in to get the job done in record time, the better to remove the party to the parlor.

And as the last dish was placed in the dishwater, a sound from the yard alerted them to more visitors. James opened the door just in time for Brace and Sarah to step inside, each of them holding a little girl. Behind them, Stephen struggled manfully with a heavy piece of luggage, and gladly gave it over to James.

"She packed everything we own," Stephen said with a grin. "And all for just a couple of days."

"I wanted to be sure we have everything we need while we're here. I don't plan on having to do any washing for the next week. It'll be time to do it when I get back home," Sarah said, aiming the boy a quelling glance.

"Yeah, you'll probably have Grandma come and help, or send it out to the laundry lady," Stephen spouted, his smile easily conquering Sarah, apparent from the way she bent on him a benevolent smile.

"Are we too late to eat?" Brace asked, and Sarah darted him a look meant to shame him into silence.

"There's no keeping these men in line," she said, looking to Loris and Alexis for their agreement.

"I live with one of them, too," Loris told her. "We try, but between Rose and me, we never manage to win the battle."

But it seemed Brace's hunger went over well with Ellen, for with little effort, she quickly brought out more bowls and they all settled around the table again to talk with the newcomers. The twins were tiny little sprites, and before long one was held on James's lap, the other on Connor's. Stephen dug into his bowl of soup, pronounced it as good as Sarah's and asked for seconds. Three slices of bread followed it into his stomach and he groaned convincingly when he turned down the applesauce.

"Couldn't eat another bite," he told Sarah, and then when the cinnamon rolls appeared, he managed to scoff down one of those.

"I'm sure glad we came to visit," he told Alexis. "My dad was excited about seeing Jamie again, but I think the food was worth the trip."

"Wait till you see our Christmas dinner," Ellen told him. 'You can get up early and help me."

"Me, too?" Rose asked, and Jacob seconded her query, waiting with anticipation as Ellen looked them over.

"I reckon you two are of a size to come in handy," she announced after a moment. "Just be down here bright and early."

"Yes, ma'am," they answered in unison, tossing triumphant looks in Stephen's direction.

"Well, with all that help you've been offered, I may just draft Stephen to give me a hand in the barn come morning," Jamie said. "I can use a good man when I shovel out the stalls."

"I don't mind, Jamie," the boy was quick to answer. "I do it at home all the time. I have my own horse, you know."

"I know, and I'll find one here for you to ride while you're with us, Stephen. They all belong to you, anyway."

His eyes widened and his mouth opened to reply, but Brace beat him to it.

"They'll be his when he's old enough to accept the responsibility. Till then, he can just concentrate on growing up and being responsible with the animals he already has at home. He's learning fast, Jamie. By the time he takes over this place, he'll be a top-notch rancher."

His eyes sent Stephen a message of pride that was duly noticed by the others, and Jamie grinned widely. "You've got quite a champion there, Stephen."

"Yeah, but he's my dad and he always thinks I'm terrific," the boy answered.

"Well, most dads feel that way about their sons," Connor said. "And their daughters, too." Rose perked up as he added the final words.

"I'd rather be a lady like my mom," she stated firmly. "She teaches me all kinds of stuff. I'll be a big help to Ellen tomorrow." She bent to her cinnamon roll and licked her fingers of frosting with deliberation. Loris shook her head as if mourning the girl's lack of etiquette, but Alexis felt a kinship with

Rose. She'd been much the same as a child, and she looked forward to spending time with the girl.

They ate heartily, and then were hustled from the table and into the parlor, Brace only making a quick detour to the buggy outside to bring in a load of packages.

Hank lit the candles on the tree, looking around the room at the gathering crowd. Connor, Brace and Jamie found extra chairs for everyone, and the children sat on the floor with Joey, who had told them of his own family and the celebration they would be having tonight. Jacob moved closer to the young man and found himself on a comfortable lap, obviously a welcome part of Joey's celebration in his new home.

"Joey's only been with us for about eight months," Alexis told Sarah and Loris. "He's from down south a ways, near San Antonio and it's too far to go home unless he plans on a month off from work. He'll probably make the trip next summer, but for now, he's a member of our family. Dad hired him through a friend nearby who knew Joey was looking to move north and work for a while."

"Well, the children sure have taken to him," Loris said.

Rose looked over at her mother as the final candles on the tree were lit and the kerosene lamp was blown out. "Can we stay here for a long time, Mama? I like it at Uncle Jamie's new house."

"For a week, Rose," Loris told her. "And maybe next year your aunt and uncle can come to visit." She bent closer to Alexis and whispered an additional comment. "After your baby is born. We'll be anxious to see it."

Alexis turned her head quickly, surprise alive in her expression. "Baby?" she whispered and then laughed. "How could you tell?"

"You have the look," Loris said, and Sarah nodded her agreement. "Men don't notice, but other women do." And from across the room, as if she knew what they spoke of, Ellen chuckled and gave the trio of women a look that smacked of feminine conspiracy.

On the floor close to the Christmas tree, Jacob, with his head resting on the cowhand's shoulder, was gazing up into the tree, pointing to various decorations, counting the candles and telling secrets to his newfound friend.

"Joey likes children, doesn't he?" Loris asked softly, her eyes glowing as she watched her son.

"He has a whole pile of younger brothers and sisters at home," Alexis said. "I suspect he misses them. His mother wrote a letter, telling Dad that she felt better knowing that Joey was with good folks."

"That you are," Loris said. "And this is a wonderful home. No wonder Jamie is so happy here. Of course, the fact that he has you might have something to do with it."

Hank went to the tree and delved beneath it for packages, handing them in turn to Rose, who delivered them to the proper recipients. When she read her own name on one, she plopped down where she stood and opened the brush and mirror Alexis had chosen for her. The wrappings fell unnoticed and she held up the mirror, peering within its depths at herself. Then the brush was put into use, setting her brown curls in order.

From across the room, Connor and Brace sat beside Stephen, who was inspecting his new bridle, and sent Alexis a grateful look, at the same time informing Loris of its designer. She grinned back at him and held up her hand-tooled purse.

Their obvious pleasure in their gifts made Alexis's day one of perfection, and watching Joey play marbles with Jacob on the parlor floor was the icing on the cake. Jamie opened the belt she'd made him, noting his name tooled into the leather, the design she'd drawn up for it a representation of a saddle on one end and that of a lariat on the other.

In a package that was bulky, wrapped in tissue and tied with blue yarn, she found two new dresses, both of them wrappers, to be worn as robes or as house dresses. Both of them with belts that tied at one side, allowing the waistline to expand if needed. She looked up at Jamie in surprise and he dissolved in laughter.

"Thought you were keeping secrets, didn't you?" he asked softly against her ear, having made his way to where she sat. He pulled her up from the sofa where she'd shared the evening with Loris and Sarah, and held her tightly in his arms. His mouth spent a multitude of kisses against her cheek and temple and he alternately hugged her and then held her away to look his fill at the woman he loved.

"How did you know?" she mouthed at him silently.

"I'm a smart fella," he said, an arrogant grin illuminating his face. "You can't keep secrets from your husband, ma'am."

"Are you pleased?" she asked quietly, holding her breath as she awaited his reply.

"Pleased as punch," he said, pulling her close again, closing his eyes quickly as though to stem the tears that threatened to flow.

"Is there something you two would like to tell the rest of us?" Connor asked, and Hank seconded his words.

"I think there's something afoot, Connor. These two have a secret, I'd say."

Jamie turned Alexis to face the rest of the family, his face glowing with pride, one arm holding his wife close. "We're gonna be Mama and Daddy next year. I'd say we have good reason to celebrate."

"I guess so," Hank boomed. "Being told you're gonna be a grandpa doesn't happen just any day of the week."

"At least I'll be well dressed," Alexis said, viewing her new dresses, admiring the dark blue plaid and the green percale with bouquets of daisies scattered over its surface.

"They'll both look pretty with your hair," Jamie said in a low voice. "And I hope the baby is a girl that looks just like her mama, with golden hair and green eyes."

"And I'm hoping for a black-haired Irish boy with flashing blue eyes like his daddy's," she told him, her words audible for the family to hear.

"I'll take whatever you give me," Hank said. And then he looked to where Ellen and Chet were sitting side by side on two dining room chairs. "Did you know about this, Ellen?" he asked.

She only nodded and smiled with feminine superiority. "I had a pretty good idea," she said. "Alexis had that look."

"That's what Loris and Sarah said," Alexis told her quickly. "I'll have to take a long look in my mirror and take note of what you mean."

Jamie grinned at her. "I think it means you're glowing and your eyes are shiny and your cheeks are rosy and you look like a happy woman."

"Well," Ellen said smartly. "That's part of it. The rest is womanly intuition."

"I guess that leaves us out," Brace told the other men.

The hired hands had been given envelopes with cash enclosed from Hank and a huge bowl of cookies to take with them to the bunkhouse from Ellen, and, happy with the new hats Connor had ordered from the catalogue at the general store for them, they donned them quickly, making a great show of modeling them for the children.

Alexis had chosen new shirts for each, pondering over colors and fabrics to be sure each would match the man it was chosen for.

The family Bible was brought from the library table and Hank read the familiar story to an eager audience, Rose and Jacob adding their own interpretation, mentioning the donkeys and sheep and cows that they knew had attended the birth that night so long ago. Apparently well versed in the words read from scripture, they announced their theory that the angels had sung songs they were familiar with, and the group were led in favorite carols by small treble voices, the twins singing words of their own as they joined in.

As if the participants were loathe to end the day, they lingered around the parlor, watching as the candles burned low, and then finally Hank decreed that they should light the lamp and remove the candle stubs before they guttered out, causing a fire.

It was with happy hearts that they all trooped to their beds, the four hands going to the bunkhouse, already arguing over the distribution of their cookies. Connor and Loris were shown their room and another with narrow cots for the children. Together they helped their young ones get into bed and sat with them for a few minutes, talking quietly of the happiness they'd found here in this house, with their family around.

Another room on the second floor held Brace and Sarah, with cots for the twins, and a small room downstairs off the kitchen served as a place for Stephen to sleep. He announced his plans for an early-morning tour of the barn, and James offered his own services as guide for the outing.

Alexis and Jamie went to their own room finally, Alexis tired and ready for sleep. She lay with her head on Jamie's shoulder, repeating the events of the day in a voice that grew softer and quieter as she spoke. Until finally her eyes could no longer remain open. Jamie turned her from him, his arms encircling her, one wide palm on her belly as he thought of the days to come and the nights when he would feel his child move within her.

The stars outside their bedroom window drew his attention and he watched them flicker and shine, felt the banked excitement in the air, knew the contentment of being with Alexis even as he thought of all their guests just down the hallway.

He'd not thought to get his life in order this way, had worried that he might never have the same closeness again with Connor. Even though they'd parted on good terms and had renewed their old relationship back in Oklahoma years ago, this day had brought it all back in focus and assured him of the love that had existed between them in earlier days. "Thank you," he whispered, not feeling foolish for such an expression of his wonder, wanting only to place a benediction on this day.

"Thank *you*, Jamie," she murmured. "You've given me a whole new family to love. And you were right, they do like me after all." Her words were muted by a yawn as she attempted to rouse from the slumber that gripped her.

James lifted to plant kisses on her cheek. She turned her head, the better to accept his gesture. "I'm not asleep," she murmured, stifling another yawn.

"You're not?" he asked hopefully, kissing her again. Accepting the gift of her love would be a perfect way to end this day, he decided, waiting till she should let him know that she was amenable to his idea.

Her hands came up to frame his face and she kissed him with a passion that filled him to overflowing with happiness. "Can we have our own celebration?" she whispered, and then anticipated his reply with caresses that drew him into her web.

He gave his approval silently, levering himself over her, his hands already busy with the buttons on her gown, his mouth seeking the warmth of her body, searching out the sensitive places on her slender frame that awaited his attention.

It was as it had been on other nights, a time of loving, of exchanging anew the vows that had formed their union. And yet, as if this were a time of rejoicing such as they'd never experienced, they found that their bodies were blessed and refreshed by the outpouring of love they experienced, each for the other.

Their whispers carried them into the long nighttime hours, their desire flaring anew as dawn approached, and when the bell on the porch rang for breakfast, they readied themselves for the day with a joyful zest that sent them to the kitchen with smiles and secret glances. James took time to visit the barns and sheds with Stephen while breakfast was being readied, and then they returned to the noisy group in the kitchen, where James quickly found his place by Alexis's side, his arm sliding around her as he led her to her chair.

If they were noticed by the others, it made no matter to Jamie. If their family looked upon them with smiles that seemed to comprehend their happiness, Alexis only gloried in it. For on this day, with the family they loved surrounding them, they knew a happiness beyond measure, exalting in an occasion that would not be duplicated at any time in the future.

For there was about them a glow, an anticipation of their first child that lent them an aura of shimmering joy, sending a message of new life. Of a joyous anticipation that seemed appropriate at this time of year, when the days were to be spent celebrating the birth of the babe of Bethlehem.

Chapter Nine

Spring 1904

The pastures were green with new growth and the lush grasses provided the horses with a nourishment they seemed to enjoy more than their rations of hay and oats that had nourished them throughout the cold weather. Although the winter had consisted more of rain than snow.

But the meadows were not only appealing to the horses, but to those who cared for them, those who had a vested interest in this place. And a part of that interest was contained in the heavily pregnant mares who were ready to deliver their foals. The birthing stalls were the ideal places for such events to take place, but many of the mares dropped their progeny in the far reaches of the pasture.

Whether it was an inborn thing or not, Jamie worried that they labored without someone to watch them, perhaps take care lest they run into trouble in the worrisome venture of birth. Although, as Hank told him, animals had been surviving for years without human help to guide their young into the world, it was still Jamie's concern. He felt responsible for these animals. Even the cows who delivered calves out on the back forty weighed heavily on his mind until he was able to ride out and be sure that all was well with the livestock he cared for.

The idea that he was a worrywart amused Hank, but to Jamie's surprise, he had a staunch champion in Alexis. She, too, fretted over the mares, worried that the colts and fillies be tended to immediately, the small creatures able to nurse, as they must, in order to survive.

But even with these worries, she bloomed. There was no other word that could describe her in Jamie's mind. She was rounding out nicely, her skin was fresh and almost translucent and her hair was growing at an amazing pace, reaching below her waist when it hung loose. Her cheeks were rosy, her arms already tanning from the spring sunshine and she looked like a woman who was thriving despite the aches and pains of pregnancy.

The baby would be born in the late summer, she thought, and announced to her father and Jamie that she would ride as long as she felt good enough to climb into a saddle. Although they turned thumbs down on her training activities, she did force a reluctant admission from them that she could walk the new colts and fillies and teach them to trust the humans who cared for them.

Keeping the records straight was a chore that Jamie gladly gave to Hank. And that gentleman was meticulous in his book work. It looked to be a prosperous time for the Double C, and Jamie's letters to Brace were glowing with reports of the new life on the ranch, of his own happiness and joy he'd found here.

A dark rumor had reached Jamie, and he'd asked the men to keep a sharp eye out for trouble, especially now that Alexis was not riding her usual fast mount, and was at a distinct disadvantage, due to her pregnancy, should she need to flee from a stranger.

And a stranger was what they feared. The news of a man answering Mick's description had been circulating over the winter months, but he'd gone from one ranch to another, so no one had known for certain where he might show up next. So long as he stayed clear of the Double C, there wasn't much they could do but watch and wait.

Jamie and Hank both made inquiries, with no results that would answer their questions, and they'd just about decided that they were worrying for nothing. The day-to-day routine on the ranch was going well. Ellen had taken charge of almost everything in the house, including the care and feeding of Alexis, who she treated as she might a child of her own. And that alone was amusing to Alexis, since Ellen only measured a dozen years older than Alexis herself.

In fact, with the attention Chet was pouring out on Ellen, Alexis would not be surprised if she were to be planning a wedding for the two of them. None of Chet's actions were public, but his concentration on the woman was obvious to those who paid any attention at all. From carrying out her wash water to the yard, to filling the wood box with kindling on a daily basis, he looked for ways to please her, and please her he did, for she flourished under his regard.

Jamie found himself at once amused and yet pleased by the drama being played out by the two who were discovering the path he had walked only a year ago. But now he had Alex, and he watched her like a hawk for he'd found a whole new side of marriage, perhaps not the most pleasant part of this endeavor. For the fear that something might happen to his beloved haunted him. And he kept close track of anyone who came near.

Her riding was limited, but Alexis insisted on making the

tour of the pastures on a daily basis. The mares had delivered a number of babies, but there were still three who eluded Slim when he attempted to bring them into the barn. They seemed to have no fear of Alexis and she sought them out daily, dismounting and checking each of them for signs of impending labor. It was a task she relished, feeling a kinship with the beautiful creatures who shared their status with her.

She smiled at her thoughts, riding from the barn and heading out into the sunshine, the horse beneath her a gelding with a gentle gait. Waving at Slim, who was working with the new batch of three-year-olds, she swallowed a sharp pang of envy that he was so proficient at doing the job she yearned to handle.

"Where you off to, Miss Alexis?" Slim called out, holding fast to the filly he was working with.

"Looking for the palomino mare," she called back. "Up north aways. I shouldn't be too long. A couple of hours maybe."

"You be careful now, you hear?"

Alexis waved her agreement, aware that Slim was doing a good job and her own preoccupation with becoming a mother was of far more importance than that of training young horses. And yet she yearned to do the work she loved.

The shade beneath the trees in the meadow was a favorite place for the newest of the colts and fillies and their mothers to laze away the morning hours, and it was to a large grove at the far end of the pasture that Alexis headed. Two of the young colts kicked up their heels and bounded across the pasture, the breeze causing their short manes and tails to fly out behind them.

Alexis laughed at the sight, understanding the exuberance of the foals, knowing that they were, even now, learning lessons from their mothers and the rest of the small herd that would stand them in good stead in the future. She approached them slowly, speaking quietly to the mares, bending to touch shiny coats with her fingertips and scanning the horses for a last mare she sought. A palomino had been bred to the sorrel stud eleven months ago and as yet had not delivered her foal.

It was of special interest to Alexis, for her father had told her she might have the colt for her own, should the sorrel and mare breed true, the mare delivering another palomino. She'd yearned for one of the golden horses for years, and when James heard of Hank's promise, he had written to Brace to let him know of the arrangement. The reply had been in Alexis's favor, Brace understanding that her work with the animals was well worth the price of a colt or filly, no matter how prized its color.

She now sat atop her gelding and looked at the mares surrounding her. The palomino was conspicuous by her absence, and Alexis felt a pang of worry. It wasn't like the mare to stray from the herd. And with her foal due momentarily, it was worrisome to think that she was off somewhere alone.

If she'd gotten out of the pasture, she could have gone north a matter of miles, for the ranch was huge and the hills in that direction would make searching for the horse a major undertaking. On the other hand, there were a few places in the pasture where she might be, and Alexis set out to make a half circle, bent on covering the area where a lone horse might be hidden.

She rode north, then east, following the fence line to the creek where she stopped for long moments of reflection. For it was north, along this same stream of shimmering water that she had first been held in Jamie's arms and felt the power of his desire turned in her direction. The memory brought a smile to her lips and it was with reluctance that she turned the gelding away, traveling north again, her eyes scanning the bushes and trees, the hollows and gentle hills that might hide a horse.

It took longer than she'd expected, for she made one detour after another, unwilling to leave any ground unseen, anxious now for a glimpse of the golden mare. The north fence of the pasture was ahead and her heart leaped to her throat as she spotted the open gate. Kept closed, it was a deterrent, lest the animals should make their way onto the range land. It stood open now, and Alexis felt her lungs seizing in her chest, her breathing an effort.

If she went on, she would be alone on the range, and Jamie would be furious should he discover that she'd traveled so far from the house. Yet, if she went back and sent two men out to look, it might be too late, should the mare be in trouble. The answer was simple. She was a big girl now, and more than capable of taking care of herself. If she kept a good eye out for trouble, she'd be fine.

And so she went through the open gate and rode in a northwest direction, to where there were a number of hollows hidden from view, places where a mare might seek out privacy. Alexis rode beyond the hills that held any number of blind alleys and box canyons, slowing her gait to peer down the length of the narrow walls. Riding a trail to the top of the mesa, she looked down at wildflower-covered meadows within the canyons, small slices of heaven, she thought, and then laughed at her flights of fancy.

Traveling north now, she circled an area that did not lend itself to easy riding, the stones on the sloping ground causing her horse to slip as she nudged him up the hill. She halted and looked around, deciding it wasn't worth the chance of damaging her animal, and went another path.

She found fresh hoofprints on a muddy patch of ground, smaller than those of her gelding, probably belonging to a mare, a small mare such as the palomino. With a thrill of discovery, she followed them into a streambed, now turned into a muddy trail, and was thankful for the fates that had left the animal's path for her to follow. It led through the bottom of a small canyon, an ideal place for a mare to hide, and Alexis felt success was right around the corner.

Instead she found herself in a dead end, with no mare in sight, and upon turning her gelding around to retrace her steps, she found she had been followed. Before her was a horseman, astride a big, black animal. And he had to be huge in order to carry the man who rode him. Whiskered, husky and taller than most men, Mick Jenson eyed her from his perch atop the black.

"Well, well, if it isn't Missy Alexis," he jeered. "And what would you be doing out here all by yourself?" As if the answer to that query was unimportant, he rode closer, and his hand reached out, snagging her shirt, almost dragging her from her saddle. She jerked back away from him, nudging her gelding into motion and the quick movement tore the yoke from the back of the garment she wore. The remainder of the shirt hung down her back, the shoulder falling forward, and as she looked down, she realized that her breast was on display.

"Well, look here what I got," Mick said with a grin. "Part of the lady's shirt. And if I'm real smart I can probably get the rest of it off real quick like."

"Don't try to frighten me, Mick," she said harshly. "You're a bully of the very worst sort, and if you hurt me, you'll be six feet under before you know it."

"And who's going to put me there? Your daddy? Or your ever-lovin' husband? Do I look scared?" His clothing was soiled, his hair long and stringy beneath his hat and he looked as if he hadn't had a bath in weeks, she thought.

"I thought you had a job, Mick," she said.

"Where'd you hear that?"

"Someone carried the news to us. Did you quit already? Or get fired?"

He looked ugly as sin as he rode a bit closer to her, his horse squeezing her leg between the two animals. "Don't you worry about my job," he said. "It's none of your damn business, or your daddy's, either. He's been askin' around about me, and I don't like it, not one little bit."

"I think you'd better get out of my way and let me ride out of here, Mick. I'm on the trail of a mare and if I don't show up right quick, there'll be four men out here looking for me."

"Wasn't that nice of me to let her out of the pasture? She was lookin' for somewhere private to drop that foal, and I gave her the whole northern section to work with. I'll bet she's found a hiding place by now."

"Do you know where she is?" And if he did, would he tell her?

"Sure I do. And if you're real nice to me, I'll show you." His eyes gleamed in a way guaranteed to strike fear to her heart, but Alexis was too angry to waste time on fear.

"Show me where she is. I have no intention of being nice to you. I'd think you'd know that already. I just want to find my mare and go home."

Mick scratched his jaw, where a growth of beard made him look even more disheveled than was usual. "Well, now," he said slowly. "Let's just go for a ride and see what we can find." He watched her with hooded eyes as he turned his horse and waited for her to follow.

At a loss as to what to do next, she reined her horse to head back out of the canyon behind him. She stood a better chance of getting away out in the open anyway, she decided, and should any of the men set off to find her, she'd be more visible on the range.

Mick rode slowly, glancing back at her frequently, his lips twisted in a grimace that offered her no comfort. He looked, she decided, like a hungry wolf, out searching for his next meal. And unless she was mightily mistaken, he had her in mind to fill that purpose. She could ride back to the barns, but escaping the man was a futile thought. His horse was capable of outrunning her gelding, and the physical risk to her child wasn't worth the chance she'd be taking.

The canyon opening gave way to the open range, where towering peaks and grassy knolls splashed the northernmost horizon. Mick turned south, back in the direction Alexis had just come, and without hesitation he found an opening she had not noticed, between two large rocks and directly in front of a sheer rock wall. As though he would pass through the barrier, he led the way and in a moment was gone from sight.

She heard his voice resound from the canyon walls ahead as he called to her. "You comin'? I thought you wanted to find that mare."

For a moment she was once more tempted to turn and run, only the knowledge that he would overtake her in moments keeping her from flight. Instead, she followed him, past the wall of stone and to one side, where tree branches shielded the opening to another Eden. She peered beyond her horse's head to where the canyon opened up into a valley she had not seen before.

And there, not more than a hundred yards away, stood her mare, the golden palomino shimmering in the sunlight. Even as Alexis watched, the mare circled, as if seeking a place to lie, and then, apparently discovering a particularly soft patch of grass, the animal lowered her heavy body to the ground.

Alexis nudged her gelding into a trot, approaching with

care, lest the mare become frightened and bolt. But it seemed that the mother-to-be had no thought for the visitors, for she ignored them both.

With an easy movement, Alexis dismounted and walked closer, her gelding standing where she left him, his reins touching the ground. The mare lifted her head and allowed her dark gaze to encompass the woman who neared. With a soft snuffling sound, she greeted Alexis, apparently scenting a familiar human and welcoming her to her chosen place.

Alexis knelt by the mare's head, rubbing and patting, whispering soft words of comfort, and gauging her readiness by the strength of the pain she was enduring. Once the spasms had passed, the great body lay inert, and Alexis moved to look beneath the animal's tail, her knowing eyes recognizing the signs of imminent birth.

"She's gonna drop her foal right quick, I'd say," Mick told her from atop a rock where he'd perched.

"Don't frighten her," Alexis said quietly.

"I know enough about horses not to do that, girlie," he told her flatly. "You just deliver us a nice little colt there, and I'll have me a pretty little palomino and colt and a girlfriend to boot."

"You'll never have me," Alexis said sharply. "I'm a married woman, Mick. You don't want to tangle with Jamie. He'll chew you up and spit you out."

"We'll see." With a complacent grin, Mick settled himself on the rock and waited.

The birthing process was sometimes long and arduous, but this time, it was as if the heavens shone upon the golden mare and offered her the ease of a short labor and a delivery that went as well as any Alexis had ever seen. The gangly legged colt was delivered readily and the mare twisted her body around in order to wash her baby, nuzzling the wet body and urging him to stand.

Within fifteen minutes, he was nursing, tilting his head in an ungainly manner to reach his mother's bag, and his spindly legs trembled as he balanced himself beside her. Alexis ignored the man who watched, her interest solely on the mare, and it wasn't until Mick called her name that she blinked and looked in his direction.

"We're not moving her," she said. "She needs to rest for a day."

"I go along with that," Mick drawled. "I'm sure we'll find something to do to keep us both occupied for a while, girlie."

As Alexis watched, the mare took careful steps, her dark, liquid gaze on her offspring. The colt followed, lured by the scent of mother's milk, and quickly found his legs to be sturdy beneath him. He fell but twice, both times rising quickly, his gangly limbs tangling a bit, until he got the knack of balancing himself.

The stream wending through the valley lured the mare closer and she drank deeply of the clear water and then grazed beside its banks, the colt beside her. Alexis followed and for a moment forgot about the man who watched her.

His hand touched her shoulder, tightening as she would have drawn away, and he growled a sound of warning, turning her to face him. "Let's see how much that fella's taught you," he muttered darkly. "I'll bet he's broke you in real good."

She pulled away, her shoulder painful where his fingers had so roughly grasped her flesh, and her free hand lifted to push him from her. "Let me go, Mick. I'm not up for grabs."

"That's what you think, lady. I didn't come all the way out here to play games. I been keepin' an eye on you for the past months, and I've spent a lot of hours keepin' track of where you go and what you do. How'd you think I knew to be handy this morning?"

Alexis felt a sharp nudge of fear as Mick allowed his gaze to sweep over her form, resting for long moments on her breasts beneath the torn shirt she wore. And then he grabbed for the remaining fabric, tearing it with ease, and she found her upper body exposed to his view, only partially covered by her vest.

"Now that's better," he said roughly, tearing at the fine fabric of her undergarment, and grasping the softness of her breast beneath.

Alexis shuddered, attempting to back away from him, but found she was no match for his brute strength. His hands were heavy as he pushed her to the ground, his body a solid weight as it pressed her into the grass beneath her and his face was a picture of evil as he bent to touch her face with his lips.

She fought him, her hands lifting to his face, her nails scratching deeply into his cheeks, her mouth opening to bite at his as he would have left his kisses on her. With an enraged growl, he lifted from her and backhanded her, the force of his blow almost knocking her unconscious.

She cried out sharply, wriggling beneath him, attempting to throw his weight from her, and all without success. He was well over two hundred pounds, a big man, tall and husky, and more than a woman's strength could hope to cope with. Yet she struggled, even knowing it would be in vain.

She shrieked aloud, screaming Jamie's name, fighting the weight that threatened to stifle her voice. And then recognized that she might very well die here, that Mick would take what he pleased from her and she might never again see the man she had married.

Jamie. His name resounded in her mind even as she tried to fight off the predator who was even now intent on stripping her clothing from her. Her belt was loosed, her boots were jerked off and the trousers she wore stripped from her legs. She screamed again, the sound shrill and anguished in the peaceful valley.

Mick crouched over her, his hands rough, his touch harsh and hurting and she fought his movements with all the strength she possessed. All to no avail. His hammy fist landed on her jaw, and he laughed at the tears she fought, jeering as he ran cruel hands over her body. And then with the power of a man whose lust has gained control over his senses, he back-handed her, her head hitting a rock that jutted up from the ground.

His big body loomed over her, his face twisted with hatred, and she closed her eyes, knowing that she might never see another sunrise. From the depths of her spirit rose a prayer, one that pled for the life of her child. And even as the soft words rose from her throat, she was crushed by the weight of the man above her, her breathing impeded by his brutish chest crushing her into the ground.

The light faded until all that remained was overpowering darkness that welcomed her and received her into its depths.

"Where's she gone?" James asked the question softly, and that alone was a warning to Slim that the boss was beyond anger.

"She told me she was gonna look for the palomino mare. That was a couple of hours ago, Jamie. She'd oughta be back right soon, I'd think."

"You seen anybody hanging around?" James asked, grasping his reins and lifting himself into the saddle.

"Not a soul," Slim told him. "Everything's quiet."

"Send Chet out after me as soon as you see him. I don't want to run into trouble out there and put Alexis at risk."

Slim nodded his agreement, and James turned his horse to the far side of the pasture where an open gate led to the range land to the north. He rode hard, some unknown fear forcing its way into his mind. The woman had no sense whatsoever, he decided, riding off on her own. And yet, he understood her reasoning, knowing that she was concerned for the mare, anxious for the animal to foal and not wanting her to be alone while she did so.

There were horses scattered over the range, but not a sign of the golden mare he sought. Riding hard, he headed for the area where box canyons offered shelter to a horse who might be in the market for a quiet spot to drop a foal. Damn horses. You couldn't count on them to trot up to the barn and into a stall to do their business. They had to go running off to a wild spot on the map instead.

And Alexis was smart enough to know that.

He followed her trail, knowing she had passed this way, recognizing the shod hoof prints of her gelding as he made his way across the meadow. The grass was crushed a bit where the horse had walked, not enough to provide a trail by tomorrow, but fresh enough to give James notice today that a rider had recently passed this way.

Ahead lay the hills and cliffs, the small valleys and box canyons that might lure a horse, and James nudged his own mount into a quicker pace. The knowledge of Alexis being on her own, alone in the far reaches of one of those canyons was enough to frighten him, and he felt the rush of dread that signaled his fear for her well-being.

And then he heard a sound, a muted shriek that might have been a woman. He rode harder toward the north, his heart pumping in his chest, his eyes pinned on the hills ahead of him.

Again he heard a cry, and his name was called aloud, faint but clear to his listening ear. *Alexis.* He'd have known that voice anywhere, and so recognized the fear that threaded through the syllables of his name. Again she called out, a faint sound on the wind, yet a cry that touched his heart.

He rode harder, urging his stud into a gallop that threw dirt from beneath the animal's shoes. Ahead of him, from what seemed to be an impenetrable spot between the rocks, a horse appeared, its rider bent low over the animal's neck, casting a look in Jamie's direction before he rode recklessly to the north.

"Mick." Jamie spoke the name aloud, certain of the man's identity, even though he had only heard a description of him. And then his heart thumped wildly in his chest as he weighed the chances of following Mick against the greater need to find Alexis.

He rode closer to the area where the rock wall appeared solid, only trees shielding it from sight. The sound of a horse caught his ear and James pushed his way through the tree branches to where the trail led between rocks into a small valley.

Ahead of him a golden mare stood by the stream, a foal by her side, and beyond that placid picture was the form of a woman on the ground. *Alexis*. The utter stillness of her being pierced Jamie to the quick and he slid from his horse, running to her side.

Alexis lay prone, her eyes closed, her arms akimbo, her clothing stripped from her and her face already darkening from the imprint of harsh blows.

James knew a moment of hatred so pure it shook him to the core. That he could despise another human being so much was frightening, and had not Mick been already beyond his reach, he would have delighted in killing him, slowly and with the strength of a man maddened beyond the point of reason.

James dismounted and approached Alexis, holding his breath as he watched for signs of life. If only she would open her eyes, he thought, even move a hand, or take a deep breath, sighing or crying out to let him know she was alive.

But it was not to be. She lay quietly, as still as if she were deeply asleep, and he knelt beside her and felt for a pulse in her throat. Bruises were making themselves known on her throat and breasts, where strong hands had squeezed and abused tender flesh.

Her breasts were uncovered, seeming to be formed of alabaster, so pale and perfect were they, all but for the scratches that marred the fragile skin. And James watched as the tears that fell from his eyes bathed the fragile skin of the woman he loved. He bent low, kissing her repeatedly, his mouth touching with reverence the soft skin of her cheeks and throat, the warm flesh of her shoulder and arm.

He stripped off his shirt and placed it over her chest, lifted her into his arms and held her firmly against himself. Her trousers slid readily up over her hips, covering the bloodstains on her inner thighs.

It was there Chet found them. His horse neighed sharply as he came in through the narrow opening to the canyon and James looked up fleetingly, recognizing the man he trusted.

"Is she alive?" Chet called out. He rode closer and slid from his horse. "Who?" he asked. And then answered his own query. "Mick Jenson. Might have known. That bastard has had it in for her for a long time." He halted next to James. "How badly did he hurt her?"

"About as bad as it gets," James said. "She's alive, but she hasn't come to yet. I suspect she's better off if she stays unconscious for now. I just want to get her home."

"What about Mick? Did you see him?"

"Yeah, I assume it was Mick I saw, riding out of the canyon. But he was out of range by the time I got my hands on my rifle." He closed his eyes, the memory of the man who'd hurt this vulnerable woman one he would never put out of his mind. "I had to reach Alexis first. It was more important to find her than to shoot the bastard, and I had to make a choice. I'll find him, somehow, some way. And that's a promise." James stood carefully, lifting Alexis in his arms, holding his shirt to cover her and then watched as Chet brought James's stud closer.

"Can you get up there on your own?" Chet asked. "Or shall I hold her?"

"Yeah, take her for a minute," James said, grudgingly relinquishing his wife to the older man. Chet held her carefully, watching as James lifted into his saddle, and then bent to take the still form in his own arms again. He tucked her against himself, adjusting her across his legs and wrapping his shirt around her naked upper body, pausing only to button the top of her trousers, holding them in place.

"Let's go," James said, sparing not a backward glance toward the place of Alexis's attack. Leading the way to the canyon's mouth, he rode slowly, nudging his horse past the opening and onto the open range once more.

Behind him, Chet tossed a lasso around the palomino's neck and led her and the newborn colt behind him. They set off to the south, James in the lead, Chet close behind him, and the mare meandering along with her colt, apparently satisfied, now that she had given birth.

It took an hour, an immeasurable length of time to James's mind, riding slowly so as not to jar the precious bundle he carried. She murmured once, his name spoken softly and with a crooning sound he recognized.

"I'm here, sweetheart," he whispered, bending low to assure her of his presence. He held her firmly, his anger at the man who had violated her still brewing in his breast like a kettle boiling on the back of the cookstove. His heart ached for the innocence of his bride, for the shame she had endured and the pain Mick had inflicted on her tender body. And beyond all of that, his mind considered the damage that might have been done to the child she carried.

He should have protected her from danger. He should have known the risk of letting her ride out alone, and forbidden her the use of a horse. He'd promised to love and cherish her, and he could not prevent his heart and soul from the overwhelming guilt that flooded him. He'd never been good enough for the woman, but by some miracle, she'd come to love him, had been willing, no, eager to bear his child. And by his own carelessness he'd caused her the pain of the attack by Mick Jenson. He had not been there when she needed him most. And for that he was filled with hatred toward himself.

The ride was long, the foal traveling at a slow pace, and lest he be set upon by Mick, Jamie wanted to stay in Chet's company. The pasture was placid, the horses within its fences standing with heads to the ground, the foals frolicking near their dams. At the house, Ellen and Hank waited on the porch, and as the horsemen approached, they ran to meet them. Hank met Jamie's hard look, recognizing the blind fury in his eyes, the harsh set of his jaw and the tenderness of his hold upon the woman in his arms.

"Is she all right?" Hank spoke the words as if he dreaded hearing the answer, but James only nodded. It would be Alexis's choice whether or not her father knew the extent of her injuries. Hank stood beside the stud and held out his arms for his daughter's weight to be shifted over to his care.

James lowered her carefully, felt Hank's strength beneath her and then watched as the older man carried his child to the house. Quickly, James followed, holding the door open, hastening ahead to their bedroom and watching as Hank lowered Alexis's form onto the bed.

"I'll take care of her," James said quietly. "Bring me a basin of hot water and some towels, Ellen, would you?"

"Right away," the woman answered, her own face somber as if she knew what was hidden beneath the shirt covering Alexis. James had tugged her trousers up in the canyon, but now he slid them down her legs and he covered her with a quilt, awaiting the water and towels with which to wash away the filth that Mick's hands had left on her.

Chapter Ten

A quilt warmed her flesh, but beneath it, her skin felt pebbled by the chill that swept over her. Alexis bolted upright, her eyes wide, her mouth opening to protest, only to see Jamie's eyes focused on hers.

Jamie. He was here, tending to her, and her cry died in her throat. "Jamie." Her voice was a whisper, a prayer of thanksgiving, a plea for his comfort, and he responded as she'd known he would.

His arms circled her, his face buried against hers, his breath whispering in her ear. "I'm here, sweetheart. I'm here." With gentle care, he moved the quilt aside and lifted his own shirt from her. His hands shook as he removed her vest, the garment torn beyond redemption, tossing it to the floor, disdaining it as soiled by Mick's hands.

She watched him, saw the multiple emotions that glittered in his eyes, the scornful glare he delivered upon the bits of clothing he took from her slender form and the ever-present love that shimmered in the look he bestowed upon her.

"Jamie…" Her pause was long, but he waited patiently, as if he knew she must tell him of her ordeal. And yet she could not. Could not bring herself to say the awful words that would soil her forever in his eyes. "Mick hurt me," she whispered finally, and that simple admission told the tale, apparently, for he only nodded and bent low to her again.

"I know, sweetheart. I've failed you miserably, letting the man get near you." His voice broke and his mouth met hers, a soft, comforting touch that offered his love, with no reservations that she could sense. "I love you, Alexis. I'm so sorry, baby. I should have had someone by your side twenty-four hours a day."

"I feel so dirty, Jamie. You can't know what he did to me."

His index finger lay against her lips, shushing the words she would have said, and she finished the words silently. *I'm soiled...stained.... I can still feel Mick's hands on me, still smell his filthy body, still feel his weight on top of me.*

"I know what he did, Alexis. I saw him leave the canyon, but I let him escape. I had to find you and make certain you were all right. I'm only sorry I didn't get there sooner. I failed you miserably and I'm sorrier than I can say. I don't know how you'll ever be able to forgive me, Alex."

She reached to clasp his head as it rested against her breasts. Her fingers ran through the soft, clean hair, traced the line of his jaw and the muscular nape of his neck. He hadn't blamed her for riding off alone, hadn't scolded her for making him worry, only taken the blame on himself, ruing the fact that he hadn't been in time to stop the man who'd sullied and torn her flesh with his own. For she felt the blood between her legs, knew that Mick had hurt her deeply and not only was she physically damaged, but her heart was aching with the loss of...what? Her girlish innocence was long gone, taken with love and care by the man who held her now.

What Mick had taken from her was the sense of rightness she'd attached to the act of loving. He'd soiled it, turned it into a sinful attack upon her body and left her to mourn the loss of her womanly dignity.

"You'll have to wash me," she said quietly, her breath soft against his skin as she made her need known.

"Would you like a bath?" he asked. "Or shall I just wash you here, in bed?"

"A bath later. For now, just clean me up, please. Or let me do it myself."

"I'll tend to you, sweet. Just lie still and let me take care of you."

And he did. With tenderness, with a gentle touch she wouldn't have thought possible by a giant of a man such as Jamie. With strong, warm hands and plenty of hot water, with towels spread beneath her and enough soap on his cloth to insure her skin's cleanliness, he washed her. His soft murmurs were of his love for her, his sorrow at her pain, the aching need for revenge that had not been satisfied by Mick's death.

The bleeding had almost stopped, and he breathed a sigh of relief, for it was the result of several small tears that gave mute evidence of Mick's brutal use of her body. To his relief, there was no flow from within her, nothing to mark any damage to the baby she held safe in her womb. And for that he was thankful. With a sense of deep gratitude, he told her the extent of the damage as he could see it, and then announced that he would send Chet for the doctor and the sheriff, in order to put this whole day behind them and go on with their lives.

With thick towels, he dried her skin, then padded her gently so that the bed would not be soiled should she shift around and bleed again. He slipped a white nightgown over her head, covering the bruises she'd gathered on her breasts, his own hands shaking as he envisioned the rough hands of a man. A man who had touched her with anger and lust. Then buttoning the front of her bodice with gentle care, his eyes dark, he took note of each abrasion, every mark she bore from the brutal touch of the man who had ravaged her body.

As if he could not leave her side, he brushed her hair, smoothed the vulnerable flesh of her belly, as if he would speak in that way to the child within her body. Stretching out on the bed beside her, he completed the task he'd begun, that of comforting her in any way he could. His hands caressed her back, turning her carefully to face him, gathering her to himself, pouring out upon her the love that filled him to overflowing.

She seemed content to lie with him, to know his touch, know the pleasure of his hands upon her. For long moments she tried desperately to put Mick from her mind, to move beyond the memory of his attack, thankful that her mind had blanked out much of the time during which he'd hurt her body so dreadfully.

The need to let Jamie know was urgent and she whispered words that she thought might comfort him. "I must have hit my head, Jamie. I don't remember much at all."

And when he sighed deeply, tightening his hold on her, she knew she had relieved his mind a bit.

"Jamie?" Her whisper was broken, tears flowing as she spoke the words that must be spoken between them. "Will you ever want me again? Knowing what happened to me out there?"

He nodded, his head moving against hers. "I want you right now, Alexis. I'll want you for the rest of my life. You're the same woman you were before all this happened. I just don't want to frighten you or make you fear me in any way. I'll leave you be until you're ready for me, no matter how long it takes. And until the doctor says it's safe for the baby."

She nodded, her head moving slowly, yet fearful that he might change his mind once he thought about the events of the day. "Does my father know?" she asked. "Or Ellen?"

"No. If you tell them, it'll be your choice, sweetheart."

"It will only cause pain for my father," she said, after a moment. "I'll tell Ellen when the time is right."

"I think they both suspect the truth anyway," Jamie said quietly. He settled her a bit more comfortably against his shoulder. "Now, just sleep if you can. I'm going to send Chet to town and then I'll be right back. I won't be going anywhere else, and I'll still be here when you wake up, babe."

And he was. Awakening when the sun was low in the sky, she murmured against his cheek, her head tilted back a bit, the better to kiss him, then fell asleep promptly once more. Hours later, curling ever closer to his body, she became aware that he'd undressed sometime during the past hours, and that now, in the darkness of midnight, he held her close. She whispered drowsy words of love, heard his response and rejoiced in it, then closed her eyes again and fell into a deep sleep, knowing he was near, that he would not leave her.

The doctor arrived early in the morning, before breakfast, while Alexis still slept in the big bed. He came into the bedroom and she wakened as he sat beside her, his kindly eyes scanning her slender form, his hands taking hers, holding them in a comforting gesture as he spoke.

"I'll have to examine you, Alexis. I need to be certain that the baby is all right, that the man didn't do any damage. I doubt that he did. Babies are resilient creatures, and once they've planted themselves, it would pretty near take a stick of dynamite to pry them from place, but we need to be certain."

She acquiesced readily, looking over his shoulder at Jamie, silently begging his presence at her side. He understood the pleading of her gaze and took the doctor's place beside her, cutting off her view of the medical man as he bent low to hold her firmly, lest she find it difficult to remain still. She clung to him, aware of the doctor's gentle hands, but able to place her trust in Jamie and all that he represented in her life.

"I don't see anything to be concerned about. You're torn a bit, but that will heal in a couple of days. The baby is firmly seated, just as I thought, and even though you'll be uncomfortable, what with all the bruising, you'll be fine, Alexis. Even this lump on your jaw will be gone soon."

He touched the place where Mick's knuckles had delivered her a heavy blow and she winced. "Put some witch hazel on it, James," the doctor said softly. "And a cool cloth to relieve the swelling. That should take care of it."

"Thank you, Doctor," Alexis said, the words breathed with a sigh. She was weary, even after a long night's sleep, and James pulled the sheet over her, tucking her in beneath its covering as he might a beloved child. He bent his head, kissing her gently, then helped her turn a bit, propping a pillow behind her back, the better to help her rest.

A visit from the sheriff the next day was all that he had expected. He only hoped that Alexis would not be required to tell of the events of her ordeal. And he was not disappointed. The lawman asked a few brief questions, and when James told him that he'd seen Mick ride away, but he intended to find him, the sheriff only nodded without surprise.

"Just be careful. He's a nasty fella, James," he said. "Is your wife badly hurt?"

James nodded briefly. "About as bad as a woman can be, Sheriff. And when I find him…" His pause was long and the sheriff nodded.

"You'll be within your rights, Webster. I doubt there'll be a problem. In fact, he won't be missed." He paused and shot James a long look. "Let's just forget about this part of our conversation."

James nodded, relief singing within him.

The sheriff shifted from one foot to the other. "How is your wife now? I doubt she'd be ready for questions, would she?"

"If you need to talk to her, she'll oblige, but I'd rather you didn't, sir." James stated his case firmly and the sheriff nodded with understanding. And then he turned a long, hard look in James's direction. "I think the world of your missus. Her pa, too. They're good folks, and God knows she didn't deserve what happened to her. She had enough trouble with Mick Jenson a few years back. So, if something should happen to Mick, no one will question the circumstances of the man's death," he said bluntly.

"I doubt anyone will come around to ask about him," James said bitterly.

"I think we're all done with this mess, for now," the lawman said, mounting his horse and turning toward the town road. "Give your wife my regards, James."

With a nod, he was gone and James felt a deep sense of relief that Alexis had not been obliged to talk to the man. She must have awakened and risen from bed for he sensed her presence behind him in the kitchen. He turned to her, her slender form faintly visible through the screened door.

"You all right, sweetheart?" he asked. "Want to come out and see the new colt?"

"Is he in the barn?" she asked, crossing the threshold and closing the door behind herself, neatly dressed in her usual garb, a pair of trousers and one of his shirts, tucked in and buttoned to the neck. As if she would not allow any of her bruised skin to show, she had managed to conceal all but the purple welt on her face. James kept his eyes from the swollen area, concentrating instead on the smile she wore.

"Slim put him in the barn last night, but he's out in the pasture with his mama now. Let's take a walk." He held out his hand and she clasped it firmly. "Do you feel well enough to walk that far?" James asked her, looking down at the golden beauty of his wife, then tucked her hand into the bend of his elbow, drawing her body as close to his side as he could manage.

"I'm fine," she answered, attempting to brighten the smile she turned in his direction. A smile that failed to lull him into a sense of belief. She wasn't *fine*. She might never be fine again, and his anger was stirred anew at the thought. He released her hand from his arm and slipped her gently into his embrace, long fingers measuring her waist, drawing her close, the urge to imprint himself upon her surging in his chest. She allowed it, gladly it seemed, for she lifted her own arm to encircle him and walked beside him, pacing herself to his longer strides, until he slowed a bit.

"I'm makin' you run to keep up," he said with a chuckle. "Why didn't you tell me to slow down?"

She dug her fingers into his ribs, finding a spot she knew to be especially ticklish, and at his jolt of surprise, she laughed aloud. "I know how to slow you down, mister," she said smartly. "All I have to do is look up at you. Slows you down every time."

"That's because I'd like to kiss you, but I don't think you'll let me, right out here in the middle of the yard, in front of God and everybody."

"God doesn't care if you kiss me," she said softly, "and neither does anyone else. We're married, remember?"

"I'll remind you of that tonight," he said, leaning down to touch her lips in a soft caress.

They walked slowly then, to the pasture fence, leaning on the top rail as they looked out over the grassy expanse where mares and foals fed on the lush grasses. The palomino mare's golden hide stood out as a beacon might in the dead of night. Her color reflected the sunlight, the small creature beside her looking like a miniature copy of his dam. His long legs were stronger now, Alexis noticed, holding him upright as he looked around the pasture as eagerly as if it were his own kingdom.

And then he sought his mother's bag and bent his body beneath her belly to suckle, taking his nourishment as the mood suited him.

"He's beautiful, isn't he?" It was a question with no answer expected, for they agreed on this one thing, if no other, and James sensed that Alexis had a real sense of ownership when she gazed on the colt. She had been there at his birth, had delivered him in the midst of turmoil and had been the first to see his gangly legs make their entrance into the world.

"What will you call him?" he asked, suspecting that she had not traveled that far in her thoughts. And he was right, for her answer was ambivalent, whispered in a voice that told him she was still looking for the perfect name for her colt. "I'll come up with something," she said slowly. "I'd like Golden in his name. His mama is Golden Lady out of Sorrel King. Seems like we ought to continue the line, don't you think?"

"Whatever you want, sweet. He's all yours, in more than one way. You delivered him, and you knew ahead of time he'd be what he is, a beauty to behold."

"If he were a filly, I'd name him that. Golden Beauty. It would fit, wouldn't it?"

As they watched, the mare spotted them, and as if drawn by invisible bonds, she approached, trotting directly to Alexis, snorting as she came to a halt, tossing her mane and then snuffling at Alexis's outstretched hand. A bit of apple had appeared there, filched from the pies Ellen was preparing in the kitchen, and James laughed at the sight.

"Did Ellen see you take that? She's pretty tight with her apples, you know."

"She saw me." Alexis grinned up at him. "I suspect she knew we were coming out here. At any rate, she didn't squawk at me."

"She wouldn't anyway. She thinks you're the best thing to come along in a cow's age. And especially since Chet started paying mind to her. She's like a spring chicken."

"You've noticed, too?" she asked, looking up at him, smiling at the thought of Chet courting the cook.

"Couldn't help but notice," he answered. "He's sweet on her."

The mare mouthed Alexis's hand again, as if searching for more treats, and with that, James dove into his own pocket where he'd managed to stash a carrot or two. "See if she'd like these." he said, passing them into Alexis's hand. The mare obliged by a sharp whinny, her nose against James's shirt. Alexis leaned across and slid one of the carrots into his pocket and then watched, laughing aloud as the horse retrieved it neatly.

"She's pretty smart," James said.

"No, she just has a good sense of smell." Alexis held out the last treat and the mare obligingly took it with care, her lips barely touching the palm of Alexis's hand. The colt stood by, his head tilted as if he puzzled over the antics of these folks, and when Alexis held out a hand to him, he stepped forward and allowed her to scratch at his ears.

"I wonder if he remembers me," she mused.

"I wouldn't be surprised." James reached for the colt and the infant horse darted from his touch, a playful move that made Alexis laugh again.

"See. He knows who his mistress is."

"Yeah. Mine, too," James said quietly.

"I'm your wife," she protested, making a face as he teased her.

"My wife, my mistress, my lover, everything I ever dreamed of," he answered, his words deep and rumbling in his chest.

Alexis turned to him, her heart beating rapidly, her eyes filling with moisture as she held his words close to her heart. If he never said them again, she would always remember this moment, his declaration of his love and the sound of his voice as he vowed his pleasure in her.

She lifted up on tiptoe, her mouth finding his with ease, her lips forming to his, her eyes closing in pure ecstasy as she reveled in his kiss. His arms were around her as if they were bands of steel, his warmth enclosed her in the heat of passion and he moved against her with a careful, sustained rhythm that told her of his arousal, and reminded her that they were in sight of half the men on the ranch.

She pulled away, breaking his hold, perhaps because he had come to the same conclusion and decided that their kiss had drawn enough attention. Yet there was within her a reticence, a withdrawing of herself, as though she must protect herself from any intimate touch.

It could not be, she decided. Jamie had cared for her, even now was aware of the damage she'd endured. And so her smile trembled on her lips, as her hands found purchase on his shirtfront, holding him firmly against herself. She could not insult him by refusing his touch.

His gaze dropped to where her breasts were outlined neatly against her bodice, filling the fabric and almost pulling the buttons asunder. His grin told her of his pleasure and she looked down, lifting her hands from his chest to cross her arms firmly across her bosom. "I shouldn't feel embarrassed, Jamie, but I do. It's as if I never before noticed my body in such a way, and now I'm almost ashamed of it."

He shook his head. "I'll never do anything to cause you shame, Alexis. I won't touch you until you're free of the fear that bastard managed to make you feel."

"I'm your wife," she said, "and I know I'm in no danger from you, but Mick caused more than physical pain."

"I know that, but I'll do my best to be patient. You've suffered because I didn't take care of you as I should have. If I have to do without your loving, so be it. You're more important to me than you know."

"I'll never hold myself from you," she said, the words a vow.

"I know that. But it won't happen until you're healed and maybe not until the baby is born. Then I'll show you all over again how much I love you, and we'll share a happiness we've never known before. Because you're a survivor, sweet, and I'm the man who plans on spending his life with you."

"I want it to be as it was before, Jamie," she told him. "I never knew I could love a man the way I love you. I hope I can be what you want me to."

Arrogant and untamed, the part of Jamie she welcomed into her arms became more visible now. As if her declaration had added fuel to the fire of his desire, his eyes shone with that same look of possession and ownership and his words reflected the promise of his passion.

"It'll be all right, babe. We'll be fine. Just wait and see."

A letter from Stephen arrived two days later, the boy enthusing about his ranch, thanking James for taking such good care of things and thanking him once again for the wonderful time they'd had at Christmas. And then he wrote a final request, a message that James pondered.

Can I come to visit for a couple of weeks? My pa and Aunt Sarah said it's all right with them, if you don't mind looking after me. Actually, I'm old enough to look after myself, but they don't seem to understand that. And then almost as an afterthought, Stephen had added another line, offering to bring his own riding horse along if it would make things easier.

James smiled as he reread the letter over again for the third time, smiling broadly. Stephen was twelve years old now, a tall boy, probably growing up faster than Sarah would have liked, but the fact was, bringing along a horse was totally unnecessary, for he owned the Double C ranch, lock, stock and barrel, including the herd of horses that occupied the barns and pastures. Bottom line was that if the boy wanted to come and visit and look things over, he shouldn't be denied the chance.

He read it aloud to Alexis and she was of the same mind, urging him to send a reply immediately in order to let Stephen know that he was welcome at the ranch. Jamie told him they would be eager to see him again and asked for details of his arrival.

Hank was given Stephen's letter to read and he nodded his head as he finished the epistle, agreeing that the boy should come to see his ranch and perhaps get to know the boundaries of the acreage he owned and the men who worked for him. "We'll fix him up with a nice room and call it his whether he's in residence or not," Hank said. "He needs to feel at home here."

And so it was that when the train chugged into the station two weeks later, the boy who climbed down from the Pullman car with an eager air and a smile of anticipation was welcomed to the Double C. The whole family had come to meet him, but if he was overwhelmed by the noisy greetings and various hugs he received, he showed no sign of it, for he seemed to fit in remarkably well.

The room he'd been assigned was viewed and pronounced to be really *swell,* and amid looks passed between Alexis and Jamie, an agreement came to be that this young man would be given every opportunity to learn about his inheritance and be trained by those who had a real interest in his future to take over the running of the ranch when he'd reached his maturity.

In the meantime, he rode daily with Jamie, or one of the men, either Chet or Slim, whichever of them had work to do in the fields and pastures. Showing a natural affinity for the horses, he soon became deeply involved with their training, and Alexis pronounced him a natural, able to communicate readily with the colts and fillies, his hands gentle and knowledgeable as he led them through their paces.

It was on a rare trip to town that Stephen met a tall, dark-haired woman in the general store, a plump, cheerful-appearing lady who approached him with a smile.

"You're one of the Clarks, ain't you?" she asked, her gaze taking in his appearance. "You've got that look about you, son."

"Yes, ma'am," he answered. "But my name is Stephen Caulfield now. My pa adopted me a while back, and I live with him and my Aunt Sarah. I'm just here visiting for a while at the Double C."

"Well, unless I'm mighty mistaken, you're my nephew, boy," she told him. "I'm Minna Scott, but I was a Clark before I got married. Hate to admit it, but your daddy, Lester, was my brother. The ranch you inherited was the place I was raised. My daddy was a rascal, and no matter how my mama tried, she couldn't make much of my brothers, but I managed to get away early on, and married a good man."

"You're my aunt?" Stephen was dumbstruck by the news. Finding a relative here, someone who knew his family, was the furthest thing from his thoughts. "My grandma was a good lady?" he asked, recalling Minna's remark about her mother.

"She was the best," Minna said vehemently. "Pa couldn't corrupt her, no matter what. She came from good stock and it was the bane of her life to see her sons turn out so badly."

Stephen stepped closer to the woman. "Do you live here-abouts? Can I come see you sometime?"

Minna hesitated, looking over Stephen's shoulder. "I think this is a friend of yours coming now, boy. Maybe we'd better ask him about my talking to you. The Clark family ain't any too welcome around here."

Jamie approached behind the boy and placed a warm hand on Stephen's shoulder. "You find a friend, son?" he asked, his eyes flashing as he took in Minna's downtrodden appearance.

"This lady is my aunt, Jamie," Stephen said staunchly. "I just told her I'd like to see her again, maybe have her visit me or I could go to her home to see her." He looked back at Minna. "This here is the man who's running the ranch for me till I get old enough to do it myself," he said. "And this is my aunt Minna," he told Jamie, a touch of pride in his voice.

Jamie took off his hat and nodded. "Pleased to meet you, ma'am. This is one fine boy. You can be proud to be his kin."

She faced Jamie directly, tilting her chin upward as if her defenses were on alert. "I am proud," she said. "He's a credit to whoever's been raising him. I'm just glad it hasn't been his daddy. Lester was a scamp of the first order, and he didn't deserve such a nice boy, let alone the poor woman who married him and lived to regret it."

"You're welcome to come visit if you like," Jamie said politely. "We all need all the family we can get, and I'll be the first to tell you that Stephen needs to know more about his background. Each of us has a right to hear about our ancestors."

"Well, most of Stephen's aren't worth the powder it took

to blow them away, including my pa and my brothers, but there were a few of the Clarks who turned out all right. My mama was a fine lady. Of course, she wasn't really a Clark. Just had the misfortune to marry one and ended up with too many odds against her."

"Where do you live, Minna?" Jamie asked.

"About five miles east of town, on a small place with my husband and four young'uns. I don't see much of my family other than the flock at my own place. There's a few cousins around and some uncles here and there, but not a one of them is worth much. You'd do well to keep Stephen away from them."

"I plan on doing that very thing," Jamie said firmly. "I'm responsible for the boy while he's here with us, and I'll take good care of him."

Minna nodded and took her leave, reaching out to touch Stephen's cheek with her index finger as she murmured a goodbye. "Come and see me," she said quietly. And Stephen nodded his agreement.

"Is it safe for him to become well acquainted with her?" Alexis asked later that same day as she sat on the porch with Jamie. "She won't hold a grudge against him, will she? Because he owns the ranch, I mean?"

Jamie shook his head. "I don't think so. I didn't get that impression of her. I think she's a good person from a bad background, and she's done her best to rise above her circumstances. I didn't know there were so many more of Lester's family hereabouts, though. Oh, I knew about some distant cousins and such, but I wasn't aware that he had a sister. It'll do Stephen good to know her, I think."

Alexis sighed and settled against Jamie's shoulder. "Life can be so complicated, can't it? Here I've been living on this place for several years and I didn't know anything about

Minna or the rest of Stephen's family, and you show up and manage to dig out details that eluded all of us."

"It wasn't me," Jamie said quickly. "It was Stephen. Apparently he looks like part of the Clark family, for Minna recognized him in the general store before she even knew who he was."

"Is he doing well with the horses?" Alexis asked. "He seemed to be a natural to me, and I know he's caught on to the training ritual. He knows how to measure their feed and he can saddle and bridle them, but on top of that, is he getting along well with the men? Do they resent being employed by a boy his age?"

"Don't seem to have any problem with anyone that I can see," Jamie said. "He was down at the road the other day, looking up at the sign Woody made, and his grin was a mile wide. He likes the idea that the name Caulfield has a part here."

"He loves his aunt and Brace, doesn't he?"

"They've given him everything a boy needs to grow up to be a man of the first order," Jamie said. "When the time comes, he'll take over here and make a success of things, and Brace can be proud of his son."

"Stephen said he misses his sisters terribly. Bree and Brenna are such sweeties."

"They lead him a merry chase at home," Jamie said with a grin. "He lugs them with him all over town, and usually has one of them up in front of him on his saddle when he rides. They vie for his attention, and he loves it."

"I'll bet Sarah and Brace miss having him at home."

"They do, I'm sure, but they know this is important to him." Jamie leaned back, hauling Alexis close to his side. "And they know we'll keep a good eye on him."

With a shout of greeting, Stephen came around the corner

of the house astride his gelding, his smile wide. "Hey there, you two. I just saw my aunt Minna on the road from town and she's coming here with her four young'uns. Have we got any extra cookies or anything?"

"Go ask Ellen," Alexis said. "I'm sure she'll come up with something."

Chapter Eleven

By the time Minna's farm wagon drew up at the back porch, Stephen was waiting with a bowl of cookies and a pitcher of foaming milk. Ellen came out with glasses enough to go around and Stephen viewed the guests with all the aplomb of a king inviting visitors into his castle.

"I'll bet you know more about this place than any of us, Aunt Minna," he said eagerly. "Being raised here and all, I'd guess you have lots of memories."

"You're right, Stephen. But not all of them are good ones. Me and my mama kinda stood together against all the menfolk in the family, and took a lot of guff from them. My pa wasn't much for manners or being nice to his womenfolk."

"Well, I suspect you've turned out to be more like your mother," Alexis said quickly. "Stephen tells us she was a good woman."

"That she was." Minna settled herself comfortably on a wide chair and accepted the glass of milk Stephen offered as he played being the host to the four youngsters who'd lined up on the steps. When all were settled with milk and cookies, he returned to his aunt.

"I'm sure glad you came over today. I've been wanting to come see you, but I didn't know where you live."

"I'll give you the directions," Minna said, and then shot an inquiring look at Jamie. "If it's all right with Mr. Webster here, you can ride by anytime you like. My mister ain't much for company, but when I told him about you being my nephew and new in these parts, he said you was welcome in our home."

"That was good of you, Minna," Alexis said quickly. "Maybe Jamie and I can ride over with Stephen for a visit."

Minna nodded at the assemblage on the steps. "My oldest boy, Jonas, is about Stephen's age. I'd heard that Lester had the first grandson, and I was sorta glad to be out of the running for this place. When I left home, I swore I'd never come back. And yet, here I am." She looked over at Stephen and smiled, her face crinkling in a manner that changed her looks into a semblance of beauty.

Alexis pondered the thought. Minna had obviously had a hard time growing up, but her marriage seemed to be a good one, and she clearly doted on her four children. All of that made her someone to be admired as far as Alexis was concerned.

The visit was not long, for less than an hour later the five of them climbed into the wagon and the eldest boy, Jonas, held the reins. "We got to be home in time for chores," he told Jamie. "But I'm glad we got to meet our cousin. Maybe Stephen and me can do some stuff together."

"That sounds like a good idea," Jamie said. "He needs a friend his own age. And there isn't much better than a flesh-and-blood kin. Cousins are good to have. Right next door to brothers."

"You got brothers?" Jonas asked, and Jamie nodded.

"Just one. His name is Connor, and he was here at Christmastime with his family."

The wagon pulled away, the horses seemingly eager to get home, and with a general waving of hands and goodbyes called out by the visitors, Minna and her children were gone.

"How does it feel to know you have family here?" Alexis asked Stephen, tugging him down on the swing beside her.

"Kinda nice," he said. "I'm glad all my kin aren't like my father."

"Do you have trouble keeping your parents set apart from your father? I understand your memories of him weren't very good."

"Naw," Stephen answered slowly, his long fingers clasping in his lap. "My first dad was a real nasty guy. When Brace got hold of me the first day I ever saw him, I knew I'd be safe with him. He let my dad know that there wasn't gonna be any more fists raised at me, and he never backed down for a minute. Him and my aunt Sarah took me in and gave me a room of my own and fought in court to adopt me."

He looked up at Alexis and she nodded. Aware that his tears were not far from the surface, and not wanting to embarrass him by making note of it, she grinned. "And they got you a horse and a dog, and made you their son, didn't they?"

"They're the best folks anybody ever had," Stephen said staunchly. "Aunt Sarah looks so much like my real mother, it's almost scary sometimes. It's almost like she died, but a part of her is in Sarah."

"It is, Stephen," Alexis said. "They were more than sisters. Being twins meant that they had shared their lives from the first moment. I think you'll find that Brenna and Bree will share the same sort of bond. And Sarah loves you the same way Sierra did. Even though she didn't give birth to you, she has the same feelings of being your mother."

"I guess I knew all that," Stephen said. "But it's good that someone else can see it, too."

From the back door a voice interrupted their words and Ellen stepped out on the porch. "I hope y'all didn't eat too many cookies. I don't want you to spoil your supper."

"Not a chance," Stephen said, grinning at the housekeeper. "And I suppose you want me to call in the men to eat with us. Maybe even Chet."

Ellen blushed a bit at the boy's words, Alexis thought, as the woman backed herself into the kitchen once more. Obviously even Stephen was not immune to the attraction between their cook and Chet. "I promised them a nice roast beef with vegetables for supper," Ellen said, "and they'll be hungry."

"Well, I know how to ring the bell when you're ready for us to come in," Jamie said. "And we'll give them plenty of time to wash up at the trough."

"Hank is in his study. I'll give him notice," Ellen said briskly. "I was surprised he didn't come out and talk to your family, Stephen."

"He's got some hard feelings toward the Clarks," Alexis said quietly. "One of these days, he'll make the effort to be friendly."

Supper was a joyous event, with Stephen elaborating on his newfound relations, especially pleased with the discovery of a cousin his own age. Jamie listened, sharing the boy's elation, and Alexis darted several looks of understanding at the lad and then Jamie, as if she shared the joy inherent in such a discovery.

"I liked having girl cousins when I was young," she said. "It's different when you have a blood tie with people. We used to lie out in the meadow and watch the clouds and tell stories and make plans for our futures."

"Sounds kinda sappy to me," Stephen murmured.

"That's what girls do," Jamie said swiftly. "Nothing like the riding and roping and chasing the bulls that keeps boys occupied."

"He'll not be chasing the bulls," Alexis said firmly. "I don't need to worry about him being gored or trampled."

"I'll bet Jamie did all kinds of stuff when he was my age," Stephen said loftily.

"You betcha," Jamie told him. "Someday we'll have a long talk."

"Not if I have anything to say about it," Alexis said. "I don't want to have to tell Sarah that her son was tossed off a horse and chased down by a bull."

"You worry too much, Alexis," Jamie said. "There's an art to it, and once Stephen learns how to handle a lariat and knows how to ride his horse with just the pressure of his knees, he'll be well equipped."

"Don't worry, Miss Alex," Chet said. "We'll look after the boy. Won't let nuthin' happen to him."

"Thanks, Chet," she said. "I appreciate having someone understand my position."

"Yes, ma'am, I surely do," he returned, sending a wink in Jamie's direction.

They undressed by moonlight, Alexis firm in her refusal when Jamie would have lit the lantern. "I can see what I'm doing," she said, picking up her gown from the bed.

And as Jamie watched, barely able to discern her features in the dim light cast by moon and stars, she lifted the gown over her head and then proceeded to remove her clothing beneath its folds.

"I hate it when you do that," he said. "Just once, I'd like to see you without all those yards of material hangin' on you."

"I've always gotten undressed this way," she said in surprise.

"That doesn't mean I have to like it," he answered. "I'd be more than willing to help you, you know."

"I'll just bet you would," she said with a laugh, and then turned her back to him. "If you can reach under my gown and undo my buttons, I'd appreciate it, sir."

He bent to his task without hesitation, lifting her gown and undoing the line of buttons that traveled up her back. With his fingers firmly enmeshed in the fabric, he tugged the dress down until it fell from her hips into a circle around her feet.

He picked it up, and she lifted her feet from the entanglement so he could toss it aside. "Now for the rest of it," he said, reaching once more beneath the sheltering folds of the white gown. His fingers undid her petticoats and they followed the same path her dress had taken. The tapes on her drawers were next and he neatly undid them with the same results.

She'd shed her shoes upon entering the bedroom and now he settled her on the side of the bed to remove her stockings. There was a hitch in her breathing as his hands settled on her thighs and rolled the white stockings downward. As if he hadn't noticed her slight withdrawal from his touch, he bent forward and touched her knees with his lips, kneeling before her as would a supplicant before his queen.

He looked up and she caught her breath at the vulnerable expression on his face. "I love you, Alexis," he said. "I want to make love to you tonight."

She shivered, unable to speak for a moment, and then her hands framed his face and she bent low to kiss the furrow that marred his brow. "I don't know if I can, Jamie."

"If you tell me no, I won't argue with you, baby. I'll just hold you in my arms till morning and be thankful for that much."

"I think you need more than that from me," she said softly, her kisses wandering to touch his cheeks and lips as she sought out the sweet hollow beneath his ear. Her breath made him shiver, as she'd known it would, and his laugh was a response to her teasing.

"You're all I need, Alex. In whatever way I can have you. I know it will be hard for you to accept me into your body after what you went through out there in the canyon. But I have to tell you, sweetheart, I'll never do anything you don't want me to, and that includes loving your body in an intimate fashion. We'll do this at your pace, just like I told you. And when you're ready for me, let me know."

She wrapped her arms around his shoulders and held him closely, her knees parting as she drew him into the embrace of the vulnerable flesh of her thighs. He sighed and shivered at the touch of silken skin and knew a moment of peace such as he hadn't felt in the long days since he'd found her, bruised and unconscious in the canyon.

His head bent low and rested against her body, inhaling the sweet scent of woman and seductive aroma of freshly washed skin that begged to be explored by his agile fingers and hands. Inhaling sharply, he slid his arms around her, drawing her closer, nestling as near to her warm and welcoming body as he could manage.

"Are you all healed?" he asked, his words muffled against her flesh.

She whispered a single word. "Yes." And then she wrapped him closer to her, nearer that place he longed to possess as his own. With a quick movement, he lifted her gown and drew it from her, over her head and thence to the foot of the bed.

Lying back on the mattress, she drew the sheet upward, covering herself, and he felt a pang of sadness as he beheld her reluctance to have his gaze upon her skin. "Your bruises are healed, sweetheart," he told her quietly, "and you're just as lovely as you ever were. Especially there where our baby is." He touched her belly through the sheet and she inhaled sharply. "I won't hurt you, Alexis. I only want to touch you," he said quietly.

Without words, she responded to him, holding her arms up, reaching for his body, and when he came to her without hesitation, she drew back the sheet, making a place for him to kneel between her thighs, turning on the bed to allow him space.

"Are you sure?" he asked, not wanting to rush her into anything that might cause harm to her tender flesh, aware that she might not accept him and trying his best to be patient.

"Love me, Jamie," she whispered, and he swiftly stripped from his clothing. Then with a look of pure male possessiveness, his gaze scanned her naked body, and he smiled. The same wolfish grin she'd come to know, the smile that signaled his desire, the twisting of his lips and the shimmering of his eyes proclaiming his need for her to surrender to him—all filling her with the pride of a woman knowing her own worth, a woman able to face with joy the man she has chosen as a lover. His eyes fed on her curving breasts, feasted on the place where his child lay, even now moving within her, and his smile was one of delight, of pleasure in her beauty.

His kisses were warm and undemanding, his hands callused, but gentle, and the caresses he offered to her supple body were welcomed with soft sighs of pleasure. "You know just how to touch me, Jamie," she whispered. "I always feel so loved when you put your hands on me, and I get shivers when you kiss my throat and…" Her hesitation was long.

"And what?" he asked, his smile well hidden by the curve of her breast.

"You know. Don't tease me."

"You like this?" he asked softly, his lips seeking and suckling the tender crest of her breast. She trembled beneath him and he knew a moment of pure joy, that this woman would so give herself to him, even though it cost her deep pain, wrapped in the memory of her too-recent assault.

"You know I do. You're a tease, Jamie Webster."

"And you're the most wonderful woman in the world, Alexis Webster." His reply was quick and he followed it with a slow and seductive journey up her throat to the lush fullness of her mouth, where he sought and found the heat of passion and desire.

"I won't hurt you," he promised, loathing the reason he must give assurance to her.

"I know that," she said. And with a trusting gesture that made him pause, she widened her legs and welcomed him to that place where he would find comfort and pleasure of his own.

That she shivered at his weight, that her hands trembled on his shoulders and her breathing was broken, she cared but little. Memories flashed through her mind and she determinedly set them aside, unwilling to refuse him his due.

"Just for now, for tonight, take me and think only of yourself, Jamie," she whispered. "I want to give you my body as a gift, my love as a promise for our future."

It was all he could do to contain himself as he heeded her words, knowing that she had good reason for withholding herself from the rapture of release he could provide. Knowing that she needed simply a memory of this time of ultimate possession, a union fashioned of love and respect to replace that of her last encounter with a man.

For it was in his power to fill her with his own essence, his own powerful body and yet gift her with the kindness and gen-

Lone Star Bride

tleness she needed for this moment. If her desire for him had made her ready for his penetration, he would be thankful. If not, he would ready her in another way. Willing to do whatever it took to accede to her wishes in this, he shushed her with tenderness as he sought out signs of her readiness. She was only damp, not yet showing signs of her passion, and he was patient, his hands and fingers exploring her, hopeful of bringing her to that place of preparation for his entry.

"I need for you to relax, sweetheart," he whispered, his movements against her lithe body forming a rhythm she could not mistake. "I won't come inside you until you can take me without pain. And if you aren't ready for this, I'll understand." He kissed her lavishly, bestowing on her the warmth and passion of his caresses as he strove to bring her to a higher level of desire.

And then she shivered in his arms, her breath seeming to catch in her throat as she spoke. "I want you, Jamie. Please."

He held her bottom in his hands, lifting her with care as his erection brushed against the fragile skin of her womanhood. "Take me, Alexis," he murmured. "Make me whole again."

"Can I do that?" she asked, her hand touching his cheek, her fingers rubbing with gentle strength against his jaw and then to the nape of his neck.

"You're like the sun in my sky, sweet. The stars I follow in my search for happiness. And best of all, you give me a new joy for living I've never had before. I want to grow old with you, and see our children and grandkids grow up in a home of our own."

She tugged at him, her hands sliding down his shoulders to join at his waist, drawing him closer to her, lifting herself, the better to contain him within her warmth. Her hands reached down his body to complete their joining, and with a groan of need, a soft exclamation of triumph, he filled her. His possession of her most delicate flesh was gentle, but smacked of a glorious triumph, as he found the source of his happiness in her arms. His tender invasion took possession of the depths of her body, and he held her firmly against himself, blending their bodies as one flesh, as if he could not imagine any pleasure greater than this. Long moments passed before he moved within her, and she lifted to him, taking his full length, causing him to shiver with delight.

Her legs wrapped him in a loving embrace, her hands sought his shoulders and the muscular planes of his back. And through it all, she filled her mind with one thought. *This is Jamie. This is Jamie.*

They fit together as they had in the past, her softness receiving the caress of his hair-roughened body, her face the recipient of his kisses. His mouth was open against her flesh, his lips finding her own, suckling the tender curve of her mouth. His lungs filled with deep gulps of air as though he ached for the next breath he would take. And then with a soft cry that spoke of a fulfillment to come, he rose and fell in the throes of passion, loving her with each thrust of his body, holding her against his muscular form, as though fearful of pressing her too firmly into the mattress. And yet unable to release her from his grasp.

It was too much for his aroused body to resist and in moments he found his release within her, his need too great to be denied any longer. And in the giving of himself, he found that her response was forthcoming, slower than his own, but bringing her with him to a surging completion that brought a cry of delight to her lips.

She buried her face in his throat, shivering and trembling against him, and hot tears coursed down her cheeks, bringing him to a fearful dilemma. "Have I hurt you?" he whispered. "Was I too rough?"

She shook her head and left the moisture of her tears on his skin. "No." Her denial was quick. "You've made me happy, Jamie. You gave me what I needed. I knew I had to feel your strength, knew that I needed the weight of you atop me to replace the horror of that day in the canyon."

"Do you remember more of it than you've told me?" he asked anxiously. "I'd hoped that the memory was buried while you were unconscious."

"I remember him pushing me to the ground and stripping off my clothing, and then when he fell on me, I…" She trembled again and laughed softly. "I'm so thankful that I hit my head on the ground, I don't know whether that was what made me faint or whether the shock of him and the vile smell of the man did me in. I only know that the rest of it is a blur, and for that I'm thankful."

"Probably not nearly as thankful as I," Jamie whispered fervently. "You might never have let me near you again if you remembered the whole mess."

"I couldn't have borne it much longer, being so separate from you."

"I know, sweetheart. I was going mad without your loving. I needed you so badly, but more than that, I wanted your healing to take place, so that you could accept me as your husband again."

She wrinkled her nose then, pushing at him in a futile effort to rise from the bed. "I need to get washed up," she said in a whisper. "I'm a mess."

"So you are," he told her, grinning wickedly. "And since I made the mess, I'd say it's up to me to clean it up." He rose from the bed, looking down at her from dark eyes that seemed to look within her soul. "Is the baby all right? I didn't hurt him, did I?"

Alexis shook her head. "No, of course not. He likes to have his daddy around."

"Well, I told him last night how lucky he was going to be, what with having the prettiest mother in the state of Texas."

"When did you tell him that?" she asked.

"When I was kissing your belly and saying good-night to my son."

"I wonder if he can hear us when we talk to him." Her smile was winsome, he thought, her face glowing in the moonlight, and he felt the luckiest of men as he looked down at the woman he loved.

"I'll be right back," he told her, walking to the basin where a pitcher of warm water awaited him. The washcloth was dipped in the basin and wrung out, and then he brought it to her and tenderly washed the evidence of his loving from her body. "Feel better?" he asked, drying her with the towel.

"I was on the verge of going to sleep, and then I caught a glimpse of that look in your eyes," she teased.

"No, not now. You're not ready for more tonight," he said with a sigh. "You've had quite a day, and you need to sleep on your husband's shoulder and let him rub your back for a while."

"I knew there was a good reason to marry you, James Webster," she announced, "and I think I've discovered what it is."

Jamie carried the linens to the dry sink where her basin and pitcher rested and then turned back to her. "Did you need a good reason?" he asked.

She nodded and scanned his naked form, as if she enjoyed the sight of him. "I had several, actually. I loved you beyond reason, and you made me feel like a woman. Then, too, my father liked you, and that was a bonus. And on top of that, you're handsome and tall and your muscles are very impressive."

"All of that?" he asked, one eyebrow wiggling as he returned her survey. "And how about you? Like the way your nice little fanny entices me." She giggled and he went on, his look pensive as he thought of that which would amuse her.

"Your bottom wiggles when you walk, and the way your hair shines like pure gold in the sunlight makes me feel rich. And then there's the way your eyes glitter when you get mad at me."

"I don't get mad at you," she denied ferociously.

He placated her easily. "Once in a while," he said, returning to the bed, lying beside her and drawing her into his arms. The sheet and quilt were pulled up to cover them and he slid his hands against her skin, one broad palm below her waist as he massaged the tired muscles there. "Feel good?" he asked, and she nodded.

"You bet it does. This is another reason I married you Jamie."

"You didn't know I'd rub your back before we got married."

"I knew you'd do anything you could to make me happy."

"Yeah. There is that," he conceded.

"Including giving me your child."

He laughed softly. "My son, you mean."

"Maybe. But it could be a girl. And then what will you do?"

His laughter faded and his words were solemn, a vow spoken from his depths. "I'll love her with all my heart." He lifted his head and sought her mouth, bending over her as he kissed her without passion, with only the sure and certain touches that reminded her of his constant, abiding affection for her. And yet, that was too mild a word, he thought.

Affection was what a man felt for his dog or horse, or even his father-in-law. For Alexis, there was a bone-deep, eternal rush of love that penetrated his heart and offered it to her as her own.

Chapter Twelve

Alexis was heavy with pregnancy. No longer able to ride as was her custom, she chose instead to walk. And walk she did. The colts and fillies in the pasture were not strangers, and they welcomed her daily pacing from one group to another, seeking out the treats she hid in her pockets, nudging her for the caresses they had come to expect from her hand. She grew to know them on a basis she'd never explored before, spending time with each, making them familiar to the touch of human hands on their bodies, holding up their hooves for inspection and brushing their manes and tails with long strokes as she whispered words of affection.

"Alexis loves those young ones, don't she?" Stephen asked, leaning with Jamie on the top rail of the corral. He'd found a stump to stand on and the added height brought them eye level. Now he pondered the pasture before him with satisfaction and finally turned to Jamie with a wide grin.

"It makes me feel rich, way inside, when I think that one day this will all be mine, and I'll be a real rancher."

"You've got a lot of learning to do first, Stephen," Jamie said bluntly, "but as bright as you are, I don't see you having any trouble picking up all the skills and knowledge you'll need to do the job."

"My pa has faith in me. He told me so." Stephen seemed to blossom as he spoke the words Brace had offered him. "He said one day I'd do a fine job of running this place. And he said if there was a man on earth to help me grow into the job it was you, Jamie."

Jamie felt a blush climb his cheeks at the words of praise offered so offhandedly by the boy. "He said that?"

"Yeah, he did. But I think he already did his part, don't you? I mean, he taught me how to ride and how to take care of my horse and all the equipment and how to have a sense of responsibility."

"Responsibility is a big part of life," Jamie told him. "It begins when you're too young to understand it, and just keeps on growing as you gain years and knowledge. Some of us take longer than others to learn responsibility, but you've got a good start already, son."

"Well, I just know that Aunt Sarah told me I should make them proud of me, and that's what I want to do, more than anything else."

"A fine aim, I'd say." Jamie nodded agreeably, his eyes never leaving the woman who paced the meadow, colts and fillies alike in her wake. One young colt butted her chest, seeking attention, and Jamie heard his breath catch as he watched, fearful of her being caught off balance.

Instead, he heard her amused laughter peal through the still morning air and knew a moment of thanksgiving that this woman was his. In all of her pregnant glory, she appealed to him as no other female had in his life. Her very existence was like a beacon to him, leading him to her side wherever she went. Which was why he'd chosen to halt his work this morning to watch her as she took her daily stroll through the pasture.

Now she raised one hand at them and Stephen waved excitedly in return. "I sure wish the horses liked me as well as they do Alexis. I want to walk with her someday and hear all the things she says to them. Do you think she could teach me how to make friends with them like she does?"

"It's worth a shot," Jamie said. And it would offer some small amount of protection to Alexis should the boy accompany her, keeping an eye out for her. An additional lesson in responsibility.

Now, Alexis turned, making her way at almost a snail's pace across the meadow, the yearlings at her back and sides, almost as if they formed a guard around her. As she approached the fence, they fell back a bit, and she turned to them, offering pats and caresses, speaking to them in low tones.

"Well, how many did you name today?" Jamie asked.

"Just two. See the spotted filly? The one with three black legs? She's going to be called Stephen's Sally, and don't ask me why. She just is. The name suits her. And she'll be a good horse for Stephen to ride one day. He can train her and break her to saddle himself in a couple of years. She's feisty and sassy but she's sweet natured."

"She'll be mine?" Stephen asked unbelievingly. "Just like that? She'll be my horse?"

"They're all yours, Stephen," Alexis said readily. "But Sally will be special to you. She's going to be one of your own riding horses. You'll need two, and she'll be a good choice to take to town and show off to the townspeople. She'll prance and skedaddle around and act like a princess. You'll love her."

"I think I do already," he said, watching with awe as the newly named filly approached him tentatively. He held out a hand and she nudged it with her muzzle.

"Here, give her this," Alexis said, holding out a bit of apple to him.

Stephen fed it to the filly, holding it on the flat of his palm so she could take it with gentle movements of her lips. His hand moved to her neck and he patted her, smoothing her mane and removing the tangles from it.

"All right," Jamie said. "Who else did you name out there today?"

"The chestnut filly, the one with white stockings on her forelegs. She's going to be Red Rose, and I'm going to train her myself. She'll be our first gift to our child."

"Why that one?" Jamie asked with a tender smile that only his wife could see.

"She's gentle and easy to handle. She'll be a fine first ride for a child. And we'll spend extra time with her so that when the baby is three or so, we can put her up in the saddle and the filly will be placid and easygoing."

Jamie reached over the fence rail and tugged Alexis closer, snatching a kiss from her rosy mouth, then thinking better of it and turning the affectionate caress into a longer, demanding blending of lips.

"Aw, come on," Stephen said from beside him. "Aunt Sarah and my pa are always doin' that kind of stuff at home. I guess all married folks act that way, don't they?"

"I don't know about *all* married folks, but I know about this one," Jamie said with a chuckle. "Kissing Alexis is one of the things I like best in the whole world." He grasped her hand and walked toward the corral gate, opening it and towing her from the pasture and into his arms.

"You've walked long enough for this morning," he said

firmly. "I think you need to go in the house and have Ellen fix you a cup of tea. You feel kinda shaky to me."

For indeed her legs were trembling beneath her as he held her close. "I was fine till just this minute," she said in a low voice. "But I think you're right. I'll go sit with Ellen in the kitchen for a while."

"Let's walk up to the house together," he said, and then shot a look at Stephen. "I'll be back in a bit and we'll take a look at the three-year-olds, Stephen. All right?"

"Can I go in the meadow and walk with the colts and fillies like you did?" Stephen asked Alexis. "I'll be careful and I won't scare them."

"Of course you can," she said. "Just talk to them as if they were your friends, and pretty soon, they will be."

With a long, strong arm about her waist, Jamie led Alexis to the house. Their path led through the barn, in the back door and out the front, and midway down the long aisle, he stopped her and turned her to face him.

"You're not getting ready to have the baby yet, are you?"

She shook her head, but he thought her look was dubious. "I don't know how to tell. I don't have any pains or anything."

He dipped his head and kissed her, longing to draw her into himself, take all the aches and cramps she suffered as his own to bear. "Have I told you how grateful I am to you for having my child?" he asked, his mouth whispering in her ear. He kissed her throat and then returned to the lure of her mouth, taking sustenance there as though he were a man thirsting in the desert and her mouth offered the only life-giving source.

"I love you, Alexis Webster," he said, feeling a rush of emotion he could not explain.

She curled into him, her belly a wedge between them as the child within her pushed in protest at being so confined.

"He kicked me," Jamie said, looking down in wonder at the rounded form of his child. "He actually kicked me." And then his lips twisted in a grin of good humor as he patted Alexis's belly. "Sorry, fella. Didn't mean to squash you that way."

Alexis looked up with a pout on her lips. "You have no idea what it's like to have those kicks and proddings going on all day and night. I don't believe this child sleeps more than six hours a day. And the middle of the night is his favorite time to give me reminders that he's there."

"Wake me up next time and I'll talk to him about it," Jamie said, his expression cunning, as if his thoughts were running on a different level.

"Fat chance. I'm not taking a chance on waking you during the night. You take too long to go back to sleep."

They turned then to the far door and continued the trek to the house, Jamie's arm holding her to his side even more firmly. Above her head, he spoke, and she shivered at his words.

"Just you wait till that baby is born and you're all healed up and ready for me, sweetheart. I'm saving up all sorts of good stuff to try."

"Well, don't get all hot to trot, James. You've got a while to wait."

"James, is it?" He squeezed her a bit and she squealed.

"You'll have me wetting all over the ground if you keep that up," she said, laughing as she spoke. "In fact, I should make a stop at the outhouse before I go in."

"I'll tell Ellen to fix your tea, then," Jamie said, halting and waiting as she walked to the vine-covered building near the corn crib.

Fixing tea and warming a cinnamon bun for Alexis was a simple task, Ellen told him, and she set about doing just that

as Jamie poured himself a cup of coffee leftover from breakfast. He'd just settled down at the table with it when he heard
a wagon pull into the yard and up to the hitching rail.

"Sounds like company," he said and reversed his movements, rising to open the back screened door.

Minna climbed down from the wagon and walked toward
the steps. "Hi there," she called out. "Thought I'd take a
chance on finding y'all home this morning."

"Come on in," Jamie said. "Alexis will be here right
shortly, and I'll be going back to find Stephen in a minute or
two."

"Actually, Stephen is one of the reasons I stopped by,"
Minna said.

"You want to see him?" Jamie asked.

"I thought he might come and spend a day with us. The
children are excited to have a cousin, and they've got all sorts
of games figured out to play if he can come for a day."

"I don't know why not," Jamie said. "But in the meantime,
I'll go round him up and sound him out about it."

Alexis came in the door and halted. "Minna." She walked
to the sink and washed quickly and then returned to the table,
bending to place a quick kiss on the woman's cheek. "I'm so
glad you stopped by. Maybe Ellen could fix you a cup of tea
and we'll have a good gab fest."

"I'm leavin'," Jamie said with vehemence. "Three women
in one kitchen is more than I can deal with." With a general
salute to all and a significant look at Alexis, he left the house,
and Ellen brought the hot teapot to the table.

"We'll just let it steep for a few minutes," she said. "I'll
put another cinnamon roll in the oven to heat for you, Minna,
and then we'll enjoy our tea."

"Are you feeling all right?" Minna asked Alexis. "When
is the baby due?"

Alexis looked up at Ellen. "We think maybe the end of the month or early August. I'm not sure what to look for. I'm real good with horses, but having a baby of my own is a different story altogether."

"So it is," Minna said. "But you'd be surprised how alike we are to the animals in the barn. Same aches and pains, same symptoms of imminent birth and the very same sort of labor pains." She sighed. "Makes me weary to think about it."

"You've got four?" Ellen asked.

"And that's enough for anyone," Minna said. "I'm happy to just sit back and give advice like an old lady these days. Sure beats having more young'uns of my own."

"Do you know of any midwives in the area?" Alexis asked. "I know I can send someone after the doctor, but I've heard that midwives are preferred by a lot of women."

"I've been delivering babies for a number of years," Minna said. "Right after my first one was born, I got called to a neighbor's place and his wife was set to have her first, and so I just pitched in and between us we managed to have a nice baby boy. If she'd waited for the doc to come from town, she'd have had that baby all by herself."

"So you've delivered lots of babies?" Alexis asked hopefully.

"A whole string of 'em. Doc has been threatening to train me, turn me into a doctor myself. But I don't want to do all the broken legs and such. I'll leave that up to him. I can do most any healing needs to be done, but babies are my first love."

"If I send for you when the time comes, will you be available?" Alexis asked.

"You bet, honey. I'll be here, quick as a minute."

"That makes me feel better," Alexis said, drinking her tea and ooking up with anticipation as Ellen brought the warm cinnamon rolls from the oven. "This may ruin my dinner, but I don't care," she said stoutly. "This baby needs to be fed right now."

"My aunt Minna is leaving now." Stephen stood at the back door, watching as his cousins and their mother climbed into the wagon. They'd come for the noon meal, and after hours of playing, the children had been gathered together, told that time was fleeting and they must get home to do the chores before supper.

Now Stephen outlined the next phase of his strategy. "I figure if I know the way to my aunt Minna's house, I can go get her when you need her to come here. You know, when it's time for the baby to be born."

Stephen had obviously kept his eyes and ears open, Alexis thought, and even though there might be an ulterior motive to his planned trip to Minna's house, she appreciated his offer of help when it should be needed.

"That sounds like a fine idea to me," she told the boy, and Stephen grinned widely, aware that his trip was all but sanctioned already.

"I can go then?" he asked hopefully. "I can follow Aunt Minna home and stay there for a bit?"

"If Minna wants you, I don't see why not. Check with Jamie first, but tell him I thought it would be fine for you to go." And no doubt it would be deemed as such by Jamie. Willing to do what he could for the boy's pleasure in being here, he was pretty open to Stephen's ideas. And Minna was apparently to be trusted.

So it was that in ten minutes Stephen had saddled his horse and was riding beside the farm wagon as it pulled from the yard. A jaunty tilt to his hat and the confident grin on his face were a pleasure to behold, Alexis thought. And Minna had

added her own words of assurance that Stephen would be jus
fine, and she'd be certain he knew his way home without any
trouble when the evening meal was over.

Yet the supper table was quiet without the boy's quick
chatter and Alexis had almost decided to be concerned abou
his homecoming by the time the meal was finished.

"He's eating at Minna's," Jamie reminded her. "It'll take
a while for him to get home."

"I don't want him riding alone in the dark," she said, her
shiver giving away the concern she felt. And then she offered
a suggestion. "Maybe you ought to saddle up and ride toward
Minna's place, kinda keep an eye out for him."

"I'll go, Miss Alexis," Chet said quickly. "I know where
the place is, and if Stephen is on his way, I'll let him think I
was goin' out visitin'. No sense in letting him think we're
checkin' up on him."

"Jonas and me had a good time," Stephen said, his mouth
working at the remains of a sugar cookie from Ellen's crock
He'd sworn that he was "fuller than a tick" upon his arrival
home, but within an hour had managed to consume a glass
of milk and two of the cookies.

"Sure was a surprise to see ol' Chet riding up towards me,"
Stephen continued. "I was pretty sure I was on the right
stretch of road, but it was just startin' to get dark, and I
couldn't see all that well."

He settled more comfortably on the swing, leaning a bit
on Alexis, his feet swinging, toes touching the porch floor.
Happily, she realized that she was having the privilege of
watching him grow from boy to youth. She'd not spent any
amount of time around young men—only the ranch hands,
and they were all older than she—as she was growing up.
Now she viewed Stephen with a mixture of motherly concern

nd appreciation for his innate sense of good humor and the
promise of the man he would become.

"You like it here, don't you Stephen?" she asked, already
knowing his answer would be positive.

"Yes, ma'am, I sure do. It's not as good as home, but pret'
near. I always liked Jamie, and he was sort of a part of the
amily anyway, so this is like bein' with relations."

"And how was your visit with your aunt and cousins?"

"Me and Jonas rode a while, out on some trails he knows
hrough the woods." He paused and Alexis held her breath,
hankful that no ill had come to the boy in a strange place.
'And then we played in the haymow a while and hid on his
sisters up there. They looked all over for us and couldn't find
side nor hair. At least that's what they told their ma when she
asked why we was late for supper." He grinned suddenly, exposing a dimple in his cheek.

"I think they was tryin' to get us in trouble, but it didn't
work. Jonas has his ma thinking he's top cream on the
bucket."

Alexis laughed aloud. "I've never heard it said that way before, but I know what you mean," she said, shooting a glance
at Jamie as he leaned against the upright post on the porch.
His pleasure in the boy was obvious and he slid to the top step,
motioning Stephen to his side.

"I'd rather you didn't go riding off into strange places,
Stephen. I know you had Jonas with you, but sometimes there
are folks intent on mischief, and I don't want you falling into
he hands of anyone with wicked thoughts in mind."

"I can ride real fast if I have to, Jamie," the boy said
quickly, as if he would show his prowess at the drop of a hat.

"I know you can. I've watched you on a horse. But the bot-
om line is, you're not a man yet, and you don't know which
are the good guys around here. I just want you to be careful."

Alexis was silent, knowing that Jamie referred to the presence of Mick Jenson. He'd not been seen in the neighboring areas, but she knew Jamie was apprehensive, worried that he would show up and seek to cause more trouble. She wondered if her husband might not be desirous of that happening, for he was never without his pistol these days, as if he must be ready for any event.

"Yessir," Stephen said, nodding his head in total agreement. "I'll do whatever you say, Jamie. I promised my dad I would when he let me come here."

Alexis smiled. It seemed that Brace had prepared the boy well. And unless she missed her guess, Stephen was used to obeying orders.

"We'll be working the yearlings in the morning, Stephen. It's time for you to make tracks up those stairs to your bedroom and get a good night's sleep."

Without a word, Stephen rose from the top step and bent to brush his lips against Jamie's cheek. Alexis thought she caught sight of a blush of color where the kiss had landed, and when Jamie looked her way, she recognized the grin of approval he offered. Stephen came to the swing where she sat and hugged her, bending to offer the caress. She gripped him firmly, kissing his forehead and then whispering a blessing that only he could hear.

"Thank you, ma'am," he whispered. "My aunt Sarah always says that when she tucks me in at night." He shrugged his shoulders and straightened. "Of course, I'm almost too big for that sort of thing, but it makes her feel better to pull the sheet up over me, so I let her."

"Maybe we can pretend that I'm your aunt Sarah, just for tonight," she offered and was pleased by his answering smile.

"That'd be all right, I guess," he said, offering her his hand, helping her arise from the swing.

"I'll be right back," she said to Jamie as she disappeared into the dimly lit kitchen. He only waved a hand in reply, but his smile was sufficient to let her know he was pleased.

It was fully dark by the time she came down the stairs and made her way back to the porch. From the darkness there, Jamie's light-colored shirt drew her to the swing where he sat, lazily pushing at the floorboards with his foot.

"Come join me," he said softly. "And take a gander at this, will you?" Near the barn, two figures walked slowly toward the pasture fence. Chet and Ellen, out for a stroll. Then the two meshed for a moment, Ellen lifting her face to Chet and accepting his kiss.

"So that's the way the wind blows," Jamie mused.

"You didn't know?" Alexis sat beside him and laughed softly. "I'd have thought it was pretty obvious by now. I'm thinking we'll have a wedding before long."

"Well, how about that. I'm gettin' kinda slow in my old age. Seems like I should have figured that situation out right off. Chet's been hangin' around the kitchen more than usual lately, hasn't he?"

Alexis laughed, smothering the sound in her palm, not wanting her mirth to carry across the yard to where Chet and Ellen stood by the corral fence. "I'd say we have a situation all right. You'd better get the barn cleaned up real good. I suspect we'll be inviting everyone in the county to a big party and they'll want to dance."

"Don't get ahead of yourself," Jamie said softly, but the gleam in his eyes told her he was delighted by the thought of Chet finding a love of his own.

Alexis watched him. His hand stretched out to her and she placed her palm in his, wondering at his motive. Without hesitation, he drew her into his arms. "I'm thinkin' old Chet has the right idea, snatchin' kisses in the moonlight," he murmured against Alexis's ear.

"You don't have to snatch," she whispered. "Mine are free for the taking. But only to you, sweetie."

"So long as you've got that straight, I'm thinking I'll keep you around, lady. In fact, I might just tote you up those stairs and we'll have us a little powwow."

"A powwow? Is that what you call it?" She snuggled closer into his arms and lifted her face for his kiss, one she knew would express his need of her. She was not disappointed, for Jamie's arms tightened around her and his lips began a foray that could only end in one way.

With an arm at her back, he rose and opened the door and led her into the house, and then easily picked her up, one strong arm beneath her knees, the other holding her against his chest.

"Be quiet now," he whispered. "Your daddy will hear us and wonder what's going on."

"I thought you were joking about carting me upstairs for a powwow," she managed to murmur, unwilling to disturb her father's work in the office.

"When it comes to loving you, I never joke. I've got the most honorable intentions in the world, and when we get into that bedroom up there, I'll spell it out for you, let you know what you're in for."

As it turned out, the result of his shenanigans were all she had expected, all she'd ever wanted.

Chapter Thirteen

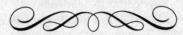

Alexis smelled the coffee and bacon through the bedroom door and sniffed with appreciation, thankful that the days of morning sickness were a thing of the past. She rose and dressed quickly, then spotted Jamie from the window, heading toward the house.

"We've got an announcement to make." Chet spoke quickly as she made her way into the kitchen, just as Jamie opened the screen door from the porch.

Chet's grin looked as if it might split his face in half, so widely did his happiness show. He seated himself at his usual place at the table and watched Jamie and Alexis for their reaction to his announcement.

Ellen crossed from her post near the stove, where she was busily dishing up pancakes onto a stack of plates, to stand behind the cowhand, her hands touching his shoulders. One of his came up to cover hers and he turned her hand to his face, kissing it softly.

"I expect y'all will be surprised by this," Chet said and Ellen laughed aloud.

"No, they won't." She winked at Alexis. "I suspect the boss

lady had her suspicions, Chet. You've been pretty obviou
lately."

Chet glanced over at Alexis. "You didn't know anything
was going on, did you?"

She only nodded and smiled. "Especially after we saw
you taking a walk last night out by the corral. And then there
were all the mornings when you showed up half an hour be
fore breakfast to lend a hand in the kitchen."

Chet's eyes widened as he pretended innocence. "Who
Me? You think I've been hanging around this woman?"

"Haven't you?" Jamie asked, reaching to clasp Alexis'
hand as they found their seats at the table.

With a sheepish grin, Chet nodded agreement. "She jus
about swept me off my feet," he admitted. "Prettiest woman
this side of Dallas. And she's agreed to be my wife."

"Well, I'd say we've got some celebrating to do," Hank
chimed in from the doorway. "How long do we have to plan
the wedding?"

"The wedding?" Chet's voice squeaked on the word.

"Yeah, the wedding," Hank repeated. "You've asked her to
marry you, so I'd say the wedding was next on the agenda."

"I thought maybe we'd go into town to see the preacher,"
Ellen said slowly. "But now that I think about it, that won'
work, will it?"

"We're gonna have the biggest party you ever saw, ma'am
not counting Alexis's wedding," Hank said firmly. "We've go
it down pat, you know, what with celebrating just last year
when these two got hitched." He motioned at Jamie and
Alexis, who were beaming, enjoying the byplay. "By the time
half the county shows up, we'll need a steer butchered and
put on a spit over the coals and a pig, too. My daughter's par
tial to pork," Hank said with a determined nod. "And we've
gotta feed that baby right well."

Jamie stood and reached out a long-fingered hand to Chet. "Congratulations, Chet. I can admit to being quite smitten by the state of matrimony myself. I'll guarantee you'll like it. I'm not sure you're good enough for Ellen, but if she wants you, you're halfway to the altar already."

Chet flushed noticeably as Ellen placed the first plate of pancakes in front of him and then bent to kiss his cheek. "Who's next in line?" she called out from where the warming oven yielded a huge platter of the round, tasty cakes.

The wedding was first and foremost in everyone's mind. Jamie rounded up all the help he could find to help set the barn to rights. The men pitched in willingly, for Chet was a favorite of all who'd worked with him. Hank put tables together for the food and Alexis wrote out invitations by hand to be delivered to the neighbors and friends in town.

"I'd guess we'll have well over a hundred folks here," she told Ellen, who seemed to be stunned by all the activity on her behalf.

"Lord a mercy," Ellen cried. "I didn't plan on such a big to-do. I'd had in mind just standing up in front of the minister and saying a few words."

"Well, you might as well get used to the idea," Alexis told her. "Once these invitations get delivered, you'll be the talk of the town, and everyone will be excited to see you wearing your bridal gown."

"I don't have one," Ellen said. "I only have my Sunday clothes I wear to church."

"Well, we'll have to get you one, or else sit down and sew up something really nice. I can do either," Alexis said. "How about taking a ride to the general store and taking a look at what they have available?"

"Wait till I get dinner going on the back of the stove, and change my dress," Ellen said, excitement lighting her eyes.

"I'll go out and have the buggy hitched up and tell Jamie where we're going," Alexis said agreeably.

Within half an hour the women were on their way to town, a shotgun stored under the buggy seat and orders from Jamie to keep a good eye out. The horse was fresh and ready to make short work of the trip, and it wasn't long before they arrived at the edge of town. The sight of a lone rider watching them as they traveled gave Alexis a stab of fear, but when she turned next to see him, he'd disappeared, and she put down her apprehension to needless worry, ridding her mind of all but the excitement of Ellen's wedding.

Alexis made several stops and handed a series of white envelopes to children playing in yards along the way, with instructions to pass them along to their mothers. Her first stop was at the post office and she left the rest of her pile of envelopes with the post master to be placed in the individual mailboxes he tended.

"Looks like a wedding coming up," he ventured to Alexis, Ellen blushing as she watched the byplay. And at her nod and wide smile, he nodded his approval. "This lady was too good lookin' to sit on the shelf much longer. And I heard Chet braggin' a few weeks back that he was lookin' into buying a wedding ring."

"Well, he's about to do that very thing," Alexis told him. "A week from Saturday. We'll be having a big party, lots of food and some music for dancing."

"Well, my missus and I will be there," he said, his own grin lighting his face. "There's nothing like a wedding to cheer the soul. Even after almost twenty years I remember mine right well." He took the envelopes from Alexis and began sorting through them. "Didn't leave anybody out, did you?"

"I hope I remembered everyone," she said, "but I'm putting one up in the general store, just in case I missed somebody."

"Your pa diggin' a pit for roasting a steer? I'll have my missus bring along some of her sauce for it and a big bowl of potato salad."

"That's wonderful," Alexis told him. "We'll be cooking up a storm, but extra is always welcome. You know that."

"I'll bet you every woman ridin' up to your place will be carrying a bowl or platter of something."

"Well, don't forget your children," Alexis said as she reached the door of the post office. "All the young'uns in town are invited, too. This is a family party."

"I'll pass the word." And with a wave at Alexis's departure, he filled the mailboxes and stuck his own invitation in his pocket.

The general store had a good supply of simple white gowns, and a large assortment of bolts of fabric, several of which would make up into a fine wedding dress, Ellen declared. She held up one garment and walked toward a mirror on the far wall.

"I declare, it doesn't even look like me, Alexis," she said with an embarrassed laugh.

"Just wait till you try a couple of them on. They'll be even prettier with you in them." Quickly Alexis sorted through the stack of dresses on the counter, finding one made of silk with flowers embroidered on the bodice and decorating the sleeves. "Take a look at this one," she called out to Ellen.

Ellen turned and her eyes lit with enthusiasm. "How beautiful," she whispered, "but too fancy for me. I'm more the type to wear gingham or muslin, don't you think?"

"Just take this one in back and put it on," Alexis ordered her, "and I'll find a new dress for me while we're at it."

Ellen took the gown from Alexis's arms and carried it

carefully to the back storeroom, where the storekeeper's wife sighed her approval.

"I'd like something in blue," Alexis said to the man behind the counter. "It'll have to be really high-waisted and full in front."

"Maybe this one would fit," the shop keeper said, lifting a pretty blue-flowered dress from the shelf. "Would you like to try it on?"

"I can pretty much tell from here that it'll do just fine," Alexis said, running her hand over the fine fabric. And then she looked up as Ellen came back into the store from her makeshift changing room.

"That's absolutely beautiful," Alexis said, her voice almost a whisper. She motioned toward the mirror and sent Ellen across the room, watching her closely. "It's even pretty from the back. There are flowers following the back seams, all the way to the floor."

"And this veil would be perfect with it," the shopowner's wife said. She shook out a filmy veil with embroidered edges and walked up behind Ellen, placing it on her head.

"I really feel like a bride," Ellen said tearfully. "But if this is too much money, I can sew up a dress."

"My father said he's paying for it, and mine, too," Alexis told her. "Jamie wasn't real pleased about that, but Daddy said he could still buy his daughter a dress, even if she was a married lady."

"Why don't I wrap them up and help you get them out to your buggy, ladies?"

Alexis turned to the woman who'd been preening over their choices, and nodded. "That would be wonderful. We really don't have time to do justice to the job of sewing up a wedding gown anyway before next week, and this way we'll be able to spend longer in the kitchen."

"Well, the whole town's excited to hear that Chet is finally getting a bride. He's kinda a favorite of the menfolk. A good man, though I suspect you've already found that out for yourself."

With deft movements, the dresses were folded in tissue and wrapped loosely in brown paper, so as not to crush them. The veil received the same treatment and the two women were ushered to the door, then helped into the buggy by the store owner. He rapped the side of the buggy after handing the reins to Ellen. "Have a good trip home, ladies."

It turned out to be a busy ride, with food and decorations being discussed. Ellen said she would make a huge pot of mashed potatoes and another of gravy to go along with the pork and beef, and Alexis said she would be responsible for the wedding cake.

"Chet has a real hankering for chocolate, you know," Ellen said. "Could you make it half and half? I sorta lean toward a white cake myself."

"We'll make whatever you like. I'd like you to make some nice boiled icing for it, too."

"My icing's a favorite of your daddy's, too. I suspect we'll have more cakes coming in anyway. Some of the ladies are a fine hand at desserts."

"It'll take a lot of food," Alexis agreed, "but they'll have all afternoon and evening to eat it up. And if my memory serves me right, there won't be a whole lot of leftovers. But probably enough so you won't have to be cooking for a couple of days."

The menfolk met the buggy and helped the two women down, then lifted the bulky, wrapped dresses, carrying them to the porch.

"We've been talking about Chet moving into the house," Jamie announced as he relinquished the light bundle into Alexis's arms.

"Well, we've got several empty rooms upstairs. If Ellen wants a bigger one than what she has, they can move her furniture before the wedding. And then Chet can move his things in with hers."

"Her bed's too small for the two of us," Chet said in an undertone.

"How would you know?" James asked from behind him.

"I was the one who moved all that furniture into her room when Ellen came here. And then she had me movin' it three times before the first week was through. Never saw a woman so persnickety about where a dresser should sit and which corner a bed should be in."

Ellen laughed. "You did good work, mister. And I've only had you change it twice since."

"Well, once I move in, it's gonna stay like it is. Only thing is, my stuff will take up half the drawers in that dresser and my britches will be hangin' on hooks behind the door."

"Chet!" Ellen almost choked as she spoke his name. "What a way to talk."

"Well, you've got till next Saturday to get it all in order, Chet," Alexis said quickly.

Hank strolled up behind them. "Old Percy Jenkins is a good hand with a fiddle. I'll see if he's free to join us again, and maybe his oldest girl will play the piano for him. We can load it up out of the parlor and haul it to the barn like we did last time somebody got hitched."

"Daddy!" Alexis turned to Hank and reached for his hand, bringing him into the impromptu gathering. "Wait till you see the dresses we bought. Your trip won't last past next Saturday, will it?"

"Naw, I'll only be gone for a day or so, but I'll be home for the wedding," he assured her.

And then he glanced at Jamie. "We need to figure out how many steers we want to sell off before winter. I've made some estimates and such, but we can talk about it tomorrow."

* * *

They sat in the office that evening, Stephen in their midst, obviously enjoying his place in the company of the menfolk. "It all depends on the price we can get," Hank said, gathering up his notes and folding them together. "I'm thinking about a hundred-and-fifty head. What do you think, Stephen?"

"Will we have to round up that many while you're gone? And do we have plenty of feed for the herd for winter?"

"Yes and yes," Hank said with a grin. "You've been payin' attention, boy. We've got a third cutting of hay to handle in a couple of weeks and our loft will be full. We planted acreage in oats this year, so we won't have to buy any. That alone is a big money saver."

"Will I be helping with the roundup?" Stephen asked, his eyes shining with excitement. "And with the haying, too?"

"We're gonna work the socks off you, son," Hank said. "You'll be sick of cows by this time next week."

"Not when I'm learning how to handle them myself."

"Well, there is that," Jamie agreed as Alexis and Ellen came to stand in the doorway.

"I don't want you to ever move, Jamie," Stephen said quickly. "There's plenty of room right here for all of us. Don't you think so, Alexis?"

"For now, anyway," she murmured. "We'll need to put off making those kind of plans until we talk to Brace and Sarah."

"I was hoping they'd be coming back to see us for a longer visit. It's been a long time since Christmas," Jamie said quietly.

"Well, we'll see about that after we have a wedding and I have this baby and we get the hay into the barn. And don't forget roundup and selling off the steers."

"And which is gonna come first?" Ellen asked, a knowing expression lighting her eyes.

Alexis shrugged. "Hard to tell. I've never had a baby before, but I'm sure I'll know when the time comes. Now, let's get supper on the table," she said to Ellen.

"I'm going to mess everything up." Alexis wailed the words even as she did her best to ignore the pain that had seized her back during the night, and was now refusing to release its grip on tender muscles.

"The wedding is at three," Ellen said soothingly, "and you've got till late tonight before this baby arrives, I'd say." She eyed Alexis closely, and only a faint bit of worry made itself known on her smiling face. "You sit yourself down there and peel those cucumbers and clean the onions while I mix up the dressing for the chickens."

Ever unflappable, the woman had not become flustered even though the wedding they prepared for was her own. "All we need to do is get the chickens in the oven. Chet said he'd rather have it fried, but I'd end up in my wedding dress, getting all splattered with grease if I did it his way."

She snatched up an onion from those Alexis was peeling and chopped it into her bowl of stuffing. "We'll help with cutting up the meat that's going around on those spits when the men tell us it's done, and that won't be too long, I'll bet. Maybe some of the neighbor ladies will be here by then to bring in their dishes and lend a hand. Mrs. Sloan always makes her hand-cut noodles and they'll be dandy in a pot of beef and gravy when I get some drippings from those steers they're cookin' out back."

For some reason, the thought of all that food wasn't sitting well with Alexis and she only nodded and bent her head over the bowl of cucumbers she was peeling and slicing. The fresh smell of the vegetable soothed her stomach a bit and she inhaled the summery aroma deeply.

"You all right, honey?" From behind her, Jamie's voice

was a welcome respite and she glanced up at him over her shoulder. His look of concern brought tears to her eyes and she brushed them away, lest they overflow. Immediately, he crouched beside her chair and one hand spread warmth and comfort across her swollen belly.

"I'm fine," she said, searching for a cheerful tone, hoping the lie would sustain her for a few hours. The thought of gaining more than her share of attention in the midst of Ellen's wedding was not to be heard of, but her backache was not getting any better.

"We're running a tight race, James Webster," Ellen said. "Between me and Alexis, we're gonna have a wedding today and a baby before midnight. I'm just hoping she'll still be on her feet long enough to stand up next to me to witness the event."

Jamie nodded, his look of concern deepening. "Well, I'd say it's a good thing the doctor and his wife are coming for the big event. He may come in right handy before the day is over."

"You two are a couple of worrywarts," Alexis said tartly. "I'll be fine and the wedding will be lovely. And I'm certainly planning to stand up with you, Ellen." She smiled then at Jamie. "And you, Mr. Webster, can sit beside me while we have us a baby."

"You're sure?" he asked breathlessly.

"No. I've never done this before, but that's what it feels like to me."

From the porch, Stephen made his presence known. "Can I go to my aunt Minna's house and tell her to come right away? I wasn't trying to snoop, but I heard what you said, Alexis, and I wanted you to know I'm ready to go if you need her now."

"I suspect she'll be here within the hour anyway," Ellen said. "She told me she'd head this way early and help with the kitchen work."

"Besides, you've done your share of riding this week," Jamie told the boy. "Herding those steers and helping get them into one place was a big job. And working at cutting the hay was enough for a grown man to do, let alone a young'un like you. You've done your share and more to help."

Stephen stood on the other side of the door and preened a little. "Everybody has to pitch in. That's what Chet told me, and he said I did all right."

"Well, he was right on the button that time." Alexis smiled her approval at the boy. "And if Minna isn't here within the hour, I'll send you out to find her. But to tell the truth, I probably won't need her for a long time yet. So long as the doctor is here, she doesn't need to do the whole thing, just lend a hand and be here for me."

"Minna will be glad to have Doc here," Ellen said. "Nobody in their right mind would argue about having the old fella around for a birthing. He's delivered half the town as it is."

"Well, hold on, sweetheart," Jamie said, his mouth close to Alexis's ear. "Let's see to the wedding and then we'll take you up to bed."

Within the hour, as if she'd known her presence was needed, Minna showed up, her husband beside her on the wagon seat, the four children behind them spiffed up in their Sunday best.

"This here is Ralph," Minna said, nudging her husband into sweeping his hat from his head as he climbed from the wagon, his hand outstretched to James. His dark eyes, crinkled at the corners with sun-squints, took James's measure.

"You're the new boss man, I hear," Ralph said. "I've always been kinda partial to Hank, but with things all in an uproar after the old man died, I could see why the boy needed someone here to watch over things for him."

"Welcome to the Double C," James said. "Haven't seen

you around before, but we've enjoyed having Minna and the young'uns here."

Ralph leaned against the farm wagon. "I helped in a couple of roundups here, a few years back. Hands were hard to come by for a couple of years and Hank hired me on for a couple of months."

"I remember you," Alexis said, stepping out onto the back porch. "You let me try out your stallion, and told me I was a first-rate rider. That made my day."

"Ma'am." Ralph nodded politely and smiled at Alexis. "You surely impressed me. I told your pa you was a whiz with those animals. You still helping with the training?"

"I'm working with them whenever I can, just not as much as I'd like," Alexis told him. Her face glowed as she spoke with Ralph, and Jamie watched closely. Next to himself, horses were the love of her life, he realized, not for the first time. He'd been fortunate to find a woman who shared his liking for life on a ranch, who had the God-given talents of a born horsewoman and the ambition it would take to make a success of their own place when the time came to move along.

Yet, he knew it would be difficult for Alexis to leave her home, the place where she'd spent her growing up years, where she'd fallen in love and become a woman. And unless they were all mighty mistaken, where she would become a mother for the first time.

Today.

Chapter Fourteen

The wedding was perfect, according to the kitchenful of ladies from town and the neighboring farms. The bride was beautiful. "The groom was bright-eyed and bushy-tailed," said one of the women, and at that Ellen blushed like the new bride she was. They were all up to their elbows in food, ready to carry it out to the yard where the menfolk and children waited.

Not willing to be left out of her own kitchen, Ellen had joined the female crew, and directed proceedings with instructions that demonstrated her long-term knowledge of such things. No stranger to feeding a yard full of men, she shooed the ladies to the back door, each of them with both hands full of food, and finally took her place beside Chet as the minister blessed the food.

His words also included phrases about the sanctity of marriage and asked the Almighty's hand to be upon the bride and groom. After Ellen dried her eyes on Chet's big handkerchief, she announced that everyone should take a plate and help themselves to the bounty before them.

Chet's chicken was a big hit, along with dressing and

mashed potatoes. Even though the dozen or so birds weren't fried, he gave every appearance of enjoying each bite. The beef and pork from the pit were soon cut into serving pieces and dished up with the noodles and gravy Ellen had readied. Crocks of shredded cabbage, dressed with homemade sauce made from cream and vinegar and a good portion of sugar were well-received, as were the rest of the vegetables served in large bowls.

The ladies had outdone themselves, Alexis decided, and whispering in Ellen's ear, she told her it was the best wedding feast she'd ever seen. Ellen blushed a bit and Chet wore a big grin, as if he were well aware of the gem he'd claimed today for his own.

Settled later beneath a tree on a quilt, Alexis watched as Jamie approached with two plates. "I hope you didn't fix too much for me," she said, accepting the overflowing dish he handed her. And then she laughed aloud. "You put all your favorites on my plate, didn't you? You knew I'd never eat all this and you'd just be able to eat seconds off my plate."

"You are a smart woman, Mrs. Webster," he said, diving into his own food. "Your pa sure does know how to barbeque beef and pork. I'll have to take some lessons for when our own kids get married and we're planning their weddings."

"And how many do you plan on marrying off, Mr. Webster?" she asked, lifting a bite of baked chicken on her fork.

"At least four or five. I figure you'll want a girl when this one turns out to be a boy, and then you'll want another boy for this one to grow up with. Brothers are a good thing, you know, sweetheart."

"Well, we'll see. Right now I'm feeling miserable and ready to deliver this load in my lap."

"We won't have any more for a couple of years, honey," he told her, his brow furrowing as he bent his gaze on her

belly. "I know you've been uncomfortable lately, and I don'
know how you do it. Up every morning and bustling aroun
that kitchen with Ellen, and doing the ironing and keepin
track of the horses and all."

"Well, I'll have you know that this has been the happie:
time of my life, Mr. Webster. Carrying your child has been
blessing. I just can't wait to get my hands on her."

"What does Ellen say? Does she think you'll have a girl?

Alexis shook her head. "She's determined it should be
son for you." She stiffened and held her breath for a long min
ute. "And unless I'm mistaken, that was a labor pain I jus
had."

"You ready to go to bed?" Jamie asked her, obviousl
ready to carry her to the house.

"Not on your life. I'm going to dance at this wedding an
then I'll present you with a baby."

"Dance?" Jamie looked dubious as he spoke the singl
word. "I can't see you doing the jig tonight, sweetheart."

"Then you'd better tell the fiddler to play a couple of slo
songs for us," she said. "Because I'm planning on dancing a
Ellen's wedding party. And now, I think I'd better stop eat
ing. I've about had enough, and I heard somewhere that
woman in labor shouldn't eat a lot."

Jamie took her plate from her and Alexis glared at him, he
fork still held upright in one hand. "I could have had a cou
ple more bites of that pork. I just meant I shouldn't eat to
much, and I've been sitting here talking and not doing justic
to my food."

"I'll take care of your food for you. I want you in goo
shape for tonight." His eyes narrowed as he examined he
face. "You're having another pain, aren't you? And it's onl
been a few minutes since the last one. You may not be dan
cing after all, sweetheart."

"Wanna bet?" she asked smartly. "I hear the fiddler tuning up right now, and the sun is almost set. I'll let the rest of the women clean up out here, and I'm heading for the barn to listen to the music."

And so she did, on a chair brought from the house by Chet, who watched over her as if she were a fragile bit of china. "Sure you don't want something else to drink, Miss Alexis?" he asked for the third time.

"You're as bad as Jamie," she told him, her grin belying her scolding. "I'm fine, Chet. Not sick, just ready to have a baby."

"Well, as soon as Ellen and I share our first wedding dance, I'll be back," he told Alexis. "I want a slow one with you, ma'am."

"It's a date," she said, smiling brightly even as she felt another pain gripping her.

"How close are they now?" Jamie asked from behind her, one hand on her shoulder as if he lent his strength to her.

"A bit closer, maybe every five minutes or so. I wish they'd start the dancing. I don't want to miss everything by trotting off to bed."

"How's it going, Miss Alexis?" The elderly gentleman, Doc Matthews, before her looked at her with keen eyes and reached to take her hand in his. "Are you gonna deliver a baby tonight?" His lips curved in a grin beneath a snowy mustache.

"Sure looks that way, Doc," she answered. "I've been aching and paining for a couple of hours now."

"How close are the aches and pains?" he asked bluntly, his eyes probing her for a reply.

"About every five minutes now."

"I'll keep an eye on you. But first I'm going to dance with my missus, then I'll be back. We might want to get you to your bed in the next hour."

"All right," she said, suddenly too weary to argue.

"Let me know when you're ready to go back to the house," Jamie said, his fingers tightening on her shoulder. "I'll carry you, honey."

"I'll walk," she insisted, and then almost thought better of it as another pain traveled from her back to the muscles below her belly. She inhaled sharply and then took shallow breaths, waiting for the pain to subside.

"About ready, girl?" Before her Minna watched her with a knowing gaze. "I'd say you're about halfway there. Maybe even more."

"You think so?" Alexis looked up at the older woman and attempted a grin. "I don't want to miss any of the fun," she said mournfully.

"You'll be having enough fun of your own to cope with," Minna said with a laugh. "But don't worry for a minute, girl. Between Doc Matthews and me, we'll take good care of you and in a few hours, you'll have a beautiful baby to show for it."

The doctor approached, the first dance completed, and held out his hand to Alexis. "I believe this is our dance," he said formally, bowing over her and lifting her to her feet. And then he glanced at Minna, who shook her head. "Well, maybe not," he conceded slowly. "How are the pains coming along?"

"Oh, they're coming along all right. I'll admit it hurts more than I thought it would, but so far, I'm doing fine."

"Why do you suppose it's called labor, young lady?" the doctor asked. "It's the hardest work you'll ever have to do, getting that baby born."

"Well, we're having our dance first," James said from behind her. "We'll do it out front, in case anything happens while I'm twirling you around, but we will dance, sweetheart."

She looked over her shoulder at him as the fiddler began another song, his daughter accompanying him with chords that supported his melody. The barn had filled with couples, everyone having lent a hand at clearing up the tables, and now the dancing began in earnest.

Without a word, he circled her waist with one long arm and led her to the wide doorway, out onto the packed dirt before the barn. His arms held her close and Alexis leaned her head against his chest as they circled in time to the music. "I love you, Jamie," she said softly. "Thank you for dancing with me."

"I feel honored, ma'am," he said, bending to speak close to her ear. "The baby doesn't seem to mind me holding both of you so close, does he?"

"No, he's been pretty quiet today, like he's getting ready for the birthing."

"He?" Jamie repeated the word she had used without thinking.

"He or she. I don't really care," Alexis told him, clinging tighter as another pain circled her and concentrated beneath her belly.

"Had enough?" Jamie asked her, bending to look into her face. "Ready to call it a night?"

"I think so. The ladies said my bag of water might break early on, and I don't want to be embarrassed."

"Better here than in the bed. Less of a mess to clean up, I'd think."

"Just full of sympathy, aren't you?" She leaned back and shot him a sour look. "I think maybe the next time, I'll let you handle the labor end of the deal and I'll say all the nice, encouraging phrases to help you along."

He laughed aloud, and from inside the barn, Doc Matthews and Minna looked their way, both of them obviously waiting for some sign that Alexis was willing to take to her bed. With a nod of his head, Jamie verified their thoughts, and within a minute he had picked up Alexis and headed for the house.

Midway across the yard, she groaned as a harsher pain gripped her and with a gush of fluid, she soaked her dress and the front of Jamie's best trousers. "You and your predictions. Now you have this mess to clean up, smartie."

"I'll strip you off inside the back door," he offered, "and then get clean clothes for myself."

"You'll have to find something for me to wear first. I'm not going upstairs naked."

"I'll run ahead," Minna said from beside them. "I'm sure I can find a quilt or a sheet to cover you, honey."

"Thanks, Minna," Alexis managed to murmur, as once more the tentacles of labor wrapped around her body and took her breath.

Behind them Doc Matthews headed for his buggy and retrieved his black bag, then hurried to catch up. "I doubt it'll be long," he said, puffing with every step. "Once the water breaks, the baby is usually ready to make an entrance."

Inside the house, Jamie stripped Alexis as Minna wrapped a sheet around her. The wet dress hit the floor and was kicked aside, then Jamie bolted for the washroom where a pair of overalls hung, clean from washday. Within seconds he had changed his trousers and was back where Alexis stood, bent over and gasping for a breath.

Without a word, he picked her up and headed for the stairway. "I'm too heavy," she whispered as he shifted her higher, the better to take the steps.

"Oh, no you're not, sweetheart. Just hang on tight and we'll make it in no time."

Edging through the bedroom doorway, he hesitated as Minna dashed ahead to pull back the quilt and top sheet, then placed Alexis carefully against her pillow.

"You want the other pillow, too?" he asked, and she shook her head as another contraction wracked her body. There was no doubt that the baby's birth was imminent.

The time went by slowly, and yet, James knew that it had been less than an hour since they'd reached the bedroom. The doctor bent over Alexis, his big hands careful as he examined her, waiting out a pain and encouraging her with a low voice, offering words of praise for the fine job she was doing.

"I haven't done anything but moan and groan so far," she told Doc Matthews.

"Ah, but it won't be long before you have to do the final deed, young lady. You'll be pushing that baby out into your husband's hands. And it won't be long now."

"Into *my* hands?" Jamie asked, feeling himself grow pale at the thought.

"It's the least you can do," the doctor told him sternly. "After all, it's your doing that she's lying here having your child. And then I'm going to tie the cord and you're going to cut it, right where I tell you to."

"Don't worry," Alexis said, reassuring him. "You can do it, Jamie. If I can do my job, then you can take care of the easy stuff."

With that, she stiffened again and as Jamie watched, she bit at her lip and held back the groan that begged for release. "Go ahead and yell if you want to," he told her, wishing he could take her pain upon himself.

"With all those people out in our barn?" Barely able to gasp out the words, she tossed him a dirty look and clenched at his hand all the tighter. He bent over her and kissed her forehead, feeling as helpless as he ever had in his life. Nothing had prepared him for watching his woman suffer as Alexis did right now.

"No more babies," he vowed softly. "This is too much for you to stand."

"She ain't the first and she won't be the last," Doc Matthews predicted. "There's something about babies that fills a woman with joy, no matter if they belong to her or somebody else."

"Ain't that the truth," Minna agreed fervently. "I'm pretty near as excited over this one as I was with my own."

"Well, she's not going through this again," Jamie said harshly. "It's too much for a woman to bear."

"We all do it though," Minna told him.

With that, Alexis groaned, her body arching on the bed, the doctor's big hand holding her still. "Just a minute now, honey," he said quietly. "You're doin' a good job, girl. I'm lookin' at a headful of dark hair right this minute."

"A girl?" Alexis gasped.

"I can't tell from this end," he said with a laugh. "But if you'll push real hard right now, we'll know in a few seconds."

Obligingly, Alexis pushed, her face reddening, her body straining with effort, and Jamie could only kneel beside her, whispering prayers that pled for her well-being.

"You're gonna miss catching this baby," Doc Matthews warned him, but Jamie shook his head.

"I'll cut the cord, but right now I need to be here with my wife, Doc. You've been catching babies for a lot of years, and if you need a hand, Minna will be glad to do the honors."

As he spoke, a piercing cry from Alexis blended with the wail of a newborn child and Jamie's heart surged, his blood seeming to fill his body with an energy he'd never known. "Is everything all right, Doc?" he asked, looking through tears at the two people who were admiring a dark-haired infant.

"Fine as frog hairs," Doc said proudly, as if he had done a good day's work. "Best lookin' little fella I've seen in years."

"A boy?" Alexis whispered the words as she tried to lift her head from the pillow. "I need to see him," she said. "Has he got all his fingers and toes?"

"Yeah," Minna said. "And the most important part he owns is ready to squirt all over the two of us, Doc."

"Won't be the first time," he said jovially. "Soon as we get this cord tied and Mr. Webster cuts it for us, we'll put a diaper on this little guy and he can pee to his heart's delight."

"What's his name?" Minna asked Alexis, holding the cord firmly so that the doctor could complete his job. With an abrupt motion, he beckoned to Jamie and handed him a pair of scissors from his black bag.

"Cut this right here, son," were his instructions, and Jamie moved to stand nearer the foot of the bed, his eyes on the tiny mite who lay in Minna's hands. No matter what he'd heard to the contrary, this was a beautiful baby. And he was perfect, with long legs and arms and a round little body, all of which gave promise of growing up to be a sturdy man one day.

"Let me see him," Alexis insisted, and the doctor nodded at Minna.

"You've got one more job to do, missy," he said. "We'll have this afterbirth out of the way in a few seconds and then you can nurse your baby."

Alexis followed his instructions and the rest of the birthing procedure went well. She held up eager arms for her child, and held him close. "Can we call him James, after you?" she asked the man who had knelt once more by her side.

"You can call him whatever you please," Jamie told her. "How about a middle name?"

"After my father," she said. "James Henry Webster. How does that sound to you?"

"Like a name to live up to," he told her. "He's gonna be a

big man, honey. With those long arms and legs, he's guaranteed to be a tall one."

"Well," she said practically. "Since I can't call him Susanna, we'll have to save that name."

"No more," Jamie said vehemently. "You've suffered enough, sweetheart. One baby is enough."

"We'll see. And it really wasn't so bad, Jamie."

"Mothers tend to forget the misery when they get their hands on that newborn," the doctor said knowingly. "I told you, there's something about the look of joy on a new mother's face that makes it all worthwhile."

"Now, you'd better go on out to that party in the barn and make an announcement, James Webster," Minna told him. "Sounds like they're breaking up anyway, so hurry and catch them before anyone leaves. Hank will be waiting to hear and so will Ellen and Chet."

"Go on," Alexis urged him, squeezing his hand a final time before she released him. "If Ellen hasn't already left, tell her to come up and see him."

The fiddler was packing his instrument into its carrying case when Jamie appeared in the wide barn door. All eyes were upon him and a hush fell over the crowd. Ellen burst through the throng to stand before him, her eyes shining with excitement.

Jamie bent and kissed her cheek and whispered against her ear. "It's a boy, Ellen. Alexis is fine." At that Ellen burst into tears and Chet hastened to stand beside her.

"Bad news?" he asked quietly.

"Not on your life," Jamie told him. He raised his voice to be heard in the far corners of the barn. "We've got us a baby boy, named James Henry, and his mama is doing just fine."

A round of applause met his words and Hank appeared out of the crowd, a wide grin on his face. "James Henry, huh? How about Henry James?"

"You'll have to argue with Alexis over that one," Jamie told him with a grin. "She gave him his name, and I found out a long time ago that it doesn't pay to argue with the woman."

"Can I go up and see him?" Ellen asked. "Who does he look like?"

"Looks just like a baby, to me," Jamie answered blithely. "You'll have to judge for yourself, I guess."

Without another word, Ellen was gone and by the time she was halfway across the yard, Chet had caught up with her, his long arm clasping her waist, his head bending to speak to her.

"Yes, you can see him, too," Ellen assured him, in a tone that carried to where Jamie still stood. He accepted the handshakes and congratulations of those who gathered around him, the ladies already planning on bringing out gifts for the new baby, the men casting him knowing glances and welcoming him into the world of fatherhood.

And then it was time for the party to dissolve, the families going to their wagons and buggies as they prepared to leave. The fiddler and his daughter had come in their own buggy and now, as they left, Jamie slipped the gentleman who had played throughout the evening an extra bonus. He received profuse thanks in return and was pleased to see the man hand his daughter some of his wages.

"She's a good girl," he told Jamie, watching as his daughter ran toward their buggy. "Always comes along to play for me. I told her we'll have to get someone else trained for when she gets hitched herself. And if the number of young men hanging around is anything to go by, it won't be too long."

"She's a pretty girl. Someone will be a lucky fella to snag her." Jamie's words were heartfelt, for indeed the young girl was a prime specimen of blossoming womanhood.

"Good night." The words rang out from folks who'd loaded up their vehicles. "I'll get my dishes later," someone called out, and another voice spoke of a visit to the new mother and child in a few days.

Jamie watched them leave and then looked up to find Chet and Ellen coming toward him from the house. "Your wife is asking for you," Ellen said. "She's worried about who's gonna cook breakfast in the morning."

"I fry bacon pretty good," Jamie said, "and we can always eat leftovers, if it comes to that."

"Well, you go on up there and tell her to rest easy. The doctor wants her to stay in bed for several days. He said ten at first, but Alexis gave him a dirty look and grumbled that she didn't have time to lie in a bed when there's so much to be done. Almost makes me wish we weren't going away for a few days."

"You go and enjoy yourselves," Jamie said firmly. "We'll be fine and when you come back, we'll be happy to see you."

"Well, we're not going very far," Ellen told him. "Just to the next town. Chet went over and reserved a room for us the other day, and just eating someone else's cooking will be a vacation for me."

"We'll be glad to have you back, but we want you to have a good time."

"Guaranteed," Chet said with a grin. "I'm planning on it."

"I'll just bet you are," Jamie said, tossing the other man a smile and holding out his hand. In the manner of men the world over, they shook hands, both of them tall and strong men, both of them pleased at their choice of a wife.

"See you both soon," Jamie called back as he strode to the porch and into the house. His stride was long as he headed for the stairway and he took two steps at a time, anxious to see his wife and child.

The doctor had packed his bag and was washing up in the basin, Minna pouring warm water to rinse his hands, and handing him a clean towel. "There you are," Doc said, spying Jamie in the doorway. "We're all settled in for the night, I think. The baby seemed to appreciate what his mama is providing for him, and he looks to be strong and sturdy to me. I'll be by tomorrow to check up on both of them, son. You must make sure she doesn't get up and start down those stairs in the morning."

"I feel wonderful," Alexis said from the bed.

"You stay right there," the doctor told her firmly. "I'll see how you are tomorrow, but in the meantime, I don't want you bleeding overmuch, and that means you'll stay off your feet."

"She'll do as I say," Jamie said, sending a look of promise to Alexis. "I'll be right here next to her all night."

"Good," Minna told him. "Then when the baby wakes up, you can be the one to change his diaper and give him to his mama for feeding."

"Change his diaper?" Jamie felt helpless as he thought of handling the tiny mite who lay in a basket beside the bed.

"Won't take long to figure it out," Minna told him, "and I'll be back in time to fix breakfast in the morning. That way, Alexis won't be trying to find the kitchen first thing after the rooster crows. I'll plan on being here for a couple of days, so long as I can go home at night to see to my family."

"Why don't you leave your boy here with Stephen while you're running back and forth?" Jamie asked.

"That sounds good to me," Alexis agreed. "Stephen would love it and Jonas is more than welcome. We have lots of room."

Minna hesitated, then nodded her acceptance of the invitation. "He can stay tonight and I'll bring him some clothes tomorrow when I come. I'll go and tell him. Probably make his day for him, he'll be so tickled."

"Stephen's, too." Alexis settled herself against the pillow

and murmured the words softly, smiling as if she imagined Stephen's glee at the discovery that his cousin would be staying for a visit.

"I'm headed back to town," the doctor said, reaching for his bag and taking a last look at Alexis. "You did a good job, missy. Wish all my first timers were as easy to tend as you were."

"Thank you," Alexis said nicely, and then smiled up at Jamie. "I couldn't have done it without Jamie being here, and Minna to look after things."

"That's what family is for," Minna told her. "And even though we're not really kin, we're still family of a sort, I'd say."

"Well, you're Stephen's kin, and that's good enough for me," Jamie told her. "You're part of our family, Minna, and all your young'uns and Ralph, too."

He thought he detected a hint of moisture in her eyes as Minna bent over to kiss Alexis on the forehead, and then turned to him, a trembling smile on her face. "Every last one of us needs all the family we can get," she said, "and I'm proud to own all of you."

Ralph had the children loaded into the wagon bed, Stephen in their midst, and when Minna joined them in the yard, Jamie heard her words clearly from the bedroom window. "Stephen and Jonas, the two of you get on out of there. Jonas, you'll be staying here tonight and I'll be back tomorrow."

"Who'll do my chores, Ma?" the boy asked, even as he clambered down and stood before her.

"The girls can pick up the slack," Minna told him, "and you'll be here to help out. Jamie has enough on his hands with a new baby and his wife to tend."

"I'll help, Ma. I'll do whatever they tell me to," her son assured her and Minna hugged him tightly for a moment before she released him and climbed up on the wagon seat. "See you

morrow," she called back, looking up at Jamie in the bed-
om window.

Jamie waved and then returned to the bed. He knelt again
the bed and encircled his wife within his embrace. "Do you
ve any idea how much I love you, sweetheart?" he asked.
You've always been a good wife, but now you've given me
hat every man wants, and what I'd never thought to have.
 son to raise. I'm so happy I could about bust with pride,
ney. I thought that marrying you was the high point of my
hole life, but this comes pretty damn close to it."

"And I love you for giving me this baby, Jamie," she said,
rning her head and grasping his hand in hers. She lifted it
 her mouth and kissed it repeatedly. "Now, can you crawl
 here with me and keep me company?"

"You bet," he told her. "I'll need to sleep fast before that
by wakes us both up."

In moments, he'd undressed and pulled back the sheet on
s side of the big bed, lying beside her and carefully lifting
r into his arms. "Are you really all right?" he asked, as if
e might break with normal handling.

"I'm as all right as I'll ever be. I have you and our baby
d our life together to look forward to. What more could I
k for?"

"I know," Jamie said, holding her in his arms and allowing
s free hand to touch her slender curves again. "You're
most skinny, Alexis. I don't know how long it will take me
 get used to you without that baby so firmly attached inside
u."

"I still feel like he's in there. I haven't gotten used to the
ea yet, that I've delivered him." She was quiet for a moment
d then she lifted her face to his. "I'm so happy, Jamie," she
ld him. "Thank you for being mine."

Chapter Fifteen

During the next few days, the house was alive with th sound of laughter, both Stephen and Jonas finding any num ber of jokes to play on unwary adults. They whispered to gether, planning an assortment of games to occupy their tim causing the menfolk on the ranch to keep a close eye on ther both.

From her room, early the first morning, Alexis heard th clatter of footsteps on the stairs, listened to the bursts c laughter from the kitchen and yearned to be a part of th household once more. Jamie was adamant about her stayin in bed the first day, and then she rebelled.

"I'll see what the doctor says when he comes out today.

What he said, several hours later, was not totally to her lil ing, confining her to the bedroom for another full day, but h reluctantly told her she could go downstairs later in the wee if Jamie carried her and then brought the baby down to slee in his basket beside her, so she wouldn't have to be on he feet to tend him.

That was good enough for Alexis. "I'm going to go dow to breakfast today," she declared, early the next morning. "

...n sit at the table and eat with everyone, and then I'll be in
...e rocking chair, just like the doctor said, watching Minna
...ean up the kitchen. Maybe she'll let me peel potatoes or
...mething for dinner."

"You don't need to be peeling anything," Jamie told her
...ernly. "I'll carry you down to the kitchen and you can spend
...e morning in the rocking chair, but just feeding this baby
...f ours is enough to use up your strength, the doctor said."

"Don't forget to bring a stack of diapers when you carry
...s basket down," she reminded him. She was eager to be up
...d about and privately determined she would lend a hand
...ith dinner.

Minna understood her problem when she explained it
...o her later. "Never could stand layin' around when my
...oung'uns were born. I always had to be up in a day or two,
...d old Doc had a fit every time, but Ralph was a big help
...d by the time I had the youngest, the other kids all pitched
... and lent a hand."

"Well, Jamie has plenty to do outdoors, but I figured if you
...uld come for a couple of days, I'd be ready to handle things
...yself."

"There's no hurry, girl. My family is taken care of. I
...oked up a mess of beans and bacon and potatoes last night
...r their dinner today, and all they have to do is heat it up.
...y oldest girl knows how to make cornbread, and biscuits,
...o, as a matter of fact. And I'll be there to help with supper."

"I don't know what I'd do without you, Minna," Alexis
...id. "I wanted Ellen to have a good time on her trip with
...het, and I knew she'd worry about leaving. It was a real load
...f her mind when you offered to come help with things."

"Well, I can keep an eye on those two boys while I'm
...ere. They're good young'uns, but I know what kind of mis-
...hief they can get into." Turning back to the stove, Minna

stirred the pan of sausage gravy and then lifted the cooke
patties from the skillet and placed them on a plate.

"Soon as these biscuits are done, we'll call the men in f
breakfast," she declared. "I thought I'd fry up some egg
while they start eating. Jamie brought in a whole crock
them this morning. Your chickens are layin' good, ain't they

"We've got more eggs than we can use. We could hard bo
a panful and fix up the yolks with cream and some pickle juic
and pepper. Ellen does them that way sometimes and the me
like them real well."

"My ma used to fix eggs thataway, too, now that I think
it. We'll do some for supper tonight. I thought about potat
salad, too. That'll use up a dozen or so. And we can slice th
beef left over from dinner. That oughta be enough to kee
them happy."

"I can peel potatoes from here," Alexis said.

"Jamie already warned me that you were bound and de
termined to help with the cooking," Minna told her with
grin. "Menfolk just don't understand what it's like to sit an
watch somebody else doing the work. I'll bet you and Elle
share the fixin' between you, don't you?"

"We have ever since she came here," Alexis said. "I'v
cooked for years, but now we just do it together."

At Alexis's side, the baby snuffled and tried to nuzzle h
fist. At the first sound from the basket, Minna was beside him
murmuring foolish sounds to the newborn infant.

"Let me get him changed for you," she said, lifting him
from his bed. "Haven't taken care of a wee one for years now
I miss having a baby around the house."

Alexis watched closely, knowing she could learn muc
from Minna's care of the baby. Changing diapers looked s
easy when someone else did it, but her own attempts had no
been as neat and well put together as what Minna managed

The baby clean and wide-awake, Minna brought him to her
nd helped her, holding the small face against her breast until
e smelled the sweet, milky scent of her milk. His mouth
pened and he suckled vigorously.

"They say the first couple of days of breast-feeding means
lot to a baby, even if they don't get a lot of milk," Minna
old her. "When Mrs. Wallace had her twins, she didn't have
nough for them both and they had to use a bottle for one.
oor little thing sickened and died. Doc said it was the cow's
ilk that didn't agree with him."

Alexis looked up at her, her mouth twisted in a grimace.
I swear I have enough for two. Doc said it wouldn't come
a for a couple of days, but it's only been two now and I'm
verflowing."

"Don't let him nurse too long at a time. It'll make you sore
nd he'll be getting the bulk of his meal in the first few min-
tes anyway."

Alexis held the tiny bundle against herself and looked
own at the tightly closed eyes and the miniature hand that
pread wide on her bosom. Tears filled her eyes and she im-
atiently brushed them away with her free hand.

"Every new mother cries when she looks at her child,"
Minna told her. "There's something about that precious mite
hat just tugs at your heart. And his little head smells so sweet.
here's no other scent like it in the world. Guess that's why
women keep on having babies. They remember how wonder-
ul it was to hold a new son or daughter and nurse them. Not
o mention enjoying all the cuddling and rocking women
ave been doing for years."

"This was worth the whole nine months it took to get him
ere. I thought some days that I was thoroughly sick of being
a the family way, but it all seems like a dream now. Even the
bor and birthing."

"The Bible says that's the way it's supposed to be, tha women forget the pain once they hold the baby."

"Well, I have a faint recollection of getting the job done, Alexis said with a laugh, "but not so much as to fear doing again." She lifted the tiny bundle in her arms and held hi over her shoulder, patting his back and waiting for the bur that was sure to follow. He accommodated her nicely, an Minna laughed at the sound.

"He's a loud one, ain't he?" She bustled over to wher Alexis sat and took the baby from her. "I'll just settle hi down here and I'll put some of the newspaper on your lap an let you peel the potatoes for me. We just won't tell Jamie."

The men made an early appearance for dinner, probabl drawn by the smell of roasting meat that flowed from th kitchen windows out onto the porch and beyond. The tw boys ran in the kitchen as Minna was making the gravy an washed up at the kitchen sink.

"The men are coming in already," Stephen said. "I wa gonna ring the dinner bell for you, but Jamie said he coul tell that dinner was ready when he walked past the corn cri and caught a whiff of what you were cookin'."

"Well, I'm not gonna mash these potatoes. I'll leave the in pieces so we can use the leftovers from dinner for the po tato salad later." Minna poured the boiling water from the ke tle, and the potatoes were dumped into a huge bowl. "I'm gla you peeled plenty," she told Alexis, just as Jamie came in th door.

"Who peeled plenty?" he asked in an ominous voice.

"I did," Alexis told him. "In between feeding your son an learning all about babies from Minna, I managed to peel a ke tleful. You need to understand that I'm strong and capabl Jamie. Just ask Minna."

"Havin' a baby don't make you an invalid," Minna offered uickly. "She didn't overdo and she hasn't been out of that ocking chair."

"Can't win this fight, can I?" Jamie asked in an undertone, aning to kiss Alexis. He bent over the baby's basket and arefully pulled the light blanket from the infant's face. "You ink he looks like me?" he asked hopefully.

"Spittin' image," Minna volunteered. "All that dark hair and iose pretty eyes. He'll be a real hand with the ladies some- ay."

"Not until his father lets him know what's what," Jamie aid. "I plan on having a lot of long talks with him, growin' p."

Taking Jamie's arm, Alexis made her way to the table, lancing out the back door to catch a glimpse of the ranch ands washing up at the horse trough. In moments they came the kitchen and offered smiles and congratulations to lexis, slapping Jamie on the back as they passed him, all of iem passing by the basket for a glimpse of the star attrac- on.

Hank's pride in his grandson was overwhelming and he ent to kiss his daughter as he passed her chair. "Your pa's ght proud of you, girl," he said quietly. "But I was thinking, ou don't want to confuse James and his daddy. Maybe you ught to call the little fella Hank or Henry, so's you can keep ieir names straight."

She laughed aloud. "I thought you'd come up with an idea ke that," she said. "But I've kinda already decided we'll call ie baby something different. I want him to be known as Jay. think the name suits him and he doesn't seem to mind when whisper it in his ear."

The men ate with gusto, Stephen and Jonas joining them passing the bowls and platters back and forth, both boys

eager to share the plans they'd been making all morning. "W
want to go camping out overnight, Jamie," Stephen said. "Ju
me and Jonas. We'll ride up north a ways to where the strean
cuts across the far pasture and take along food to cook ov
the campfire. Do you think it'll be okay?"

"What I think is that Jonas needs to check with his m
first," Jamie said firmly. "And you had better see if Alexi
thinks it's good idea. I don't want these womenfolk worry
ing about the pair of you."

"There's nothing out there to hurt us, Ma," Jonas told hi
mother, throwing her a pleading look. "We'll just be gon
overnight and come back tomorrow before supper."

"What do you think, Minna?" Jamie apparently was giv
ing Jonas's mother the right to speak her opinion first.

"Should be all right. Ellen and Chet will be back here i
another day or so, and I'll be taking Jonas home with me. I
the boys promise to be careful, I suspect it'll be all right."

Alexis felt a finger of doubt crawl the length of her spin
and shivered. "You know more about such things than I d
Minna," she said after a moment. "I guess I'm a little protec
tive of Stephen. I like him right handy so I know he's a
right."

"Well, we'll think about it this afternoon. Maybe w
should plan it for tomorrow instead of today," Jamie saic
shooting an inquiring look at Alexis. "We don't want to tak
any chances of someone hanging around and causing troubl
with these boys."

Stephen looked a bit disappointed, but shrugged it o
quickly. "That'll be all right. It'll give us more time to plar
won't it Jonas?"

And so it was postponed for a day, and Alexis was able t
rest easy. The fact that Brace and Sarah had entrusted thei
son to Jamie and Alexis for a matter of months weighe

eavily on her shoulders. A sense of responsibility for his
vell-being was constantly at the forefront of her mind, and
he determined to speak about it to Jamie tonight. The idea
f Mick Jenson still on the loose worried her, even though she
ealized her uneasiness was probably just her natural fear of
he man surfacing.

Jamie listened to her theory and nodded, but she knew that
rivately, he had reservations about the man's presence in the
icinity. The questions were still unanswered, but they both
efused to live in fear of what might happen in the uncertain-
ies of life.

"We're going to have company," Jamie announced the next
ay. "One of our neighbors just dropped off the mail and
here's a letter from Brace and Sarah. They're missing
tephen and want to know if we're ready to get rid of him
et." He laughed at that idea and the look on Alexis's face as
e spoke the words.

"They were just teasing, honey. But, they are serious about
oming here and taking Stephen home with them. They want
im back in school, there in Benning, and Sarah thinks
tephen should be with his sisters."

"I'll love having them come here," Alexis said quickly.
But I hate the idea of Stephen leaving us. He's fit in so well,
nd he's enjoying the work here. It's been a real education for
im. He'll have need of all he's learned one day in the future."
he paused and looked up at Jamie, and her smile vied with
he tears in her eyes. "I hate to be selfish. I know if he were
ly boy, I'd want him home, too. I don't blame Sarah a bit."

"Well, they'll be here in a couple of days if I don't wire
hem differently," Jamie said. "They'll take the train and ar-
ve day after tomorrow, if it's all right with us."

"Who gets to tell Stephen?" Alexis asked, privately hop-

ing she didn't have to be the bearer of news that Stephe
might not be happy with.

"I'll talk to him," Jamie said. "He may surprise us and b
ready to go home. I'm sure he misses his family."

"Well, I won't be able to do much to get ready for then
If I'm to be stuck in this rocking chair for another three c
four days, I'm pretty much limited to holding a conversatio
with them. You'll have to help get cots for the babies out c
the attic, Jamie, and set them up in the back bedroom."

"Don't worry about a thing, sweetheart," he told her, bend
ing over the rocking chair where she sat. "You just rest an
take care of the baby and the work will be handled by the re
of us."

"Don't forget, Ellen's gonna be back tomorrow," Minna r
minded her. "There'll be the two of us to make up beds an
dust things up. We'll be ready for them."

"I hate to keep you from your family so long, Minna,
Alexis said. "I've loved having you here, but I know they mus
miss you."

"They do," Minna answered with satisfaction. "When
walk in the back door at night, they're all over me, like flie
on honey. Makes me feel good to know I'm important to m
family. But they're doin' all right on their own. My girls ar
gettin' big enough to handle things right well."

Alexis relaxed and shot Jamie a wide smile. "Well, I'll qu
worrying and just look forward to the visit. I know you're anx
ious to see Brace again."

Jamie bent and kissed her, a lingering blend of lips tha
clung together. Alexis lifted her arms to encircle his neck an
he knelt by the rocker. "Did I remember to thank you for m
son?" he asked in a low murmur.

"A dozen times over," Alexis answered, holding tightly t
him and brushing numerous kisses against his cheek an

hroat. "But I like to hear it anyway. When I hold him and look at him, it's like seeing you as you must have been as a baby. I wish your brother and Loris could see him, and your mother, oo."

"Yeah," Jamie agreed. "It's hard to be so far from family, sn't it? But I'm sure glad this is where I landed, else I'd never have met you, sweetheart, and look what I'd have missed."

"I think we've got everything we need, Jamie." Stephen ooked pleased as punch with himself, Jamie decided. Next o the back door was a stack of bedrolls, two burlap sacks of oodstuffs and even two towels, added to the list of supplies o that the boys could bathe in the stream if they wanted to.

"Do you have enough food?" Alexis had watched the vari- ous items Minna provided for the trek, but knowing the appe- ite of both boys, she wondered if they shouldn't add a few tems.

"I gave 'em over a dozen cookies, a bunch of biscuits for breakfast and meat to heat up for their supper tonight," Minna aid, reassuring Alexis somewhat.

"How about vegetables?" Alexis asked. "And what will hey have to drink?"

Stephen rolled his eyes at Jonas. "You like vegetables?" ie asked.

"Not so's you could notice," Jonas murmured with a glance at his mother. "We could take some milk along, though. It houldn't spoil before morning."

"You're going to need a packhorse to carry all this stuff," Alexis said. "Why don't you take along one of the geldings?"

"We'll get it all on our horses," Stephen assured her. "Once ve get everything together, we'll let you look at it and see if t isn't all right."

Alexis subsided with a fretful look at Jamie, who was try-

ing desperately not to smile at her worries. "They'll be fine,
he told her. "As long as they stay near the stream and build
good fire to keep the critters away—"

"We know all that," Stephen told Jamie. "There's lots of
firewood up there, and we both know how to build a fire, and
we'll be fine."

"All right." Alexis gave her consent to the outing and was
echoed by Minna.

"Y'all be right careful now, you hear?" Turning to both
boys, Minna hugged one, then the other. "Be sure you wash
out your skillet in the stream tonight, so there won't be any
animals sniffing around. And I put six slices of bread in a dish
towel for you. They're all buttered and ready to eat."

Within a half hour, both horses were weighed down with
packs, tied securely behind their saddles. The two boys were
so excited, they could barely stand still and their eyes flashed
with the knowledge that they were setting off on a real adven-
ture.

"I wish I wasn't worried about them," Alexis said as she
peered out the window, watching them leave. They both sat
erect in their saddles, hats pulled down to shade their eyes
and headed for the far pasture.

"They'll be fine," Jamie told her. "If you want me to, I'll
ride out there after dark and check on them."

"No, they'd be highly insulted," Alexis said with a laugh.
"I just keep thinking how hard it will be to let our baby grow
up and do the sort of stuff those two are always plotting."

"It's part of being a parent, I guess." Jamie crouched beside her, the better to see the boys as they rode across the pasture.

"You got that right," Minna offered from the doorway.
"But they're both good boys and pretty smart to boot. They'll
do fine."

"Well, tomorrow is the big day for all of us," Alexis said. "When that afternoon train comes in, we'll need to be ready for company. When do you expect Chet and Ellen to be here?" she asked Jamie.

"Maybe late tonight. Chet told me they'd be back by tomorrow, and if I know him, he'll want to start out the morning full tilt. They're probably on their way home right now."

His prediction turned out to be on target when the buggy containing the newlyweds pulled up into the yard just as Minna was putting supper on the table. Ellen was lifted down from the seat and Alexis smiled as she watched Chet hold her closely for a moment, only releasing his bride after he planted a long kiss on her mouth.

"I'd say they had a good time," she murmured, and Jamie laughed, heading for the door to welcome the couple. Slim came from the barn and took the buggy, leading the horse toward the barn. "Here they come," Jamie announced, opening the screen door and waving Chet into the house.

"Just in time for supper," Minna told them. "We'll only be having leftovers, but it looks pretty good. I made beef stew out of the roast we had yesterday and put dumplings on top."

"It looks wonderful," Ellen told her, one arm squeezing Minna's shoulder. "I can't tell you how much I appreciate you being here while we were gone. I'd have been tempted to just stay here myself if you hadn't volunteered to help Alexis."

"Well we got along just fine. Alexis has been sitting in that rocker and keeping me company while I cooked, and between us we took care of the baby."

"The baby! Where is he?" Ellen asked, her eyes darting around the kitchen till they caught sight of the wicker basket beside Alexis's rocking chair. With a soft, crooning melody, she bent low over the infant and lifted him from his bed. "What a sweetie," she whispered, bending to kiss his head.

"And such dark hair. I swear it's the exact same color a
Jamie's. And would you look at that cute little nose and thos
nice flat ears."

Chet grinned at Jamie. "I'm afraid you'll have my brid
thinking about babies."

"Well, if flat ears and a cute little nose are the signs o
beauty in a newborn, ours qualifies as a success," Jamie sai
proudly. "I have to admit that I've never been so proud of any
thing in my life."

Minna stood watching the proceedings with a proprietar
air. "You ought to hear that child howlin' in the middle of th
night," she told Ellen. "Got a pair of lungs like a hound dog.'

"I imagine I'll hear him tonight," Ellen said. She turned t
Alexis. "Do you need me to get up and change him for you
before you feed him?"

Jamie shook his head. "We've got that all figured out. I'n
getting pretty good at the diaper thing."

Minna opened the oven door and brought out a dish o
baked beans. "The dumplings are about done. One of yo
fellas can ring the dinner bell."

Chet turned back to the porch and did as she asked and the
returned to the kitchen to wash up at the sink. "We haven'
eaten since noon," he announced, "just before we headed fo
home."

"Well, it sure took you long enough to get here," Minn
said. "It ain't that far away, just the next town down the road.'

"We stopped by the waterfall and took a walk," Chet began
as if he had a tale to tell.

"Never mind that," Ellen said quickly. "Just suffice to say
we didn't hurry. Just kinda lollygagged along."

Jamie turned to the back door, as if the sight of the men a
the watering trough was fascinating, but failed miserably a
hiding his laughter.

Ellen darted a look at Chet that only served to bring a broad smile to his face, and then she took plates from the kitchen dresser and set the table quickly. The butter dish and a container of jam were placed in the center of the table, and then she turned to Minna. "Should I slice some more bread?" she asked, receiving a quick nod in reply.

A jar of applesauce was opened and poured into a bowl and Minna put hot pads on the table before she brought the hot dishes from the stove. "Don't want to ruin that new oilcloth," she said as Ellen lent a hand, placing a large serving spoon in the kettle of stew and dumplings.

The men trooped in and they settled down to eat, Hank joining them from his study. He looked more than satisfied with his afternoon's work, and gave Jamie a short report on the profit they'd made selling off the steers.

"You've breathed new life into this place," he said firmly. "We're sure to come out way ahead this year, what with the bumper crop of oats and hay we've stored up for winter. We'll have the smokehouse full when we butcher next month, and Ellen's gonna need another lard barrel for the pork we don't hang to smoke."

"That's easy to fix," Ellen said. "How many hogs you going to butcher?"

"Probably six or eight," Hank said. "We'll butcher a steer as we need to. Once it gets cold enough, we can hang that meat in the corn crib and let it freeze."

"Alexis and Ellen put up more jars of food than I want to count," Jamie said, tossing a proud look at his wife. "We'll eat good this winter."

The stew and dumplings were dished up and disappeared in a hurry. The men had seconds all around and scraped the crock of baked beans clean. The bread was spread with a layer of golden butter and lavishly coated with jam, vanishing in mere minutes as the men finished up their meal with the freshly baked offering.

"I don't suppose any of you would be interested in a piece o pie, would you?" Minna asked, and was overwhelmed with the affirmative vote from the ranch hands, who loudly expressed their approval of the idea. She rose and brought two pies from the pantry, placed them on the table and cut them into generou pieces.

Ellen cleared the empty serving dishes to make room fo dessert, and brought smaller plates to serve it on. "They' be wanting you to stay on here," she told Minna. "I don' have a good hand with custard pie, and they go for it in big way."

"I'll tell you the secret after we eat," Minna said. "M family is right fond of this, and pumpkin, too."

Both pie pans were empty in minutes and the men rose to return to the barn, ready to finish up their chores. Slim turned back to Jamie upon reaching the door and proposed a suggestion, his brow furrowed, his concern apparent.

"You want me to take a quick ride out to the stream and check on those boys?" he asked. "I know they're probabl having a good time, but it wouldn't hurt to take a gander an make sure they're all right."

Jamie hesitated, glancing at Alexis, then Minna, as if asking their opinion of the idea. Apparently seeing no protest ing frown from either of them, he nodded his approval at Slim "Just wait till it's almost dark. If they don't catch sight of you so much the better," he said. "They'll have a fire going b then, I suspect, and there's enough cover out there, so you ca get a good look without them knowing."

Slim nodded and took his hat from the rack by the door touching the brim with his index finger as he put it on hi head. "I'd feel better knowing there's no mischief going on

ll take care of it, boss," he said, and with a word of thanks
or the meal directed at Minna, he was gone.

"Slim hasn't come back yet," Chet told Jamie in an under-
one. It was fully dark and the two men stood near the barn,
aking a final survey of the animals before they locked things
p for the night.

"Should have been here by now," Jamie mused. "I sure
ope he didn't run into any trouble out there. Alexis will be
vorried sick if I tell her he hasn't come back yet."

"Want me to take a ride out?" Chet asked quickly.

"You've got a bride in the house waiting for you," Jamie
old him with a grin. "I think we can wait a while before we
et too worried. And it could be that Slim just kept his dis-
ance and is keeping an eye on things for a while." He looked
oward the house where two of the upstairs bedroom windows
vere lit from within. "I'd say your wife has gone up to bed,"
e told Chet. "And it looks as if mine has, too. I told her I'd
arry her up, but the woman is dratted independent. Just so
ong as she had one of the others carry the baby up, I guess I
von't be too mad, though. I kinda like a strong woman, and
Alexis qualifies."

"That she does," Chet said agreeably. "My Ellen has a
nind of her own, too. But she sure is— Well, never mind."
Covering his lapse with a wide grin, Chet turned to the house.

"Now there goes a happy man." Jamie laughed softly and
is words were a harbinger for the years to come.

As he watched, the lamp in one of the rooms upstairs was
xtinguished. The room he shared with Alexis drew him like
beacon as he hastened into the house.

Chapter Sixteen

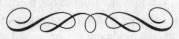

"Where do you suppose Slim could be?" Alexis asked the question of the men who sat around the breakfast table. "I'm getting a little worried, what with him gone all night."

"He may have decided to hang around out there, keeping an eye on things," Jamie said. "At any rate, he'll probably show up here right quick. He'll know you women are concerned."

And the women weren't the only ones, he thought privately. Slim's return was past being a minor thing, and Jamie had begun to feel a deep sense of uneasiness early on in the morning when he'd found it impossible to sleep. Now, he faced a dilemma, knowing they shouldn't wait any longer to check up on things, but yet, sending the men out looking would upset Alexis, and she was worried enough already.

"I think the fencing in the north pasture needs some help," he told Chet. "Might be a good idea for you and Woody to take a ride up there with a hammer and some staples to see about it."

Chet's mouth tightened and his glance at Jamie was neutral as he shrugged and agreed. "Yeah, I noticed myself thother day that the wire is sagging in a few places. Me and Woody will take a look and get it fixed up."

"While you're up that way, could you check on the boys?" Alexis asked.

"I reckon it wouldn't hurt any," Chet allowed. "We won't be far from them, anyway."

"I was thinking maybe we shouldn't have let them go all alone," Alexis said quietly. "They're only boys, and good boys at that, but they could have run across something dangerous up there, like snakes or wildcats or whatever." *And the whatever is what worries me.*

"You're probably stewin' for nothing," Jamie told her. "But it won't hurt for Chet and Woody to take a look so long as they're in the vicinity."

The men rode off within the hour, and Ellen and Minna set about making up beds for the expected company and cooking food enough for a small army. Alexis sat in the rocking chair, fretting and peering out the window until Minna halted on one trip through the kitchen to look at Alexis with knowing eyes.

"You're gonna lose your milk if you're not careful, girl. Worrying about those young'uns ain't doing a bit of good, and that baby needs his mama's milk. So, just quiet yourself down and think about that little fella." She stepped closer and picked up the tiny bundle from his basket, handing him to Alexis.

"Here. You just hold him and rock him a bit, and think good thoughts, you hear? It's about time for him to eat anyway, and it'll relax you to hold him."

Alexis looked up with gratitude at her friend. "You always seem to know the right thing to say to me, Minna. I appreciate you so much."

"Well, having four of my own, I know some of the secrets of being a new mother. And another thing we need to do is

start you drinking a cup of tea every once in a while through
out the day. My mama and grandma always said that tea
makes milk, and I do believe they were right. I about floated
away on the tea my mama had me drinking when I first started
nursing my babies."

"You know better than I," Alexis admitted. "I'll drink any
thing you give me, but I prefer the green tea to black."

"We can handle that," Minna said with a grin. "You just
give me fifteen minutes to finish up with Ellen in the back
bedroom, and I'll fix all three of us a cup."

Alexis nodded absently as she looked down at the babe in
her arms. Snuggled in a light blanket, his miniature features
so like those of his father she could scarcely believe it, he was
a precious sight. And the idea that her fretting could damage
her milk supply was not to be heard of.

Her thoughts went to Brace and Sarah and the twins, who
would be arriving in just a few hours, and she tried to imag
ine how much the little girls had grown since Christmastime.
And then the thought of Brace's face when he discovered that
his son had gone overnight and had not returned yet made her
shudder. She and Jamie had promised to take care of the boy.

Not for the first time since midnight she closed her eyes
in silent petition to the Almighty, trying her best to think pos
itive thoughts, and asking only for the safe return of the two
young boys. Tears overflowed in her eyes and she used a cor
ner of the baby's blanket to wipe them away. He snuffled in
her arms, turning his head from one side to the other, and his
mouth seemed to be searching for sustenance. Tiny, but still
so much like Jamie's, with a tiny bow accenting his top lip,
it made her heart churn in her chest. And the knowledge that
she alone could feed and nourish this child gave her a sense
of delight she could barely contain.

A sound of voices coming closer alerted her to Minna and

Ellen's entry back into the kitchen and they both looked at her warily, her tears obvious to them.

"What you been cryin' about?" Ellen asked abruptly. "Don't be gettin' all upset over those boys, you hear? Chet and Woody will be up there checking on them in no time. Probably there already." Her eyes shifted to watch the baby Alexis held. "And it looks to me like that little one you're rockin' is getting hungry. You'd better let me take a look at his diaper and then you can feed him."

"All right." Alexis was agreeable, feeling somehow more secure with the two older women in the same room with her. She watched as Minna found the metal box of green tea and measured an amount into the teapot, then added boiling water from the teakettle on the stove. Ellen was cooing and whispering to the baby as she changed his diaper, and both women seemed intent on soothing her worries.

"You get that baby settled at your breast, and I'll put your tea on a chair beside you," Minna said. "Milk and sugar both, ain't it?"

Alexis nodded. "A good teaspoon of sugar, please. My mama used to drink hers that way, too." She watched as Minna brought the tea to her, sliding a chair from the table to sit beside the rocking chair.

"I'll just rest my weary bones right here beside you for a few minutes," she said, depositing herself on the chair, holding the teacup carefully. "This ain't too hot, but I'll put a towel on your front, so's it won't drip on the baby."

"Thank you, Minna," Alexis said, holding the cup and sipping the fragrant brew. "I won't find it a hardship, drinking this every few hours. Tea is a comfort drink, you know. Not like coffee. Tea makes you feel all warm and snugly inside."

In her arms, the bundle she held began to squirm in earnest, his tiny mouth opening, his head turning toward his mother. "He smells your milk," Minna said. "Give me that cup and get him situated."

Alexis opened her dress and did as Minna told her, feeling a comfort at the older woman's words. It was good to be pampered, and she could not help but be encouraged by the two women who shared her kitchen with her.

The baby suckled strongly and settled down to nurse. Minna gave her back her tea and Alexis drank it eagerly. Whether it really would help make her milk supply more abundant or not, the taste was good and she felt its warmth slide down her throat and settle in her stomach.

"There's enough beef left over from the other night to make up a quick pot of soup for our dinner here," Minna said. "I'll just cut up some carrots and onions and pour in a jar of stewed tomatoes and see what we come up with." She went to the pantry to retrieve the beef and found the large butcher knife. In a few moments she had made a pile of neatly chopped bits of beef and scraped them from her cutting board into a kettle.

Next came the onion and carrots from the supply kept in the pantry and with the addition of the tomatoes, the soup began to cook in earnest, filling the kitchen with a redolent smell that enticed Alexis's senses.

"What did you put into the oven?" she asked Minna. "I saw you get out the big roaster, but I didn't pay any attention to what you put in it."

"Just a couple slabs of ribs from the lard barrel. Though we could open up a jar or two of sauerkraut and put it in later on, along with some potatoes. Makes a good supper for the company. Hope they like pork and kraut."

"Well, I'll almost guarantee it," Ellen said from the doorway. "My mama used to make it and we'd clean it up in no time. When I was little, the sauerkraut took some getting used to, but I think it's something that kind of grows on you."

"Well, we'll have some soup left from noontime in case
the little ones don't like the pork and kraut," Minna said eas-
ly. "Might sit better on their stomachs, anyway."

Ellen walked across the kitchen to look out the window.
"I wonder when those men are coming back? Jamie will be
ucky to make it into town for the train if he doesn't hurry up."

As if her words had called up his image, she laughed aloud
and pointed to the north where a single rider could be seen,
heading for the barns and house. "There he is now, I'll war-
ant. Sure looks like his horse."

Minna stepped up behind her. "I declare, you must have
some kind of power, Ellen. You sure enough drummed him
up out of thin air."

The rider rode at a fast pace to the corral and then disappeared behind the barn. In a few moments, Jamie came out
the wide front door and headed for the house. If Minna or
Ellen thought he looked upset or worried, they did not men-
ion it aloud, and Alexis hoped silently that all was well in
the north pasture.

It was not to be. Jamie came in the back door and removed
his hat. "I came back to harness the buggy," he said. "Either
that or the wagon. I don't know how much baggage Brace is
bringing with them. There isn't a heck of a lot of room in the
buggy for anything but people."

"They won't mind riding in the wagon," Alexis said, "and it'll
certainly be simpler to put their belongings in the wagon bed."

"Well, you made that choice easy," Jamie said, crossing to
where she sat and bending to kiss her.

"You'd better have yourself a bowl of soup before you go
back to the barn," Minna said. "It's about done anyway, and
you've gotta be hungry. Been a long time since breakfast."

"What's going on, Jamie?" Alexis asked quietly. "Did you
find any trace of the boys or Slim?"

"Not hide nor hair. We searched the whole area, but the problem is that there are a heap of box canyons just a bit north of there, and for whatever reason, they may have gone in that direction." He glanced over at Minna. "Don't be frettin' over this too much, Minna. The boys are both smart and I have a notion that Slim is with them. They'll be all right. I just hate to tell Brace that we lost his son."

The expected visitors stepped down from the train looking a bit worse for wear, but to Jamie's eye, they were the most welcome sight of the day. Sarah and Brace each carrying one of the twins stood before him, smiles glowing and gazes darting behind Jamie, as if they sought out another person waiting to greet them.

Brace approached Jamie, Bree held tightly in his left arm, and held out his right hand. With a grin, Jamie seized it and then dropped it in favor of a back-slapping hug. Bree leaned into the embrace with all the enthusiasm of a child who is familiar with such things, and received a loud kiss on the cheek from Jamie.

Sarah watched, her eyes misting as she took stock of the deep affection felt by the two men. "Do I get a hug, too?" she asked, shifting the little girl she held, whose weight was evidently getting heavier by the minute.

"Sure do, ma'am," Jamie said, taking Brenna from her and then including both of them in the warmth of his clasp as he encircled them with a long arm.

"I'm so happy to be out of that train," Sarah said. "It wasn't really a long trip, but these two kept us hopping."

The little girls looked suitably innocent as their mother spoke, Brenna turning her head to nuzzle in Sarah's neck.

"I'll bet they're scamps," Jamie said with a genuine laugh, and then sobered quickly as Brace spoke the words he'd dreaded.

"Where's Stephen? We thought he might come to the train station with you."

"That's a long story," Jamie said. "Let's load your baggage in the wagon and we'll talk on the way to the ranch."

The wide board seat held the three adults easily, and the twins sat on their parents' laps, bouncing joyfully as they waved at the horses and the watching townsfolk who greeted them with neighborly gestures. "Now, let's talk," Brace said, eyeing Jamie with curiosity.

"Stephen and his cousin, Jonas, went on a camping outing last night," Jamie began, "and they're not back yet."

"When did you tell them to get home?" Brace asked, a touch of concern in his voice.

"That's the thing," Jamie continued. "I sent one of the men out last night to take a peek and make sure everything was all right, but now he's gone missing and so have the boys."

"Now what do we do?" Brace asked, while Sarah sat beside him, her eyes wide and filling with a look of panic.

"I sent two other men out this morning to take a look and went, too, but their campsite was deserted and there wasn't any sign of the boys."

"We'll head that way as soon as we get there," Brace told him. "I suspect they've gone off exploring, but you never know. It won't hurt to set up a search for them."

"My thoughts exactly," Jamie said. The reins cracked over the backs of his team and they broke into a fast trot, heading for home.

They arrived at the ranch in record time, Jamie pushing the team to their limit, knowing that Brace was as impatient as he to begin the hunt. Sarah and the twins were welcomed with a profusion of hugs and kisses by the women who had been waiting for them, and after seeing to his wife's comfort, Brace nodded at Jamie and the two of them headed for the barn.

There they released the team into the pasture and set about saddling two horses for their trek to the north pasture.

"The problem is," Jamie began, "there are a lot of canyons up there and a large wooded area not far from where they camped. We may have a lot of scouting and tracking ahead of us."

"Doesn't matter," Brace said vehemently. "If it takes forever, we'll find them. I'm not the kind to give up easy, you know that."

Jamie nodded in acknowledgment, and his words spoke his confidence in his friend. "I know that, Brace. I can't think of a better man I'd take along on a hunt like this one."

The men were persuaded to take time for soup before they left and sat down at the table to eat. Minna sliced fresh bread to accompany the soup, and both men ate heartily.

"I turned this down before, when I left for the train station," Jamie said. "If I'd known it was this good, I might have taken five minutes to eat some then." He smiled at Minna, an obvious attempt at easing her worry. "We'll leave you ladies now, but I'll bet we'll be back by suppertime."

"Well, that's only three hours away," Minna said. "You might want to rethink that promise."

"We can always push supper till seven or eight," Sarah said. "If the twins eat soup now, they won't be hungry for a good long time. And I won't, either." She settled the little girls at the table and took the small bowls Minna offered. "It sure looks good, Minna. I'll bet I could eat a bowlful right now," she said.

"Well, get yourself up to the table," Minna told her with a grin. "Just look at those babies diggin' in. Are they high enough to the table sitting on those pillows?"

Sarah nodded in reply and then pulled out a chair across from the bench where the twins were diligently spooning their food into their mouths.

Brace and Jamie headed for the back door, Jamie making short detour to drop a kiss on Alexis's forehead. Brace shot s wife a look that made her smile, and then they were gone their way to the barn.

In five minutes' time, they could be seen riding across the sture, their horses moving at a fast clip, as if they sensed e tension their riders felt. Alexis watched in silence from e window, and then closed her eyes to send up a prayer for eir success and the safety of all concerned.

"You coming to the table, Alexis?" Minna asked. "Or shall ring you a bowl over there?"

Alexis rose from her rocking chair. "I'll sit at the table. u've done enough waiting on me."

"Well, as soon as I finish eating, I'm going to pick that by up, whether he's asleep or awake," Sarah warned her. 've been itching to get my hands on him ever since Jamie ired us that he was born. Looking at him all wrapped up in e basket isn't good enough. I need a good cuddle."

"He loves to be held tight," Alexis told her. "That's why I ep him wrapped in that light blanket. It seems to frighten m when his arms and legs are free. He kicks and carries on I I pick him up and hold him close. But, believe me, that's hardship for me. I can't think of anything I enjoy more than ddling that little sweetie."

"Unless it's cuddling his father," said Ellen in an under-ne that brought laughter from the other three women.

"Well, there is that," Alexis conceded. "But then, that's hat got me in trouble in the first place."

"Well, you can't tell me you don't enjoy that man of urs," Minna said, her smile wide. "After all, a woman's bed-om should be a safe place for her, sort of a haven, I think," e said, continuing her line of thought. "Ralph don't look ry romantic, I know, but he's a strong man and keeps me

safe and happy. And he's a good cuddler, too. That's abo
all a wife can ask for, if you want my opinion."

"You may just be right," Ellen said softly. "Chet is big an
tough and strong, but he treats me like a china doll. Can't sa
I mind going to bed in my room every night, so long as he
there."

Sarah only nodded at the opinions expressed, as if sh
possessed secrets she was not willing to share, and then sh
looked over to where the baby slept. "Well, just know that I'
planning on getting in my share of snuggling with that bab
this evening, Alexis. Haven't held a newborn in a long time

"That's easily fixed," Minna said with a grin. "Just hav
yourself another one. You need a brother for Stephen, anyway

There was silence for a moment at the mention of Stephe
and all four women wore worried looks as they thought of th
two boys who were, even now, the subjects of a grand searc
by the menfolk.

"Do you suppose there were mischief-makers around la
night?" Ellen asked musingly. "Or maybe a cougar scared th
boys into hiding. Chet says he's seen more than one of thos
big cats."

"I prefer the cougar to men who are up to no good," Minn
told her. "A big cat can be mighty dangerous, but evil huma
beings are even more so. Ever since Mick Jenson showed u
hereabouts a few months ago, I've kept a close eye on thing
especially in those woods my young'uns like to play in."

She shrugged, feigning nonchalance. "But, to tell the trut
I'd lay money that those boys got scared by some animal an
they're hiding out in one of those box canyons. There's a hea
of caves in the hills, some of them just a bitty little hole i
the side of a hill, but the boys wouldn't have had a proble
finding one big enough to curl up in and sleep. And it's m
bet they lit a fire to keep the animals away."

"Sounds like you've been thinking about this," Alexis said, eling relief at Minna's theory.

"Only all night long," Minna said, lifting a hand to wipe her eyes. "There's nothin' worse than worryin' about a ung'un. And in this case, there's two of them to fret over. ems like Stephen is pretty near my own, being blood kin d all."

"Well, he surely loves you, Minna, and your family, too. pecially Jonas."

"Those men said they'd be back by suppertime," Ellen id. "We'd better be ready for them. They'll be hungry."

"That meat is about done," Minna said. "All we need to do cook up some vegetables to go with it and make up a pan cobbler for dessert. There's plenty of fresh bread."

"We'll be ready whenever they show up, then," Ellen said. 'robably be a couple of hours at least."

And it was. In fact, the sun was setting by the time Jamie d Brace showed up, and the womenfolk had begun look-g for them in earnest, all four of them relieved when the two en came in from the barn after caring for their horses.

"Looks like they went north to one of the box canyons," mie said as the women waited for their report. "We tracked em into the woods and then Slim must have caught up with em and all three headed north. So long as he's with them, von't worry so much."

Brace hung his hat by the door and went to the sink to ash. "Chet will be here shortly," he said. "Woody wanted go on farther and see if he could track them down, but we rsuaded Chet to head for home right behind us."

"We'll go back early in the morning, when there's enough ylight to make out a trail," Jamie said. "I'd be willing to t they're just fine for now, with Slim along."

"Chet's coming across the pasture," Ellen said, looking

from the doorway to where her husband rode toward the ba
"We'll set a plate for him." The table was full by the time s
had rearranged the plates and put out bowls for the babi
There was an abundance of chairs for the adults to sit on, a
even though the women were still digesting their dinner, th
sat down to share in the meal with the men.

Minna dished up the ribs and sauerkraut and put the ne
potatoes in a separate bowl. Quart jars of green beans h
been heated and soon joined the assortment of food. The pu
gent scent of sauerkraut permeated the air and Jamie seem
to get his second wind when he sat down by Alexis.

"Sure smells good," he said, eyeing the big platt
"Haven't had kraut for a long time."

"Well, Ellen canned this last year," Alexis said. "I reme
ber cutting up the cabbage for her. We had it in a crock fo
while and then after a couple of weeks it was ready to can
in jars. I've learned a lot from Ellen, and now from Minn
They'll turn me into a good ranch wife yet."

Jamie squeezed her hand under the tablecloth. "You're
wonderful wife already," he murmured in her ear.

"Just think how wonderful I'll be in a couple of yea
when those two get finished with me," she told him.

He bent to her and planted a kiss on her cheek. "I love y
just the way you are. You don't need to improve any to s
me, sweetheart."

The meal was enjoyed by the adults but the twins turn
up their nose at the scent of sauerkraut and settled for mo
soup. Alexis laughed. "I think this is an acquired taste," s
said easily. "The soup's better for them, anyway."

Kitchen duty was handled quickly, and the little ones we
prepared for bed by lamplight. "I think I'm going to jo
them," Alexis said with a yawn. "I'm tired out, and I haven
even done anything today but sit there and rock." She look

at the rocking chair, a spot Sarah had claimed as her own after supper was over. The bundle in her arms was nestled against her, and her soft voice hummed a lullaby.

In Alexis's considered opinion it might not be too long before Sarah found herself well on her way to motherhood again. Some women were born to have children, and it was Alexis's thought that Sarah was one of them. Her obvious love for her own two and her ability to take her sister's child as her own were ample proof of that. She went to where Sarah sat and knelt by her side.

"If you want me to take him now, I'll go on up with him and settle us both down for the night."

But before Alexis could take the baby from Sarah's arms, a sound from the backyard caught her attention, and she rose to her feet.

"Won't any of us be going to bed anytime soon," Jamie said, standing quickly and striding to the back door. "Unless I miss my guess there's some sort of a hullabaloo going on out by the back of the barn. I heard voices."

"Is it the boys?" Sarah asked in a hushed tone, as though she feared getting her hopes up. She rose with Jay in her arms and silent tears fell from her eyes.

"Can't tell for sure, but it sounds like a bunch of them are back," Jamie said. "Too dark to see what's going on, but I'll fix that in a hurry."

He was out the door and across the yard in mere seconds, and the women went out to the porch, the better to see. The big barn door slid open as Jamie neared it and he went on inside.

"I'm about prayed out," Minna said quietly. "If I don't see that boy of mine in the next few minutes, I'm about done for." Her shoulders slumped as she spoke, and then, as Alexis wrapped her arms around Minna's shoulders, a shout rang out from the barn.

"Both of them?" It was Jamie's voice and Slim who an swered.

"Hell, yes. Did you think we'd bring back one without the other?" He laughed and the sound brought tears to the eye of the women who listened intently. "They're comin' in fron the corral now," Slim shouted.

Jamie added his voice to the sudden rumble of men's and boy's voices as he greeted them, the sound carrying easily t the back porch. "Get yourselves up to the house, the both o you. You've about scared the dickens out of your mothers an everyone else, too."

He came out the wide door, shooing the two boys ahead of him, and both ran pell-mell toward the house.

"We're back," Jonas called. "And boy did we have a time."

Minna was down the steps, running at full tilt, and then he arms were full of Jonas, even as one hand reached out to sna Stephen's arm, hauling him into her wide embrace. Besid Alexis, Sarah sobbed quietly.

"I knew they'd be all right," she whispered between wip ing her eyes and digging for her hankie.

"Give me that baby," Alexis said with a laugh, "and go t your son, Sarah."

Chapter Seventeen

Stephen tried valiantly to subdue the tears that surfaced as Sarah caught him in an embrace. Taller now than she, he shuddered visibly as he clasped her tightly. And then laughed aloud as she scolded him roundly, dragging him with her toward the house.

"Didn't you know how worried we'd be?" She asked the question, and then failed to await an answer, as if she realized that she stood little chance of receiving one from the boy. "You boys have had four women crying and praying for you, not knowing where you were, or if you were even alive."

Stephen swiped his fist against his eyes and stood tall beside her as they reached the porch. "We didn't mean to worry anyone. Things just happened. There was a cougar and he wouldn't go away, no matter how big our fire was. So when he finally did, we decided to hide in the woods."

The faulty logic made Alexis smile—unwillingly, to be sure, but hiding in the woods had made the boys a perfect target for the big cat, had they but known it.

"When Slim came riding through the woods all hell had broken loose, we hollered at him to let him know where we were," Stephen continued. He looked chagrined for a moment. "He told us we were crazy to leave the fire and hide out in the dark. Said the cougar had a better chance at us, because they can see in the dark so good."

"So then what did you do?" Sarah asked.

"Slim said we'd wait till daylight and then see if the big cat had gone. So we went back to our camp and built up the fire again. And when it got light enough, we saw the cougar south of us, and Slim said we'd better find a better spot someplace where the cougar couldn't get to us so easy. He said there'd probably be someone out looking for us right shortly anyway. So we went north a ways to the first box canyon and climbed the side of the cliff to a cave he knew about."

Relief swept through Alexis at Stephen's explanation and she let out a breath. She waved Minna and Jonas toward the porch, and included Sarah in her command. "These boys need some food in their bellies, unless I miss my guess."

"So do that bunch out in the barn," Ellen said. "We'd better get the food on the table for them." She bustled back into the kitchen and began heating up the big pot of leftovers for the hungry men. Slim and Woody stopped at the horse trough and washed, splashing water on their faces and laughing. Their relief was evident, their triumph at finding the lost boys was a visible bond between them and they entered the kitchen with enthusiasm, sniffing the air and finding their seats at the table.

"Smells like kraut to me," Slim said. "Haven't had anything to eat since early on this morning. I feel like I could eat you out of house and home, Jamie."

"Well, sit down and have a shot at it," Jamie said, laughing at Slim's vote of appreciation for the meal. Stephen and Jonas had already scooped food onto their plates, and were halted, forks halfway to their mouths, when Minna announced at somebody better say some words over the food and the oys' safe recovery.

"I can do that," Hank said, watching from the doorway. e'd been in his office, and done his own share of worrying, the circles under his eyes were anything to go by, Alexis ecided. He walked to the table and placed a big hand on each f the boys' shoulders, then spoke a brief prayer of thanks-iving. At his final word, Stephen and Jonas began eating, and lim laughed aloud.

"You young'uns act like you haven't seen hide nor hair of yything fit to eat in a cow's age," he said, "and I saw you oth gnawin' on a biscuit early this morning."

"It didn't last long," Stephen said, scooting over as Brace ime in the door and looked for a seat at the table.

"Sit here, Pa," the boy told him, making room on the bench or his father.

"Reckon I will," Brace told him. "I've missed having you our dinner table back home, son." His hand clasped the oy's shoulder as he sat beside him, and Alexis thought she w a tear in Brace's eye. Stephen was his pride and joy, if e knew anything about it. His baby girls were precious, but s son…now that was another story.

The food disappeared rapidly, and the bowls were scraped ean. "When y'all get done eating, bring your plates to the nk," Minna directed them. "We already cleaned up once, and ou can all pitch in to help."

Chet stood, holding his plate and looking over at Ellen, ho was busy pouring hot water into the big metal dishpan. 'll give Ellen a hand here. You just go sit and listen to your oy, Minna."

Ellen glanced at him and then smiled. "We'll get these ashed up in no time," she said. "And then everyone can get emselves off to bed."

Chet went to where she stood and whispered in her ear an
she elbowed him in the ribs, muttering a muffled word th
made him laugh aloud.

"Well, I'm ready to go upstairs," Alexis said, gathering
her son and holding him close against her breast.

"I'll take him, sweetheart," Jamie said. "Do you want h
basket along? Or should we leave it here for morning?"

"I'll just put a quilt in a dresser drawer for tonight," s
said, covering a yawn with one hand as Jamie took the chi
from her arms. "He can sleep next to the bed so I can rea
him when he wakes up." Then, remembering her duties, s
searched out Sarah and smiled. "You'll find your rooms read
for you. Same place you slept at Christmastime."

Sarah waved her thanks and shooed Jamie up the stairs b
hind Alexis.

They made their way up, calling back a good-night
those below and Alexis almost stumbled as she reached t
bedroom door. Jamie reached his free hand to grasp her arm

"Are you all right? I think this day has been too much f
you, sweetheart."

"Probably," she agreed. "But it ended up well, didn't it"

"You can't imagine how happy we were to find Slim wi
the boys in that cave. He'd built a big fire on a flat spot in fro
of it and we saw the smoke before we got there. He wasn
taking any chances with any more wildlife sniffing them ou
Jamie paused for a moment, and then cleared his throat.

"There's something else, Alex," he said quietly.

She turned to him, noting the frown on his face, the tigh
ening of his lips as he spoke. He placed the baby on their be
and turned to her.

"There was more than a cougar out there," he said harshl

"What are you saying, Jamie? Another animal?"

"You could say that," he allowed. "Mick Jenson was in t

canyon, too. He rode out while we were getting the boys and Slim. I followed him." His eyes were flat, the brilliant blue faded and chilled as he faced her, as if he hesitated at completing his story.

"Are you all right?" she asked, her instincts on alert, sensing already that his words would tell a tale she dreaded for his sake, for he seemed haunted and distraught.

"Better off than Mick is. I chased him down and made him face me."

"He's dead?" She felt a shiver run down her spine, and opened her arms to Jamie, wanting to comfort him.

He stepped into her embrace and shuddered. "He's dead, sweetheart. I'll send someone out to bury him tomorrow." He squared his shoulders and his eyes were dark as the midnight sky as he stepped back to face her. "He won't ever bother any of us again."

"You killed him because of me, didn't you?"

"I shot him down without thinking twice. It was like executing a lobo wolf or a madman set on destruction." His love for her gleamed from his gaze. "Yeah, I killed him, without a moment's hesitation. Because he touched my wife and caused her pain and because his gun was aimed at me and I had no choice."

She went to him, wrapping her arms around his waist and holding him tightly. His heartbeat was strong against her ear and she whispered a quick word of thanksgiving that he was safe and sound and in her arms. As mean as he'd been, Mick had been someone's son and Alexis felt remorse that his life had been so futile. And perhaps his death might bring pain to his family.

"Where will we put the baby to sleep?" James said, happy to change the subject. "What dresser drawer were you talking about?"

Alexis released him from her grip and smothered a yawn. "This one. Ellen got it out and emptied it earlier today for me." Pulling it close to her side of the bed, she fluffed a quilt, placing it in the enclosed space. A clean towel from the wash-stand followed, tucked over the quilt, and the baby's bed was ready. Jamie placed him there gently, then retrieved a small blanket from a stack on a table. With tender touches, he covered his son, tucking him in for the night.

"Now, to take care of you, sweetheart," he said in a low tone. "Crawl into bed and I'll put you to sleep."

"And how are you planning to do that?" Alexis lifted an eyebrow and shot him a teasing look.

He showed her, curling up behind her and rubbing her shoulders with his strong fingers. "How's that?" Amusement touched his words as he worked out the stiffness from sore muscles.

"You know it's wonderful," she whispered. "I'm half asleep already." And then she yawned again and shut her eyes.

"It's gonna be awful quiet around here," Jamie said several days later. It was hard to acknowledge the fact that Stephen would be traveling home with Brace and Sarah. Even though Jamie had expected this farewell for weeks, he found it more difficult than he'd imagined.

"I'll bet you'll miss him, won't you?" Brace stood by his side as they watched Stephen roping a horse in the pasture, then drawing the animal closer, his arm reaching to encircle the young colt's neck.

"Yeah, and so will that colt out there. Stephen has spent more time than you can imagine with that animal, and he's mighty smitten with him."

"Don't sell him," Brace said, stuffing his hands into hi

ockets as he watched his son. "I have a notion he'll want that olt for his own in a couple of years."

"They're all his, Brace," Jamie reminded him. "And I vouldn't think of selling that one. It would break Stephen's teart. He's already planning on coming back next summer to vork with him."

Brace looked questioningly at his friend. "What are you nd Alexis going to do now?"

"Stay on here for a few years, probably, at least until Stephen is old enough to learn the ropes and take over the place. Alexis and I have talked about a place of our own and 've been considering a piece of land about fifteen miles from tere. Good pasture and a nice house on it. I may make an offer nd then Alexis and I can work on it in our spare time, get it eady for us to move our family in later on."

"Will Hank stay on here?" Brace sounded mildly curious, ut Jamie wasn't fooled by the casual query.

"As long as you need him. Or, I should say, as long as Stephen needs him. He's a valuable asset to the ranch."

"It sounds like things are right on track, then," Brace said. He grimaced as he looked once more toward his son and the torse he appeared to be talking to in the pasture. "Now, how do I get him out of here?"

"You call his name and he'll come running," Jamie said vith a smile. "Don't you know you're the most important person in his life?"

"More likely it's Sarah," Brace said quietly. "He dotes on ter."

Jamie laughed aloud. "Yeah, well so do you, big fella."

"We're a lucky pair, aren't we, Jamie? Alexis is the woman or you, and Sarah is just right for me, even if she is a spunky ittle outfit."

"You love it. And seeing you with her for the years before

I left Benning gave me a good example to follow when married Alexis. I've tried to be the kind of husband you are Brace."

Brace coughed, clearing his throat and looking aside "Didn't know I had that much influence on you, son."

"More than you'll ever know. I'll never be able to thank you enough for this chance to put my life together and fin the woman I love."

"It will all work out, you'll see," Brace said. "Wish I coul look ahead a few years and see how things go."

Epilogue

spring 1914

"Excited?" Jamie's grin revealed his own thoughts as he looked down at his wife. After years of hard work, their new home was ready.

"You bet," she said quickly. A shout from the rear of the wagon caught her ear and she turned on the wide board seat, the better to see the three children who tussled on the quilt their father had placed them on.

"Y'all behave, you hear?" she said, her voice just loud enough to be heard by the small girl and her two brothers. They subsided, giggling softly as they untangled themselves and sat upright. "We're going to be home in just a few minutes," Alexis said. "You can be good for that long."

"We will, Mama," Jay said, shooting a warning glance at his brother and sister. Used to his leadership, they sat quietly, even though their whispers carried to the wagon seat where Alexis held her newest child, a tiny girl with eyes like new leaves in the spring, as her father was fond of saying. He doted on this child, her golden curls and delicate features so like her mother's.

"Will Stephen be all right?" she asked Jamie, her mind o
the young man they'd left to run the ranch.

"He's a man, full grown," Jamie told her. "You just can'
imagine that he's over twenty years old, can you?"

Alexis smiled ruefully. "You're right. I still think of hir
as a young boy."

"Well, with Jonas there, working alongside him, he'll d
just fine. Between them, and with the older men to back then
up, they make quite a pair."

"I worry about him, though, with that newfangled automo
bile he bought." She was silent for a minute and then leane
closer to Jamie. "Did you know he's courting one of the girl
from town? Took her out motoring twice last week."

"Who do you think gave him instructions on how to be
have himself?" Jamie's smile lit his face.

"A fine example you are," Alexis spouted. "You had me i
the tack room that first time, with the door locked, before
knew what was happening."

"Well, I didn't tell Stephen about that sort of thing.
With a glint of mischief in his eye, Jamie slid his arr
around Alexis's shoulder. "Some things he'll have to fin
out for himself."

"I'm sure he will."

Ahead of them, a well-worn lane led off to the right, an
at its end sat a white farmhouse, with assorted buildings sca
tered beyond it. A large barn, wearing two coats of red pain
sat at the far side of the wide yard, and Jay pointed at it, mov
ing to lean on his father's shoulder.

"Pa, can we play in the hayloft?" he asked.

"Not today, son. You get to put your bedroom in orde
and help your mama with things while I get these horses se
tled in."

"Who's gonna help us, Pa? You can't do everything by yourself." Jay sounded a bit worried, Alexis thought.

"Chet and Ellen are moving in next week," Jamie said. "We've got lots of bedrooms and Chet will run things for me pretty much. I'll hire a boy from town to lend a hand, too."

"And Ellen will take care of the house," Alexis added, thankful for that fact.

The wagon pulled up around the back of the house and Jamie jumped down, then reached to Alexis, taking the baby first, then helping his wife to the ground. They went up to the porch, the three youngsters following them closely.

"Here, Jay. Hold the baby for a minute," his father said. Alexis frowned.

"What's going on?" Her voice was high-pitched as Jamie scooped her up in his arms. "What are you doing?"

"What does it look like?" he said, his lips against her ear. "I'm carrying you over the threshold. This is our new home, Alexis, and you're my bride."

"I haven't been a bride for a lot of years," she said, laughing at his foolishness. And then he silenced her with his usual method. His mouth was warm against hers, his kiss a promise of more to come, and from the porch she heard little Lexy whisper loudly, "They're always doing that, ain't they?"

Jay laughed. "Might as well get used to it, sis. They'll probably be kissing and hugging for the rest of their lives."

"Now that boy is one smart fella," Jamie said, lifting his head to wink at his eldest son. He looked down at Alexis and his heart was in his eyes as he bent to her again.

"Welcome home, sweetheart," he whispered. "Welcome home."

* * * * *

MILLS & BOON

Historical

On sale 7th May 2010

UNTAMED ROGUE, SCANDALOUS MISTRESS
by Bronwyn Scott

Self-made Miss Aurora Calhoun is shocked when, minutes after colliding with Lord Ramsden's carriage, she's kissing the incorrigible rogue! Their mutual passion is uncontrollable and Society is rocked by this outrageous couple. Can these two wild hearts find a place to belong?

THE VISCOUNT'S UNCONVENTIONAL BRIDE
by Mary Nichols

As a member of the renowned Piccadilly Gentlemen's Club, Jonathan Leinster must ensure the return of a runaway. Spirited Louise has fled to her birthplace, hoping to find her family – but charming Jonathan stops her in her tracks! His task is simple: escort Louise promptly home. Yet all he wants to do is claim her as his own!

0410/04b

MILLS & BOON
Historical
On sale 7th May 2010

COMPROMISING MISS MILTON
by *Michelle Styles*

Buttoned-up governess Daisy Milton buries dreams of marriage and family life. But Viscount Ravensworth shakes Daisy's safe, stable existence up. Could the tightly laced miss ever forgo society's strict code of conduct…and come undone in the arms of a reformed rake?

FORBIDDEN LADY by *Anne Herries*

Sir Robert came to claim his lady honourably. But Melissa denied their love and her father had him whipped from the house. Then, as the Wars of the Roses ravage England, Melissa falls into Rob's power. He should not trust her – but can he resist such vulnerable, innocent beauty?

STETSONS, SPRING AND WEDDING RINGS
by *Jillian Hart, Judith Stacy, Stacey Kayne*

Clara, Brynn and Constance are heading West, looking for new lives, and three forceful men are determined to keep these courageous women where they belong – in their towns, in their hearts and, most of all, in their beds!

millsandboon.co.uk Community

Join Us!

The Community is the perfect place to meet and chat to kindred spirits who love books and reading as much as you do, but it's also the place to:

- Get the inside scoop from authors about their latest books
- Learn how to write a romance book with advice from our editor
- Help us to continue publishing the best in women's fiction
- Share your thoughts on the books we publish
- Befriend other users

Forums: Interact with each other as well as authors, editors and a whole host of other users worldwide.

Blogs: Every registered community member has their own blog to tell the world what they're up to and what's on their mind.

Book Challenge: We're aiming to read 5,000 books and have joined forces with The Reading Agency in our inaugural Book Challenge.

Profile Page: Showcase yourself and keep a record of your recent community activity.

Social Networking: We've added buttons at the end of every post to share via digg, Facebook, Google, Yahoo, technorati and de.licio.us.

www.millsandboon.co.uk

2 FREE BOOKS
AND A SURPRISE GIFT

We would like to take this opportunity to thank you for reading this Mills & Boon® book by offering you the chance to take TWO specially selected books from the Historical series absolutely FREE We're also making this offer to introduce you to the benefits of the Mills & Boon® Book Club™—

- **FREE home delivery**
- **FREE gifts and competitions**
- **FREE monthly Newsletter**
- **Exclusive Mills & Boon Book Club offers**
- **Books available before they're in the shops**

Accepting these FREE books and gift places you under no obligation to buy, you may cancel at any time, even after receiving your free books. Simply complete your details below and return the entire page to the address below. You don't even need a stamp!

YES Please send me 2 free Historical books and a surprise gift. I understand that unless you hear from me, I will receive 4 superb new books every month for just £3.79 each, postage and packing free. I am under no obligation to purchase any books and may cancel my subscription at any time. The free books and gift will be mine to keep in any case.

Ms/Mrs/Miss/Mr ——————— Initials ———————

Surname ————————————————————
Address ————————————————————
————————————————————————
——————————————— Postcode ———————
E-mail ————————————————————

Send this whole page to: Mills & Boon Book Club, Free Book Offer, FREEPOST NAT 10298, Richmond, TW9 1BR